TURKISH
EYE

BY
BEATRICE
JAMES

**MYS
Pbk**

First published in Great Britain in 2014 by:
OBILIUM Ltd
Manchester House - 113 Northgate Street
Bury St Edmunds - IP33 1HP
ISBN 978-1-909868-08-3

For
those who
fall in love
with Turkey's
Aegean coast
and stay a while…

Acknowledgements

Thank you to:

Jill Baker; Simon & Yvonne Mitchell; Chris Chatten.

Bengi Yuceer.

Special mention to everybody at
The Foreign Citizen's Advice Centre
in Kuşadasi, for all the help and support they provide.

theEgeEye.com

And to all at Obilium, for their continued support and patience.

BEATRICE JAMES

ALSO BY BEATRICE JAMES

THE 'RETRIBUTION FANTASIES'

AN ARTIST'S IMPRESSION
SENTENCE EXPIRY DATE
BAYBE & ME (Acts of Charity - Act 1)
HELL, FIRE AND WHISKEY (Act 2)
THE COLDEST DISH (Act 3)
THERE BUT FOR THE GRACE OF GOD (Act 4)

'Everything we see in the world
is the creative work of women'

- Mustafa Kemal Atatürk
*First President and Founder of the
Turkish Republic*

Foreword

K ușadası is a port on the Aegean sea in the west of Turkey. It's a growing town and its population of ninety thousand is on the increase, as new developments appear on the surrounding hillsides, often blasted out of the rock face. Literally pushing the place outwards, in three directions and becoming more upmarket in the process. Changing from a haphazard, chaotic place to something a little more defined and planned. But only up to a point. It is Turkey after all and nothing is ever quite what it appears to be. It'll draw you in and before you know it you will be wanting to come back, as soon as you've left.

Principally a seaside resort, it is popular with the Turkish people, English and Irish alike. Flights have been arriving from Southern Ireland and the north of England since the early eighties. The expanded town centres on the original old one where the archways and buildings look as if they could tell a tale or two. It's got character that's for sure and the bars, shops and restaurants have everything a tourist could want and at a price that you can haggle for, for as long as you want. Take your time, drink a glass of apple tea, it's all part of the charm. It's a friendly place, 'no hassle.... Ok?'

Do you want a rug? A designer handbag? Or even a genuine fake watch? No problem. Enjoy the experience and don't expect it to be quick. The merchants enjoy it as much as you. It's their livelihood and they're born to it. They work long hours in the heat and don't complain. It's the life they know and love.

Kușadasi is where 'East' meets 'West' in a positive

way. The warm air is heavy with the smell of fragrant spices and the market stalls are ablaze with colour, displaying locally grown fruits and vegetables; aubergines, tomatoes, peppers glisten in the bright light and the locals fill up their baskets and trollies in a bustle of activity. Their traditional clothes, heavy skirts and headscarves, contrasting with the shorts and skimpy T-shirts of the tourists unused to the midday sun. Somehow the two merge and walk side by side in the busy streets and alleyways that make up the town centre.

There's an exotic feel to it all and you can't help but admire the waiters and restaurateurs who manage to look immaculate in their white cotton shirts and black trousers, perfectly groomed and fragrant despite the sometimes oppressive heat. They constantly try to entice you into their restaurant with promises of free drinks and a platter of exotic fruit. Go in once, and you will return a friend. They will remember your face and your name for years to come. Like family. You feel part of it all and it's a genuine welcome. Not the rehearsed interest of other nations' resorts. These people want you to have a good time. They have learnt the languages of their visitors, particularly English and Dutch. Certainly better than efforts at the Turkish language. We might manage 'merhaba' (hello) or maybe 'teşekkür' (thank you), that's usually about it. The English and Irish who live in Kuşadasi don't know much more. Then again, they don't need to.

Don't forget the Port. Set on the southern end of the bay at the opposite end to the impressive new Marina. The huge floating hotels or Cruise liners dock for the day to visit Ephesus, the great Roman theatre that the Americans make a Taxi dash for. They used to dock a couple of times a week, before they redeveloped it, digging it out to be extra deep and adding more berths, now two or three ships are in every day bringing more prosperity to the town. The Turks aren't stupid. The shops and stalls around the Port will have their own price structure if they think they can get away with it. They will try their hardest to sell their more expensive wares, the intricately woven rugs, resplendent in colour texture and style. Beautiful designs and patterns, leather coats and handbags, with the quality expected by the discerning eye. Those passengers from the ships have no time to hone their bartering skills or grasp the value of the Turkish Lira before they are lured in the shops that line the entrance to the Port itself. Still they are usually happy with their 'bargains.' They don't see the real Turkey though, it's just a flavour before they get back on board and off to wherever, for the next day's adventure.

The sound of Kuşadasi, can be heard from the central Mosques and the call to prayer throughout the day and night. It's a backdrop for all the other noises; the Turkish and English music; the shouting from the merchants; the sounds of the birds and crickets in the heat. It's a unique sound and quite comforting. It's not at all a quiet town.

Kuşadasi, means 'Bird Island.' The 'island' itself isn't an island though. A short walk from the Port along the front and a walkway filled with day boats and excursions leads you onto the peninsula, which is bird shaped if viewed from above. It has still got the very impressive walled fortification, now an ancient monument converted into a museum. It's changed many times over the years to suit the mood of the town. In the eighties and nineties it was used as a nightclub but now beautiful after years of restoration, with a walkway to stroll around and watch the town from a distance. The view is amazing. The bars and restaurants have gone, no sunbeds for the tourists now, it's back to its original form and the council wants it to stay that way. Well for now anyway, until you come back next year and it may have become something else. That is the nature of the place, forever changing and moving, not always forward, but you can't get bored here, that is for sure.

Am I selling it to you? That's not my purpose here. I am trying to set the scene for you. This is a special place. A bustling vibrant town, but in essence with a village feel to it. Everyone knows everyone particularly in the bars, restaurants and shops. The staff, mainly waiters and kitchen hands migrate to Kuşadasi for the summer season eager to escape the villages and towns from which they originate. They often move around, changing their pitch, hoping for a better restaurant, better job, and better money each time. Making the most of the summer months, the bright lights, the excitement of a new season until late October, when the nights draw in and it's time to go home. Back to the land and to their families for the winter months.

They seem to genuinely like the tourists, well most of them. The young women from England and Ireland hoping for their first holiday romance. Their English is good, perhaps they learn it in school. They are keen to learn, to flatter and tease the girls who are sometimes easy prey. They have dark eyes, smouldering good looks, and a cheeky grin, whatever is your fancy. Sometimes their patter is good, if not they can make you laugh anyway. Bar Street for the madness, the foolish, and the craziness of youth. It doesn't get going until at least midnight and the revellers are still going at five. It's not for the faint hearted though and certainly not everyone's cup of tea, but all comers are catered for here;

and you can always find what you are looking for.

The local men have an easy way with the ladies and not just the young ladies. The older women, who should know better, sit gazing in to the eyes of the younger beaux. You can see many unlikely couples sitting in the bars and restaurants. Hardly able to believe their luck, sometimes they can be persuaded to make their lives here. To sell up and find a place in the sun and start again. The men can enjoy some financial security and the women can find a new lease of life. It's a strange phenomenon, but it works for some. Who are we to judge?

You can have a good life here if you are willing to take a risk. Maybe not so much of a risk really. The climate is warm and sunny, the winters are bright and warm during the day. There may have been snow in 2004, but that was a freak event. The cost of living is lower than in England, without frightening gas and electricity bills and your savings are safe in the Turkish banks that offer great rates of interest. It's a good life and easy to take for granted.

You can find the expats here without trying too hard. They could be English women now married to Turkish men, maybe running a business and adapted to Turkish ways more than most. Some of the women here have a Turkish boyfriend who has persuaded them to make their lives here. Though many still want their Satellite TV and their home comforts despite the change in climate and culture. The couples and singles who haven't been romanced by the locals, have probably made the decision to stay for economic reasons.

Perhaps I am being cynical. They may have simply fallen for the charm of the place and want to linger.

1

Mary

M ary tottered precariously down the narrow cobbled alley, trying to aim her four inch narrow heels onto the larger stones and not get them caught in the joints. She cursed to herself as she nearly lost her balance. An old Turkish man gave her a toothless grin from his regular spot; a pile of plastic and cardboard, outside a T-shirt shop that had closed for the night.

His job was to protect the owner's stock for the few short hours that the shop was actually closed. It was too laborious to pack everything away that was outside, now covered in plastic. Particularly because a Cruise ship would be docking in three hours' time and an onslaught of American or European tourists would be wandering up the alleys on their way to the centre of town. He could watch five or six shops from his vantage point and the owners trusted him.

As he stared at Mary, by now nearly out of sight, he muttered to himself about her appearance. Her cheetah print shift mini dress with a silver diamante cardigan was, in his view, not even suitable for someone of half her years. The dress rode up high as she took big ungainly strides, resulting in an unattractive display of thigh and cellulite.

Selim had seen worse of course. In his almost forty years of working in the town from the seventies until now, he was saddened to see a steady decline in the quality of visiting tourists. An old fashioned man, he could remember the days when women of Mary's age were appropriately clothed, albeit in tasteless holiday wear, but at least they hadn't tried to kid themselves that they'd ever see fifty again. 'This one probably had grandchildren,' the old man thought to himself. He didn't know her name, but he had seen her many times before, mostly outside Adem's bar, drinking and smoking with the other expats. Selim considered himself a liberal, having spent so long with the tourists, but even he had to turn his head away at some of the sights he'd witnessed in this alley.

The old town's streets are cobbled, unevenly paved and very narrow. They appear to be a maze of random paths, weaving a route from the seafront and port to the centre of the old town. You could easily go round in circles if you don't know your way around, but Selim knew these streets better than the back of his hand. Regular visitors are often confused as shops and bars change owners and change names, but intrinsically they pretty much stay the same business. Landmarks though are much slower to be things that are altered and the locals didn't seem to notice the subtle differences.

Selim's mind wandered back to the halcyon days of the seventies. He had travelled to Kuşadasi from his village Selçuk, approximately twenty kilometres away inland. Not a great distance, but to Ali, it was a different world, exotic and exciting. He had been young, just seventeen and a tall good looking boy. He was fifty six now, but looked and felt two decades older. It was and is, he thought a hard life. He looked down at his weary body and shivered. It wasn't cold by any means, still more than twenty degrees, but his bones ached and he knew that at his age, he should at home with his wife, tucked up in bed and sleeping. Not lying under cardboard like a feral beggar.

He had no choice, when his days as a waiter came to

an end. He wasn't quick enough anymore. Hundreds of younger men found their way to the town every year to find work, earn some money for their families, and to have some fun along the way. When he first came to the town he had worked at a restaurant on the seafront and did so, every summer season, for years after. His father had known the proprietor's family and it hadn't been too difficult to settle in to the room they had provided for him. He had been popular with his regular customers who returned each year and he looked forward to the generosity of their tips.

When the owner decided to sell up, and return to Söke, a richer man, Selim was devastated. The new owner had plenty of sons and nephews to work for him and they didn't need him anymore. After a few stints in other restaurants, he found himself without any permanent work and the jobs he coveted were being taken by his younger counterparts.

He started selling flowers and would see some of his old customers along the way. He liked to think of them as friends. He sold them roses and wished them well in the new restaurants and bars springing up along the front and the new Marina. He didn't fit into the new world. Long nights and days had taken their toll on his looks and energy and he aged badly, almost overnight. A tear came into his eye as he remembered the look on his wife's face on the days when he couldn't make enough for them to eat and pay their meagre rent. He felt deep shame that he couldn't provide for her and for a brief moment was grateful he had not been blessed with children, money had been so tight.

An old acquaintance from the restaurant and the owner of several shops in the alleys asked him to mind the shops and he gratefully accepted. Earning less than he would have received in tips, from his restaurant career, at least the money was regular and they could survive. His wife cleaned in one of the hotels and they managed. He had already forgotten Mary who was now making her way down a side alley. The clipping noise made by her heels could still be heard as she disappeared into the darkness.

Mary was wishing she hadn't had that last vodka and coke at Adem's bar. Well the last two or three actually. Feeling quite woozy, she recalled Adem urging her to stay and have another.

She normally walked back to her apartment with Val, her friend from the neighbouring flat. But Val had struck lucky that night and left earlier with a tall Dutchman that she had been talking to in Adem's. 'Good luck to her,' Mary thought, 'you only live once' and Val seemed quite keen on him. They had gone for food somewhere and Mary wished she had eaten something as well. She hiccupped, feeling silly, but there was no one around to hear her. Mary didn't wear a watch and she wasn't sure of the time. It must be after five she thought. It was quiet, unusually so, there was always someone around. This was a town that never sleeps. The shops and stalls stay open nearly as long as the bars. As long as there were potential customers the spirit of optimism remained. Perhaps it was later than she thought.

Mary was used to her late nights. Funny really, when she thought back to her home city of Cork, where she had lived all her life until she moved to Kuşadasi six years ago. She had always been in bed by ten in Ireland. Tucked up with her book listening to Seamus, her husband snoring away. She didn't go out until after ten now, sometimes nearer eleven. Her body clock had adjusted and she now slept late. At home she would have been up at six in the morning. How life changes she mused.

Deep in thought and still under the influence of the vodka, she didn't see or hear the figure emerge from the shadows behind her.

2

Charlie

C harlie Davison stretched out her body slowly like a cat. Her long limbs were still entwined with her lover Anthony and she felt the heat from him pressed against her. He wasn't just her lover, he was her boss and her mentor. She pulled herself from under him as he murmured in his sleep.

She looked at him as he slept, oblivious to her scrutiny. He looked peaceful and composed. No stress lines or worries evident on his smooth features. Jet black hair, cut close to his head and an aquiline nose, he looked almost angelic, Charlie thought. Christ that's far from the truth. They had been sleeping together for almost a year, but the luxury of having him in her bed was still quite rare. She savoured the moment as he slept.

His phone rang from his trouser pocket in the living room. The trousers that had come off in a hurry earlier in the evening as they clawed at each other's clothing. She had no complaints in that department. He was a great lover and an enthusiastic one, with her anyway. Last night had been a combination of desire, and the champagne they'd consumed in quantity. Most of their couplings happened after they'd both been drinking. It was all energy and heightened desire.

"Fuck!" Anthony said as he stirred, alerted to the mobile's annoying ringtone and looking at his watch. He jumped up and ran naked into the living room to retrieve his phone. It rang off before he could get to it and now he was cursing again, loudly.

As he looked down at the missed number, Charlie snapped, "don't tell me," already feeling a different mood forming than when she had awoken, "Alice?"

"Sorry Charlie, I didn't realise the time. You're such a vixen." He smiled not wanting to upset his fiery Geordie girl. He couldn't ignore his wife Alice for long though, she was also a force to be reckoned with. He thought, not for the first time, 'what am I doing?'

He knew Charlie wanted more. He could see it in her face. Now and when she sometimes looked at him at work that way. The sex was amazing, but it had taken a lot of persuasion to get this woman. She wouldn't even agree to go for a drink with him. She had her morals and her principles and she knew he was a married man. He had promised her more than a fling. That was his style, it was all about the chase. He liked to think he couldn't help himself. But Charlie had also had the 'hots' for her boss Anthony. Big time. Six foot three, ex-public-schoolboy, little boy lost expression, and completely ruthless. She played hard to get for him, but she had fallen and fallen hard.

Charlie liked to think of herself as a feminist, a woman's woman and she believed in the power of the sisterhood. Brought up for most of her teenage years by her single parent mother, she viewed women as the stronger sex, ready to take on the world. This relationship had made her question the strength of her values, after all Anthony had a wife. Deep down she wasn't proud of herself but something drove her on.

"Charlie," he groaned, "don't do this." He wanted to be inside her again, but the thought of Alice pacing the floor, ringing again and again was enough to make his erection subside.

"I have to go Sweetheart, you know what she's like. I

didn't know we were coming back here last night. I can't make any more excuses, she isn't stupid."

Charlie had persuaded him back to her place after they had attended the opening night of a small gallery together. It was work, but a few too many glasses of free champagne later and they were in the back of a black cab acting as if they were teenagers.

Charlotte Davison wasn't a teenager. She was nearly thirty. Well twenty eight and three quarters to be exact. Anthony was forty in a month's time. They were both old enough to know better. Charlie already regretted drinking too much. She had shown weakness and despised herself for it. For the sake of her sanity she had been trying to end the relationship with Anthony for the last week, albeit half-heartedly.

Charlie was sharp and sassy and knew in her heart, without a shadow of a doubt that Ant wouldn't leave Alice or his two 'spoilt brat' daughters. She had wanted to believe though, like many women before her, that they had a future. She was also aware that she had justified her own behaviour by choosing to believe in him and even vilifying his wife, it was part of the act, the charade. She had to hate Alice in order to do what she was doing now.

Staring at her lover coldly, the passion subsiding in an instant. She initiated the next scene in the play she had mistaken for a relationship.

"Fuck off home then Ant, if you haven't got the bottle to stay that's fine. I don't need a man in my life despite what you may think."

He tried to kiss her, to make it ok. Though he too knew that the eleven months of secret trysts and great sex were coming to an end. She was fun and feisty and he loved her, but just not quite enough to leave his wife and split up the family for. His own parents would disown him. Alice's family were his family, their lives were too entwined now. It was a cliché, but it was true.

He couldn't be honest if he tried.

"You pursued me Ant, for nearly a year before we started this. You're a bastard, do you know that? A selfish spineless bastard!"

"Stop it Charlie, I'll make it up to you. I'll book us a weekend somewhere, Rome? Paris? You name it and I'll sort it. Soon. I promise. We're good together, don't spoil it." He looked desperate now. His life would be so dull without her. He didn't want it to end like this.

"Me spoil it?" Charlie's voice was becoming higher pitched now and her Newcastle accent more pronounced. She was seething. "You're full of empty promises Ant and I am sick of it all. Believe me when I say, I have had enough."

"Look, don't be hasty Charlie, let's go away for a few days, then we can spend some proper time together, relax, eat, drink, talk, fuck, anything you want."

"I wanted you Ant." Charlie almost spat at him. Holding back tears that were threatening to come and show weakness that he would exploit. He would worm his way back in, with his persuasive words, making her feel she was special. A thought flashed through her mind, remembering how she had been her dad's 'special girl'. Was she so insecure? She had loved her dad with all her heart, but he had left her too. Was this what it was about? Charlie could be a deep thinker, but this wasn't the time or place.

Anthony dressed quickly and went into the bathroom to call Alice. He shut the door. When he came out he had another look on his face, anxiety.

"It's Erin," he said staring down at Charlie who was

still lying in bed motionless. "She's in hospital. Alice thinks it may be meningitis." He called a cab, kissed Charlie as a second thought and left to wait outside.

Charlie hadn't spoken a word. She felt as if she was a prize bitch now. It was all wrong. She looked around her swanky London flat. Docklands' splendour. 'Swanky' is such a Geordie expression. Her posh London existence envied by her school-friends and family still living in Newcastle was also a sham. It didn't make her happy, not really. The large wall to floor windows had a terrific view over London, well the East end of London anyway. The balcony where she sat and drank her morning coffee, the one that inspired her to start her working day. The city gave her energy, but it had drained from her in an instant as Anthony banged the door behind him.

She looked at the interior of her home that should have been a source of pleasure and pride. The oak floorboards, the sofa from Heals that cost a month's salary and had made her mam gasp when she told her the price. The shiny kitchen with the array of appliances that she rarely used. It meant nothing, she realised. She wasn't happy and she hadn't been for a while. It wasn't just Ant. It was her. She had strived so hard to get what she thought she wanted, to only realise she didn't want it at all.

She picked up the phone and rang her mother. It went straight to voicemail. She hardly ever rang her mother. Her mother always rang her. Every month to be exact. It felt like a duty call. Was she ok? How was London life? Was she eating and looking after herself?' Her mother's dulcet Geordie tones used to make her feel safe. She represented home, Newcastle, her roots, her safety net; but not anymore. Deidre had moved to Turkey to live, permanently, three years ago. Charlie had been horrified. They'd argued constantly for weeks and had nearly fallen out with their own friends about it. Yet her mother, Deidre Davison, sensible and reliable old Deidre, went and morphed into Dee. And Dee was someone Charlie didn't know or like much.

Charlie ignored her calls for months. Dee came to see Charlie in London and they resumed a form of contact mainly on her mother's part. Charlie had promised to visit her in Kuşadasi, the town in Turkey she had moved to, but that hadn't happened either. Their contact had shrunk to the monthly phone calls.

Charlie rang her again a few minutes later. She just wanted to hear her voice. She felt bereft, but she didn't know why. Voicemail again and not even her mother's voice, but a recording. Charlie felt a sense of rejection that she knew was ridiculous, but felt it nonetheless. Perhaps her mother had got a new phone. She had been cut off before because she hadn't topped up frequently enough. Those Turkish Sim cards? It had never been a problem until today, as she had left the contacting to her mam. After all Charlie was the wronged party, wasn't she?

She went back to bed with a glass of water and some painkillers. She'd had too much red wine on top of champagne last night, after Ant had fallen asleep, as she sat on the balcony in the dark assessing her life. She knew at the time that she would be paying for it in the morning.

She took the phone with her and rang her mother again.

It went straight to a Turkish recorded message.

3

Val

V al Neville lived 'downtown' in a typical Turkish apartment near the Friday market in the town of Kuşadasi. That's not an actual area, but everyone knows it as that. Near enough to town to walk in and out and cheap enough for English expats to buy or rent without breaking the bank. The apartments are built close enough together to know your neighbours and their neighbours too and to watch a slice of Turkish life on your doorstep. Locals live alongside and mix with the English and they seem to rub along quite well. What they quite make of their European cousins, remains to be seen, but they seem to be pretty tolerant.

The Friday market is now on a Wednesday. It's a large clothes market visited by tourists and locals alike, apart from in the winter when it's cheaper and less manic. The new market on a Friday is now a fruit and vegetable market held further down into town. Confusing and slightly random that's the Turkish way.

Val loves her apartment. It has a small balcony, with enough space to sit out and enjoy the sun, read her books or just watch the world go by. Room for a table, two chairs and a shelf unit full of plants and flowers. She painted the balcony a sunny yellow and paid a local handyman to lay some blue and white ceramic tiles. It's her sanctuary and her window on the world.

Its location is in a noisy area and Val doesn't mind. It makes her feel less lonely. The blocks are all closely packed next to other apartment blocks, all different shapes and sizes. Anywhere there's a bit of land would eventually be filled. It is a mismatch that somehow works. Close to town and the seafront, Val likes to watch the Turkish families with their children on the nearby balconies. They smile shyly and acknowledge each other in the way that women do and she made an effort to improve her Turkish so that she could make some conversation other than greetings.

She watched the families in the evenings, the dynamics changing as the men returned and the families ate dinner on their balconies, taking up most of the outside space. The women would heave pans of bubbling tomatoes and fresh herbs outside and Val would watch with interest as they poured bright red sauces into separate jars. They were industrious, she thought. Most don't have much money and the mothers seem not to work outside the home much, but they're clever in their housekeeping. They return from the Friday fruit and vegetable market with shopping trolleys overflowing with enough provisions for the week. Meat and poultry sourced from the local butcher, they make some fantastic smelling dishes served up with steaming rice and salads so colourful it seems a shame to eat them.

Val soon realised she was a people watcher and that her flat was an ideal place to do so without looking too weird. She tried to emulate the thriftiness of the women around her, but mostly failed. She tended to shop in the supermarket rather than the Friday market because it left her too hot and bothered and she could use up the food in time before it went off. No preservatives meant fresh organic produce, but it also meant a short shelf life. She certainly lived more cheaply than in Newcastle her home town even if she still bought wine and chocolate. Old habits die hard. She had given up the ciggies though, so maybe her life was healthier now. She tried to swim at least four times a week and walked everywhere in town.

Val looked over her balcony's edge, where she could balance to see if her neighbour and friend Mary had re-surfaced. Mary would usually be sitting out by this time having a cigarette and a coffee, both of which Val could smell. The way the properties were built meant that from this one angle they could talk almost as if they were over the proverbial garden wall. Mostly Mary came up or Val went down, which was easier than getting neck ache.

She heard Mary's cat Alfie crying loudly on the ground below, near the bushes and shrubs. When she went downstairs to let him in, he sprang up on the landing making more noise than a five year old child. She let him into her flat and opened a tin of tuna she found in the cupboard. Cats ran riot in this town, breeding and creating more kittens than there are homes for. Alfie had been a feral stray when Mary took him from Karen, the cat woman, who spent most of her time collecting strays and having them neutered, raising the money in 'Chatterbox,' one of the local 'English' style bars, through raffles and bingo to fund the operations. Alfie was happy with Mary, she spoilt him rotten and he seemed to forget he had once been a Turkish stray. She fed him very well and he didn't need to scavenge in the bins like his cousins.

"Where's your mam pet?" Val asked Alfie, almost absentmindedly expecting a reply.

"That dirty stop-out," Val laughed. They usually have coffee around this time and catch up with any gossip. Especially if they had been out separately, for the evening, which wasn't that often. More normally, they both frequented Adem's bar in one of the alleys near the front. Adem was a charismatic Turkish man, tall and powerfully built. He was gregarious and loud and had the ability to get on with most people, Turkish, English and Irish alike. He also encouraged the students from the University to the bar, making an eclectic mix. He opened the business with very little money and steadily built it up. It was one of the few bars with enough custom to open in the winter months, so courting the students was a sensible strategy. It was similar to most of the bars in the alleys, a stone structure without a proper roof and a walled garden where everyone sat out during the oppressive summer sun and hot evenings. During the winter, a makeshift roof went up and the inside bar came into its own with an open fire. Adem liked to get in local musicians, mainly singing guitarists to liven up the place and give it some atmosphere.

Last night wasn't particularly full when Val arrived. Mary had gone out before her, as she had been taking a phone call from England. When she arrived at Adem's after the usual fifteen minute walk, Mary was in her usual corner with a vodka and coke and Val had chatted to her for a while. Both women were softly spoken and Val loved the Irish lilt in Mary's voice and found it quite relaxing to listen to, particularly when she was telling a story about her life, or someone else's. They had some things in common, Mary was sixty-two and Val a year and a few months younger. They had first met when they were on holiday, some ten years previously. They exchanged pleasantries and chatted with each other and subsequently they met up in Kuşadasi for a few holidays before both took the plunge and moved to the town permanently.

Mary had lived in the flat below for five years and Val had had her flat almost four years. It had been a bargain in Val's eyes when she bought it, but Mary still rented hers from an Irishman who owned a few properties in the area. Mary didn't have the capital to buy a place outright, but her pension and savings and the cheap rent meant she had a decent standard of living. Certainly better than she would have done in Cork, where tourism and the introduction of the Euro have forced up the prices of everything and Mary had found it hard to manage.

Val and Mary still found plenty to talk about despite their long standing friendship. Last night they had discussed the changes in the town, particularly the ones on the front, and how some of the little restaurants they liked had been pulled down due to the council's new regulations. Mary had joked, 'it was getting just like Ireland,' with all the bureaucracy and they both chatted about when they had first discovered the town.

While Val was at the bar she got talking to an interesting Dutchman. Ron was in Kuşadasi on business and it was his first time at Adem's bar. Val left Mary chatting to others in their group and joined Ron at another table. She liked his openness and his smile and a couple of hours later agreed to go for a bite to eat. It wasn't unusual to do this so late in Turkey and Val remembered it would have been around one thirtyish when they left for the restaurant. Val took Ron to one of her favourite haunts, a few alleys away, with an outside garden still full of people eating and drinking. She smiled to herself as she remembered the evening. They had eaten roasted lamb and herbs on skewers with local bread and salad.

She had also introduced Ron to 'Raki' the local spirit, usually drunk with water, but in Val's case she liked a drop of cherry juice. Ron winced a bit at the first mouthful, but soon got used to it, and likened it to a brand of mouthwash sold in Holland. They'd chatted and laughed together quite naturally. Ron walked Val back to her apartment around four and set off for his hotel. She noticed Mary's lights were off. She would have knocked if they'd still been on, but assumed that Mary was back by now and sleeping.

Val slept deeply that night and woke feeling happy. It was a long time since she had such a good evening with a man and it had put a spring in her step. She looked at the clock in the bedroom and saw it was already eleven. Shame on her; she had agreed to meet Ron at one. Val had a shower and dressed quickly. It was still hot, although the season was coming to an end, and she settled for a sleeveless shift dress. After feeding Alfie and wondering where Mary had got to, she set off to meet Ron. Mary was a big girl, she had probably gone back to someone's house and stayed over. She wouldn't put it past her.

Val headed off to meet Ron. After a long walk along the front, she guided him up some steps near the fish market where some local men sat outside on metal seats with some rough looking tables. He looked quizzically at Val, she shook her head and guided him up a flight of steps to the real restaurant. It overlooked the whole harbour, including the cruise liners and the blue Aegean views took his breath away. No tourists, it was full of local people and by the time their order of sardines and calamari arrived, he realised what a find the place was. They enjoyed a leisurely lunch washed down with some Efes, the local beer and they chatted about themselves and their lives. He was good company and when Val looked up at the clock she realised they had been talking for more than three hours.

By the time Val got back to her apartment it was after six. She spotted Alfie before he spotted her and he followed her up the stairs. She gave him her last tin of tuna and vowed to use her spare key to check the apartment if Mary wasn't back by tomorrow.

Meanwhile her mind was on other things as she decided what to wear for an evening with Ron. He was taking her to a restaurant further along the Marina that was quite expensive and upmarket by Turkish standards. They weren't meeting until nine, so she had time for a nap. Val smiled to herself, well she needed one at her age.

4

Dee

D ee was petrified. Not much could frighten her; she was a tough cookie. She had to be; she'd had a childhood that could have been drawn from the pages of a Catherine Cookson novel. Born in South Shields, her own mam Elaine had died giving birth to her. Women did in those days. Even in the early fifties, antenatal care wasn't what it is now and scans were a thing of the future. Deidre had been born in a breech position, the cord wrapped around her neck. It must have been agony for her mother, she was her seventh child. Not a lucky seven for her mother, who died after the botched up caesarean performed by an off-duty doctor, called to the house from the pub and was probably seven sheets to the wind. The bleeding wouldn't stop and Deidre was never to know her mother who had died giving her life.

Photos, tattered around the edges, in black and white showed a handsome woman, dark curly hair, with large dark eyes that seemed to stare into the camera in a knowing way. She looked serious, as she held the hands of her brothers and sisters in their well-tended garden. Clearly her father took the photos, he was rarely in any of the pictures. Their wedding day pictures were an exception with a happy looking couple holding glasses and cutting cake. Her father Jack was tall dark and handsome, at least when he was younger and they looked good together. Seven children in the following ten years, she still looked young and hopeful, with her young family growing, keeping house and her husband happy.

Deidre had been raised by her siblings, her eldest sister Joan had been eleven when she was born. Already used to a bit of mothering, she had taken over the care of little Deidre. Her father had continued to go to work in the solicitors' office, but his grief had been palpable. His Elaine was gone and he was left to support four girls and three boys without the tower of strength he had married. He tried not to blame little Deidre, but he had little to do with her in terms of her day to day care. Joan was supposed to go to school, but after a couple of years of leaving Deidre with a neighbour during the day, she stopped going. She was due to leave when she was fourteen anyway, what difference did a few months matter.

Deidre remembered the Christmases, the birthdays, the family knitting together in a tight pattern, so not to let anything else pull them apart. But Elaine was always missing. Nothing was ever quite right. Jack tried his best, as did Joan who was a little mother to them all. They all made a fuss of little Deidre but they all had their needs as well. Her twin sisters Judith and Jane were very close, and mostly communicated with each other. Her brothers Thomas, Jim and Andrew were hardly in the house, out playing and just being boys. She couldn't describe what was missing. She had never had a mother to know. She loved Joan and felt loved in return, but it couldn't replace the bond she would have had with Elaine and she would cry herself to sleep if she thought about it, too much.

They didn't have a lot of money. Jack provided what he could and they were never starving. It was a grey childhood with few splashes of colour. They couldn't afford holidays apart from the odd week in Whitley Bay in a caravan, but it became too much of a squeeze as they all grew taller. Deidre remembered her father kissing her goodnight, but couldn't recall a cuddle or sitting on his knee. She never felt quite comfortable in his presence, she wanted to please him, but felt that by virtue of her birth, she had ruined his life. Jack in his way tried to be kind, to his youngest daughter and he was a good man at heart. He didn't show his emotions easily; men of his generation didn't show weakness. His mother helped out, but he didn't want to rely on anyone. They were all his children and his responsibility.

Deidre and Joan, in their own way, held the family together. Joan taught Deidre the skills needed to run a home from an early age. She could make cakes and pastry by the time she was six or seven. She could sew and mend the boys' trousers from a similar age. It was an old fashioned life in some ways, even as they moved into the swinging sixties.

Dee tried to speak. Something was over her mouth and face. She hated the sensation. Why couldn't she talk? Panic started to rise in her stomach and it wouldn't subside.

5

Charlie

C harlie still had the headache she'd tried to sleep off. She slowly moved to get out of bed without jolting her head. It didn't feel as if it was actually attached to her body. A combination of champagne, red wine and no food wasn't a good one.

She remembered the argument with Anthony, the empty promises and then the phone call. She hoped they were wrong about Erin, his daughter. Charlie suspected that Alice had a touch of the 'Munchausen by proxy' syndrome. She always seemed to be taking one of the girls to hospital. It was attention seeking of the worst kind, but then Alice was good at it, she had obviously had years of practice.

Still moving very slowly into the living room, she picked up her phone from the coffee table. Anthony had sent a message at just before eight.

'Erin ok, a chest infection, sorry about last night- will see you Monday love u xxxxxx.'

It was now lunchtime Saturday. Charlie had met Alice on two occasions. The first when the Company organised a charity event and she turned up with Anthony and children in tow. Charlie remembered that Ant was pursuing her back then, but she hadn't responded and nothing had yet happened between them. She was interested however, to see what kind of woman he was married to. The way he had previously described Alice hinted that it was almost an arranged marriage. Their parents were close, they had grown up in the same Surrey village on the commuter belt. Charlie was working class through and through and resented the wealth and privilege of the upper middle classes, with their booming voices and sense of superiority and arrogance.

Despite that she had fallen for the charms of Anthony, whose 'mockney' cockney had initially almost fooled her into thinking that he was 'one of us'. He had cleverly played down his education and back ground at first. He was a prize winning chameleon she now realised. He could be anything to anyone and in his line of work this skill served him well. He never seemed to talk down to anyone, even the cleaning staff loved him. Charlie was beginning to realise that she was one in a long line of women who had fallen for his patter and his ability to know what to say and how to say it.

Alice was the horsey type, she associated with the upper classes; all 'Mwah,' 'Mwah,' 'darling,' 'sweetie,' as if she was cast in 'Ab Fab.' She was on the plump side but curvy, with yellowy blond hair, well-scrubbed looking face, not much make up and with an air of self-confidence that Charlie had never felt. Her dress was amazing, probably a vintage Halston, but her shoes were scuffed and her handbag was the wrong colour. She wasn't well groomed despite her horsey air, Charlie thought, somewhat meanly.

Smiling Anthony introduced Charlie to Alice, as 'the Company Finance Director.' "Oh you mean the accountant darling," smirked Alice, surveying Charlie from head to foot very quickly. "You keep trying to make that company of yours sound as if it's a Conglomerate." Her husband winced and Charlie responded in her strongest Geordie accent, the one she tried to tone down since she'd been accused of sounding like Cheryl Cole.

"Hello pet, lovely to meet you, yes I'm just the lowly accountant me, luckily your Anthony's taken me under his wing." She smiled at Anthony, all teeth and hair for that split second as she looked his wife in the eye. She'd learnt from her mother that she was as good as anyone, and her words were effective as she squared up to Mrs Alice Adams.

Alice looked at Charlie again, differently this time and registered the tousled caramel curls, dark brown eyes, the long lashes and the steely expression. She would be one to watch; common just how Anthony liked them. God knows she was well aware of her husband's weakness for the fairer sex, especially the feisty ones.

Alice moved on swiftly, without introducing Erin and Ellie, the two strawberry blond chips from their mother's block. Anthony had the decency to look embarrassed. Despite that he hadn't managed to persuade her to go out with him, she was certainly the current target for his attentions and fantasies; and had been for some time.

Charlie couldn't see how the fabulous looking Anthony had produced such pasty and podgy children. Somehow instead of putting her off the idea of an affair with him, it had the opposite effect. She had seen the way, the other woman had looked at her, initially with indifference then contempt. She felt sorry for Anthony, as well as fancying the pants off him, it was probably what pushed her into the decision she would later regret.

Anthony apologised for his wife, at work the next day. He said that Alice didn't always think before she spoke and could be a 'bit insensitive.' 'He obviously doesn't know women as well as he thinks he does,' thought Charlie smiling to herself. Then decided to accept his invitation to lunch. And so began her downfall into adultery.

She arranged to meet Anthony outside the tube station and casually left the office alone, at twelve. She didn't want her colleagues to know she was going out with the boss. They had seen them flirting for months, but hopefully thought it was just that and wasn't leading anywhere. Charlie had dressed more carefully than usual that morning, wearing a plunge neckline dress that showed off her cleavage. As soon as she'd removed the scarf she'd worn in the office and pinned on a diamante brooch; put on stockings and high, black Jimmy Choo's; she at least felt the part. If she was going to be the mistress of her boss, she would be the best. She had made up her mind that she was going for it. Anthony had made it clear he wanted her and she had no other current love interest. Mind you with the hours she was working she didn't have time to socialise.

He was waiting when she got to the tube. He looked at her appreciatively. He was wearing a charcoal suit and a light blue shirt. She loved a man in a suit. Her father had been a mechanic in a big factory and had always gone to work in overalls. Anthony represented success and her new life. Or so she thought.

She thought they were going into the tube. He looked at her and laughed. He hailed a cab, and took her to the Oxo tower for lunch. The surroundings were opulent and she didn't know if she was comfortable or not. She ate soft-shell crab and lobster risotto and drank a vintage champagne. There were no prices. The conversation was playful and they didn't mention work or his wife. She was smitten. Was it the surroundings, the food, or the gentle seduction? She wasn't sure. Her senses were heightened and when they stumbled out three hours later, slightly heady, she asked him without irony.

"Your place or mine?"

"Better make it yours." He laughed and knew he had landed the prize he had been waiting months for. It hadn't been a waste of time after all.

The next time she saw Anthony's wife, it was totally unexpected. She was shopping in Harvey Nicholls and sitting in the shoe department trying on suede boots. By that time the affair with Ant had progressed and she was still in the throes of lust and the belief she would eventually be the second Mrs Anthony Adams. She had even practised the signature whilst sitting at her desk, preoccupied with their activities of the night before. No one had gone down on her in the way he had, he had spent what seemed like hours pleasuring her. She could think of nothing else. She was literally glowing from the sex, the attention, the excitement. The last person she wanted to see was the first Mrs Adams.

As she sat in the shoe department, she noticed the large blond figure to her left. Then she heard the familiar booming voice ordering the cowed shop assistant to, "get these pumps in a six and a half, in all three colours." Charlie looked around and froze. She knew what she should do; make polite conversation and ask about the children. Chat mindlessly for a few minutes and then make an escape.

She knew what she wanted to do; stand and look her in the eye and say. 'Actually pet, I've been promoted to Finance director because I am fucking your rather tasty, upper-class, wealthy husband at every opportunity and very soon he is going to dump you!'

She did neither. She pulled off the brown suede boot,

slipped on her shoes. Got up and turned away without looking up or back. Ignoring the, "Charlotte, hi. Charlotte? Charlotte, it's Alice Adams…"

And ignoring the woman herself, as if she didn't exist, she strode out of the shoe department into the lift. Alice (I can't believe anyone could ignore me) Adams followed quickly, but the doors closed and Charlie was gone. This episode hadn't gone unannounced. When Anthony got home his wife had complained that the 'stuck up Geordie bitch' must have seen me. He assured her that wouldn't be the case since Charlotte was not without manners.

Charlie wished she had been a fly on the wall for that conversation. She related the tale to one of her closest girlfriends in Newcastle, later that day. The silence on the other end of the phone suggested disapproval? She didn't know or care at that stage. Sophie was just jealous, her loser boyfriend didn't even have a job. She didn't like Sophie's parting words. "Charlie you're changing. Think about what you're doing. Your mam's worried about you too." Charlie hung up with her friend's words ringing in her ears. Her mum was in Turkey doing her own thing, what did she care?

Now, months later, something had changed that made her question her current lifestyle and existence. How had she become so obsessed with Anthony? He wasn't the man for her and she knew it. Her career bored her half to death, even London bored her. She was stuck and didn't believe that she would ever feel like this. She knew that her mother was proud of her achievements. It didn't mean she was happy that she was having a relationship with a married man. Dee had tried to talk her out of it, every time she rang. Charlie frowned to herself. 'Why do mothers always end up being right?'

That reminded her, before she went back to sleep, she had tried to ring her mother for the first time in ages. She picked up her phone and rang her number. As she pressed call, some part of her already knew it would go straight to message. She felt aggrieved despite the fact she had ignored her mother for months. Mothers are just supposed to be there when you want them. Aren't they?

Charlie went out to get some fresh air to clear her head and allow her to think. She looked at her phone's contact list and realised there was no one in London that she really wanted to see. Her crowd of girlfriends were okay for a night out, a few drinks and dinner occasionally, but no one she could have a proper heart to heart with. She guessed that her position at the company and intimate relationship with the boss prevented deeper relationships forming.

She thought of how she was perceived by others. They didn't know the real Charlie. Fun, yes, but ambitious and probably not to be trusted. After all she was sleeping with the boss who was married with two young children.

Her real friends Sophie and Elsie were still in Tyne & Wear. Elsie short (or long) for Lauren Cross (LC), but always Elsie since their school days at Gosforth High. What if she got on a train now? No it was ridiculous. Both girls have partners and other lives. 'I can't just show up on their doorstep.' She dismissed the thought. She would plan a weekend in a few weeks' time and fly up to see them. They needed to re-bond. Especially now, she and Anthony were over.

She realised she didn't want to lose face after all. Admit her life was a bit of a sham and that Ant was a waste of time and space. Could she tell Sophie and Elsie the truth? That London wasn't all it's cracked up to be, the flat is lonely most of the time, and she doesn't know any of her neighbours. Instead waiting around for a married man to call round and treat her like an unpaid whore.

'Am I becoming a caricature of myself?' She didn't know the answer to that question. Her head hurt.

Back to the more immediate question. What to do today? She showered and found a clean pair of jeans. With her hair tied back and wearing a plain black hooded top, she looked nothing like the Company Director she was during the week. Was it a role she played? All suits and sensible shirts with maybe a cheeky pair of Laboutins to liven up the outfit. Charlie had always been the sporty one at school, even a bit geeky with her glasses and long hair parted in the middle. How had she morphed into this boring accountant with the corporate wardrobe? Even though the company was a laid back type of business she still had to look the part. Finance was a serious business. Too serious mostly.

Elsie her friend from Newcastle was the mad one; ripped jeans, bodice tops and full Goth make up. She could be relied upon to cause mayhem. Especially on some of their nights out. She thought about the time they were nearly arrested. Elsie liked a protest march and they had taken on the Police after drinking too much real ale one afternoon. Luckily she didn't wear designer shoes then and they could both run faster than the overweight policeman who they'd been shouting at.

Sophie was more middle ground. First to try the vodka smuggled into the prom night, but sensible enough to make sure everyone got home safely. The three musketeers found enough common ground to become close friends.

Elsie had threatened to move to London and set up her own market stall in Camden, but instead settled for becoming a successful stage manager at the Theatre Royal in Newcastle. She was still wildly avant-garde in her own north eastern kind of way. Her flat was the loudest mixture of colours and styles that could live side by side. Her flamboyant friends dropped by and she seemed to embrace the alternative lifestyle.

Sophie ended up staying in Newcastle after University as well. She became a nurse at the Royal Victoria Infirmary and would regale Elsie and Charlie with tales that were both horrific and funny at the same time. She was now engaged to Raul, an anaesthetist at the hospital.

Charlie finished her accountancy course and a prestigious company in Durham offered her a post. She declined and wanted to spread her wings, to everyone's surprise. She ended up in London working for a well-known, but dull company in the City. After three years she couldn't stand it anymore and went to an agency to find something more exciting. She wondered if there was anything more exciting out there in the world of corporate finance. They lined her up with some interviews and at that time Anthony Adams and Co was a small media company looking for an accountant. She liked the place, the location in the West end, and the people seemed lively and more interesting, Mr Adams in particular. The rest as they say is history.

So why four years later is she looking at the phone book on her mobile and wanting to cry. She longs to be back in Newcastle with her girls. Wine, chocolate and some advice is what she needs. She doesn't cry though. She takes her bag and her keys and walks to the station at Canada Square. She isn't dressed for retail therapy and she heads for her favourite place, the Serpentine in Hyde Park. Swimming costume and a towel in her bag, the weather holds up in a late summer kind of way. It's mid-September, but still warm enough to swim. She is of hard Geordie stock after all. After an hour of strong strokes up and down, she'd blown away the cobwebs of the previous night. Afterwards as she sips coffee in the café, she wonders how it will all turn out.

6

Val

V al started to worry. A small seed of discomfort in the pit of her stomach was turning into a knot of anxiety and it related to Mary. She hadn't been back to her apartment for the last two days. Alfie is going mad and Val makes the decision to enter the sanctuary that is Mary's apartment.

Feeling slightly like an intruder she took the spare key to Mary's flat and ventured down the stairs. Alfie has followed her hoping to find his English cat mother. She opens the heavy metal door and pushes it open. "Mary pet, it's me," she calls out in case Mary has sneaked back and is asleep. The apartment smells a bit musty and she knows Mary is not one to leave any windows open if she goes out despite the weather. She had been burgled once back at home in Cork and was more security conscious than Val.

It doesn't take long to look around. The living room is cluttered with Mary's stuff. 'She's an untidy mare,' thought Val, as she saw the makeup on the coffee table, magazines, ashtray, dirty glasses and the remains of a sandwich on a plate, now covered in ants.

Clothes scattered on the sofa and easy chair. Val knew Mary tended to get ready in the living room, not bedroom, because the light is better for putting on her makeup. Consequently the coffee table doubles as a dressing table. Which is why Val prefers it if Mary comes up to hers for coffee, so that they don't waste time clearing up before they sit down.

Val knew straight away that Mary hadn't been back

since Saturday night and it was now Monday. She felt the tightening in her stomach again, as she looked again at the ants. Something was definitely wrong. Val saw Mary's phone on the sideboard. Val had rang her a couple of times and left a message when Mary hadn't returned, but didn't really expect her to have the phone with her as Mary rarely took it out. She was old school, using the phone to ring family and sending a few texts, but not as the young ones do, texting and Facebooking all the time. She was also worried that if she did take it out, she would leave it in a bar or lose it altogether.

Val picked up the mobile. It was an outdated Nokia and would have been laughed out of town in England. But Mary liked the weight of it and it suited her. Val tried to remember how to operate it, it had been a long time since she had used one like it. She flipped through missed calls and could only see her own number. It seemed as though she was the only one who had missed Mary during the last couple of days. There was a text from a Dolly, one of her Irish relatives, saying she had booked to come out in a couple of weeks' time and would like to meet up with Mary. I shouldn't be reading this thought Val. Mary will wonder what I am doing going through her phone like a suspicious partner.

Val tried not to panic and thought about what to do. She knew a lot of people in Kuşadasi, someone must have seen her. Friendships were strange things out here. It was more casual. You could meet up with someone three nights in a row, have a really good time and then not see them for two or three weeks. People came for weeks on end and then went back to England for a while, or had family over to stay and would go off the radar for a while. People met up at Adem's or other bars knowing that there would usually be someone there to talk to. It wasn't an arranged thing. Unless you were going out for a meal or something special you knew that you wouldn't be alone. It was all quite impromptu out here and Val liked it that way. It also meant that if you didn't feel like going out, you weren't going to let anyone down. Basically, you could do as you please.

It was slightly different with Mary. They were closer and looked out for each other and generally met up every day even for a quick coffee. They had keys to each other's apartments and secrets they had shared over a bottle of wine or two. Where is she?

Val felt a pang of guilt, as she realised she had been pre-occupied with Ron rather than looking out for her friend. She decided to walk down to town and see if anyone else could shed some light on where Mary might be. She knew her friend could be reckless at times she had seen it. The good catholic girl from Cork had shown a different side in this town and she wasn't against a dalliance or two with men a lot younger than herself and at times had her fingers burnt.

Val worried that she might have made another mistake and gone off with someone on Saturday night. Val decided though that she wouldn't have left Alfie, and she would have let her know she was ok.

Where to start looking? That was the question. Val headed for Adem's, the most logical choice since that was where she had seen her last. It was around noon and the bar was deserted. A woman in a headscarf and traditional dress was watering the banana plants and cleaning the tables. Val went into the bar itself and breathed the stale smell of the remains of Raki and beer that had been consumed the night before. It wasn't like the North East of England thought Val, Saturday night didn't mean anything more than Sunday or Wednesday.

There was no weekend as such. Last night, Sunday must have been a heavy one, judging by the state of Adem, sleeping on the padded seating that was fitted around the bar and covered in heavy Turkish brocade fabric. He was snoring gently, grabbing what sleep he could before the next night started again.

She touched his arm gently and he sat up abruptly. The smell in the room changed to the musty odour of an unwashed armpit as he opened his eyes. He saw Val and got up to give her a hug, as was his way. She ignored the smell and hugged him back. "What's up?" Adem said seeing the look of anxiety on her face.

"Adem, I'm probably being stupid, but have you seen Mary? I mean since Saturday night when I was in here?"

He looked puzzled, probably because he had just woken up. "Let me think," he said and went behind the bar and started making some strong Turkish coffee. As he poured the water into the metal unit, he paused.

"I don't think so, she was here till late on Saturday, after you left."

Val pulled a face, "and you haven't seen her since?"

He had to think, sometimes the nights all roll into one, such was his schedule for serving and partying.

"No she wasn't here last night."

"I left around two Adem, with the Dutch guy Ron, you remember?" Val was prompting in case it helped.

"Yes I remember Val, it was a late one. Tarkan turned up and sang for an hour or so, that must have been about three." Val knew Tarkan well, he was the singer in the Cactus bar on the corner in the main town. He liked to come to Adem's to wind down and 'unplug and unwind'. Adem continued, "he stayed and there was a group in the garden maybe nine or ten people. I think

Mary left around four thirty, maybe five? You know I don't watch the clock hunny, I would go mad."

"Did she leave on her own?" Val was surprised. There was always someone to walk back with, well nearly always. This wasn't what she expected to hear.

"I think so. She was a bit drunk maybe." Adem shrugged his shoulders. "I was serving, I remember her paying for her bill, I don't think she was with anyone."

He knew Mary though and remembered a few evenings when she'd left with young waiters after meeting them earlier in the evening. Val knew that he thought Mary could look after herself. Turkish men often perceive the English and Irish women to be strong and independent, such was their lifestyle out there. It was a compliment of a kind, although Val wasn't so sure that Mary fell into that category. She was vulnerable in a different kind of way, but she just didn't show it.

"What should I do Adem?" Her voice faltering. She felt upset and slightly panicked.

"I don't know hunny. Maybe go and see Tarkan at the Cactus later? See if he was paying more attention than me. I was busy you know. She may have gone off with someone he knows."

'Between here and home?' Val thought to herself. 'Hardly likely, but possible, she may have gone on to another bar? There would have been a few still open at that time.'

Adem promised to text, or ring round some of the people who had been in the bar, he knew everyone in the town, if anyone could locate Mary he could. He was texting as she left. He seemed less worried than Val expected. Then why would he worry, this was a safe town. She would turn up sooner or later.

Val went back home and opened the door to Mary's

apartment again. She fed Alfie from the box of food Mary kept on top of the fridge. Her first instinct was to tidy up and clean the place, but something stopped her. She sat on Mary's balcony, in the easy chair she had bought from a second hand shop. 'Stop it,' she said to herself, this is silly, go out and see what is happening. Someone will know something.

She went back to her own place and rang round their mutual friends. No one had seen Mary since Saturday, some hadn't seen her for a few days. No one seemed unduly worried such was the life they led. Val led by a feeling of uneasiness went to see if she could find Tarkan at the Cactus bar.

It was early evening by now and Tarkan was already singing. The cactus was the busiest and the brightest restaurant in Kuşadasi. She didn't often go there to eat. It was a bit expensive for her, but sometimes later in the evening she may stop by for a drink. She loved to hear Tarkan sing, but the over enthusiastic clapping of the waiters and noisy dancing were not for those who like their music soothingly acoustic. The place itself ran as if it were clockwork and was immaculately kept and maintained.

Aimed directly at the town's tourists, the cuisine ranged from Mexican, to Chinese, to Italian, to Indian and finally Turkish. Hotel guests from outside the town came in by taxis paid for by the restaurant. It was a marketing dream Val thought. Posters for the restaurant were everywhere even on the small dolmuş buses that drove around the town. Val wondered if the smaller businesses nearby selling authentic Turkish food lost out because of it.

As she turned the corner, Tarkan was singing Tom Jones version of Delilah and parties of tourists were waving white serviettes around. Val tried not to wince. She brought to mind the set of songs from the early days when she had visited Kuşadasi on holiday. The singer was different, but the songs were the same. She remembered Symmon, the resident entertainer before Tarkan, singing 'Living next door to Alice;' 'Sex Bomb;' and other essential numbers that the audiences never seem to want to change.

Tarkan was a much better singer though and Val didn't like hearing him doing all this corny stuff. She preferred it when he was working in a small but popular bar in the alleys, called East meets West. He sang his own stuff there and the sort of music that Val enjoyed such as Santana, the Doors, Van Morrison and other similar classic artist covers. Val still went into the bar, but the singers didn't quite match Tarkan's standards.

Now he had a fixed smile on his face as the crowd joined in 'Why, why, why Delilah?'

He smiled at Val as she sat down at a table near the stage and ordered a glass of wine. Tarkan liked Val and felt he had known her for many years since his first year as a young singer at East meets West. She waited for him to finish his set and he came over to speak to her. At six foot one, with pale skin and shoulder length dark hair and dark brown eyes he looked more Greek than Turkish. She remembered the shy singer she had first met who wouldn't look at the audience or make eye contact. He now had an air of confidence about him. Young women stood around the stage, giggling and flirting and he always made time for everyone making him a very popular man.

Now nearly thirty he probably knew he wasn't going to be big time. But he was very good and he wasn't arrogant like some become. He didn't go to East meets

West or sing in there anymore. Val knew it was a sore subject with him, but didn't pry. He does still go on to Adem's at least once or twice a week after he finishes at the Cactus, including last Saturday night when Mary was there.

After exchanging kisses and pleasantries the Turkish way, Val cut straight to the chase that was the Geordie way. She asked Tarkan if he had seen Mary leave, or know what might have happened to her on Saturday night. He didn't. He knew Mary of course, everyone did. He had sung a few traditional Irish songs on her birthdays over the years and knew her to talk to. He said he'd said hello to her on Saturday, but didn't have a proper conversation with her. He said he sang from around half past two, for an hour or so in Adem's and had a few Rakis. Afterwards he had a discussion with Symmon, who used to sing at the Cactus before the owner decided he liked the sound of Tarkan better; apparently it got a bit heated. He left shortly afterwards about four with two friends and they went back to his flat. Tarkan said he was sure Mary was still there. Yes he remembered her saying 'good night' to him.

Tarkan was a caring guy and he could see Val was worried. He said that he too would ask around, but had to get back to his set. It was time for 'living next door to Alice,' he said with a sigh.

7

Josie

J osie lay back on her sunbed and lit a cigarette. Exhaling a plume of smoke, she thought to herself I must cut down. The sunbeds were so close to each other, the woman on one side of her started coughing. Josie sat up annoyed. She looked at Ömer lying on the sunbed next to her. He had one of those stupid giant headsets on and his eyes shut, oblivious to her and the rest of the world. He was twenty nine and probably just past his prime. Turkish men age quickly thought Josie. Ömer had been twenty four when they first met. He wasn't tall, around five feet eight, but powerfully built and his dark eyes were his most attractive feature. They had once gazed longingly into Josie's as they danced together in the Orange bar when they first met.

Josie had been on holiday with her sister. She had fallen hard for Ömer's charms. Over the week he relentlessly pursued her and she felt like the most desirable woman in the world. By the time she ended up in his bed she was in love, or so she thought. Everything else was forgotten.

She had never had attention like it in her life. She sat on a stool in the Orange bar where he worked, a dark and atmospheric place. A small intimate bar leading out to a large open dance floor with lighting and cosy corners for couples. Ömer served drinks and kept her supplied with her favourite brandy and lemonade. At every opportunity he brushed her lips with his, squeezed her bottom and whispered in her ear, telling her what he would be doing to her later. The sun and the sex was a heady combination for a woman from Bolton. She was in a constant state of arousal and her breasts would tingle the minute he touched her. She would wait patiently until the bar shut, sometimes at four or five in the morning before they could leave together. He was worth the wait. He had a dingy room a few streets away in a shared house. Lots of the waiters and bar staff lived there, but by the time they got back they saw no one. She would spend the night, what was left of it and go back to her hotel at the following lunchtime. Her thighs and her groin aching from the pounding she had received. She loved it and she felt twenty-five again. He became like a drug. She needed more.

Back at the hotel, her sister Sandra would be waiting, if she hadn't already gone to the beach or the pool. She was angry with Josie and wasn't afraid of saying something. She had met Ömer the first night, but hadn't liked him. She called him 'shifty.' Josie called her a jealous cow. It caused a tension between the two sisters that would never be mended. The holiday had been planned as a getaway. Neither had been to Turkey before and they were looking forward to having some time together. After Ömer, this went out the window and Josie spent the rest of the day sleeping, smoking sunbathing and ignoring her sister.

Until it was time to have a nap, have a shower and get ready for the night. She would spend hours on her hair and makeup, wanting to look her best. She knew she was a lot older than Ömer, but if it didn't worry him, it certainly didn't worry her.

Their mother had died a few weeks earlier and both women had nursed her through the last few months. The cancer finally won and she gave up the fight. Josie was showing her grief in a very different way to her sister. It brought with it a kind of recklessness that she couldn't explain. She would never have behaved like this in the past and Sandra knew they were both missing their mum.

Sandra called Josie selfish, due to her continual absence both emotionally and physically and said she had spoilt her holiday. Josie didn't care. She was dealing with the grief of losing her mum in her own way. All hell broke loose on her return to Lancashire and to her old life working in the local supermarket. And to Barry, her nice but dull husband. She couldn't stand it, couldn't live that life anymore. She missed Ömer like crazy, ringing him at every opportunity and planning her escape. She felt like a caged bird ready to fly the nest. She was soon planning her escape. With or without Sandra's blessing, her mum would want her to be happy. Everyone else thought she was crazy.

She left Barry, her husband of twenty one years, after starting divorce proceedings as soon as she was back. He complied, but with a sense of bewilderment and shock. He thought they were happy. Well most of the time. Like all married couples they had their ups and downs, mainly about money or the lack of it. Being childless had also been an issue. Barry blamed himself, but neither went for tests. Nothing happened and the years passed.

Their small terrace went on the market and was soon snapped up by a young couple eager to start their lives together. Josie and Barry had been that couple once, thought Barry as he showed them round the place.

"Are you going somewhere nice?" Enquired the young woman, politely wondering if they would be stuck in a long chain of sales.

"Back to my mother's." Barry said looking at his feet.

"My wife's moving to Turkey to shack up with a

twenty five year old barman." He spat the words out.

The young woman looked mortified. "I'm so sorry."

"Me too," said Barry with a mournful tone.

So she left. Josie had her inheritance from her mother and her share of the house. Barry didn't contest anything. He still loved her and wanted her to be happy. Josie returned to Kuşadasi and to Ömer. He was overjoyed to see her and she felt she was finally home, back in his arms. "You're my woman Josie," he smiled.

She bought an apartment for them both to live in. It was easier than she thought. Cash is king and the exchange rate was good. Ömer's job at the Orange bar didn't pay much. She felt like a queen. A kindly benevolent queen. They furnished the place lavishly and it was nothing like the home she had left behind.

The apartment overlooking the Marina was perfect. In a fit of generosity, or madness, or both she instructed the Turkish solicitor to put the deeds in both their names. He was her man, she wanted him to be happy. He worked long hours, and was tired a lot of the time. They would be happy in the apartment, big telly, surround system, they could spend time in the huge bed, instead of the smelly single room in Ömer's old place.

It was perfect. Josie couldn't understand why she wasn't happier. The weather was fabulous unlike cold damp Bolton and she didn't have to spend hours on the till at the checkout until her back ached. She didn't have to go round to her mum's every day and look after her. She didn't have to worry about Barry anymore, his back, his feet or his work worries. Ömer didn't say much. His English wasn't as good as she'd first thought, unless he was speaking the language of love. She tried to teach him new words, but he would always revert back to

Turkish especially when he was talking to his friends or family.

Josie applied more lotion to her arms and chest. Her skin felt leathery after too many hours in the sun. She wished her skin had the elasticity it once had when she was young. She gazed at a group of young Turkish girls with some envy. Their slim, toned bodies, brown and taut. Confident as they moved around the beach in their tiny bikinis. Nineteen maybe twenty they had a vibrancy and energy she envied. As they splashed and threw a ball in the water she wished for the umpteenth time she had learnt to swim. Ömer was a powerful swimmer. He loved the beach here. Ladies Beach. What a strange name Josie thought. It wasn't exclusively for ladies at all. Today was the usual sardines in a row, the Irish leaving and the Turkish arriving as the sun started to cool. They may be native, but they don't bake in the midday sun.

Ömer pulled off his headphones and stretched. His body glistened in the sun and Josie thought it was still an object of beauty. They had a good life didn't they? Ömer had given up his job at the Orange bar apart from the weekends when it was busy. It was so he could spend more time with her. She ignored the rumours about other women. She loved him. He was her man.

She saw him looking at the group of girls. Well he can look she thought, who could blame him. She was probably thirty years older than most of them at least. She looked down at her stomach and thighs. At least she hadn't had children. No stretch marks. She thought about the miscarriages in the early years and Barry blinking back tears. It was probably for the best.

Later that evening Josie left Ömer at the Orange bar to walk home. He was making cocktails and flirting madly with a group of Irish girls. Sitting in her usual seat, she saw one of the girls look her up and down. She whispered something to her friend and they both started laughing. It wasn't the first time. She saw a bruise on the girl's neck. Perhaps that was why he had been so late home last night.

She sipped her brandy and it seemed to turn to acid in her mouth. She picked up her keys and cigarettes and put them in her bag. Ömer didn't even notice her leave. As she walked along the alleys towards the seafront, her mind was elsewhere. She thought about what she had just witnessed. Her father's words echoed in her head as a figure moved silently from a side alley behind her. 'There's no fool like an old fool.'

The sound of Santana echoed from the nearby East meets West bar.

'There's a monster, living under your bed. Leave the light on, leave the light on.'

She didn't hear any more than that.

8

Dee

D ee's head also hurts. She can't see a thing and her eyes feel as if they are stuck together. She wonders why she feels so befuddled. Her mind has been going backwards and forward and she wonders if she has been administered some kind of truth drug. Her mind slips back to her childhood and she is back in the kitchen in Heaton, Newcastle.

Her sister Joan is stirring something in the large pan on the stove. Probably soup. It smells good and Deidre is doing her homework on the kitchen table. It's a peaceful scene. Joan is a calm kind of girl who enjoyed baking and feeding people long before 'the Great British Bake-off' made it fashionable. The phone on the sideboard starts ringing and Joan answers it with one hand holding a tea towel and a wooden spoon in the other. Deidre wonders how the brain remembers this stuff. Her sister's face turns white and she drops what she's holding on to the floor. In her head Deidre is re-living the scene and watching as if it were an episode of a soap opera on television. It's a surreal experience and she knows the script, word for word.

"No. You must have made a mistake. No! No, no. What do you mean? No go away leave us alone.'

Joan does not make another sound. Silent screams threaten to fill the air as she opens her mouth, as if to swallow air. Tears are running down her face. Deidre is terrified, she has never seen her sister like this.

Nothing is said for several minutes as the sisters sit at the kitchen table. It's not a companionable silence.

Deidre wants to ask the question, but she doesn't want to know the answer.

"Is it dad?" She finally speaks. Her mouth is sticking together and she can't form the words properly.

Joan looks at her little sister. She is wearing an old school uniform that used to be hers and is too big for her. She looks vulnerable and small sitting behind the big pine kitchen table surrounded by books.

"Yes pet, he collapsed at work today. They think it's a heart attack."

"Is he dead?"

"Yes pet." Joan picks up the wooden spoon and rinses it under the tap. She goes into automatic pilot and starts to stir the soup.

Dee's crying now. She can feel the tears behind whatever is covering her face. All this emotion brought to the forefront. She can feel the tremors running through her body. 'What's happening to her? Where is she?' She still can't see anything. 'Have her eyes been glued? How long has she been here?'

9

Charlie

As the plane's internal lights dimmed for landing, Charlie again wondered what she was doing on a flight to Izmir. The decision, made at the last minute, to take a fortnight off work and book a trip to Turkey had for Charlie been a rash one. She normally planned and organised herself well in advance.

She told Anthony that her mother was ill and she needed to go out to Kuşadasi. He accepted this without question. Well she might be ill, reasoned Charlie. I wouldn't know as she won't answer her bloody phone. Anger and anxiety are not a good mix of emotions and Charlie was used to being in control of her feelings.

The plane's landing was smooth and polished and Charlie was soon reaching for her hand luggage and travel documents. She was used to foreign travel, but mainly the kind of all-inclusive resorts that don't require much effort and mean you could have been staying anywhere; the gated communities being cut off from the country, the culture and the people.

She had never been to Turkey. After her mother moved there more than three years ago, she had promised to visit, mainly when she had been drinking and her mam phoned her. She would agree to come then make excuses. She didn't really know why. Spite? Petulance? Disapproval? Probably all three.

She found her passport and the entry visa she had printed. Ever the accountant she had found a cheap flight and reasonable taxi transfer and hotel. She had been tempted to use the credit card Anthony had given her, but suspected he may have cancelled it, when he realised that they were over. Perhaps she wouldn't be tax deductible any more.

As she stepped off the plane the air was balmy. Turkish time was after midnight, but it felt like a tropical climate after rainy London. It may have been September, but the plane was still quite full of people hoping for a break in the sun or returning to their homes, after visiting England during the hottest months. Dee had said she would do that when she first moved, but apart from the first year she had never come back. Charlie suddenly realised that she may have gone back to Newcastle, but she hadn't told her if she had. Charlie suspected this was mainly to do with her. Some of her mam's friends from Newcastle had flown out to see her and had a whale of a time apparently.

She sat a seat apart from a young Turkish girl on the plane. She didn't speak a word of English and Charlie was grateful for that. She had her own thoughts and didn't want to make polite conversation with a stranger. She was too pre-occupied for that.

She collected her case from the carousel. She now firmly believed it was first on, last off. She had arrived at Gatwick far too early and was one of the first to check in. Once she had made the decision to go, she just wanted to get here. Half of her suitcase was filled with items she had bought at the airport. It was for Charlie quite liberating.

Waiting patiently as all her fellow passengers took their cases and bags, her red spotty suitcase finally made its appearance. A solitary flash of colour on an empty carousel. Charlie lifted it off quickly before it could do another round on its own.

Heading out to the entrance of the airport, she saw a

group of dark skinned men dressed in light shirts and dark trousers. They were holding various names up written on bits of card. She almost laughed aloud at some of the spelling. 'Jeem Brun' she suspected was Jim Brown. She wondered if Mista Cheesi would ever turn up or even recognise his name if he did. She eventually spotted a board with Charley Davison on and guessed this was her man.

She approached him, saying, "I'm Charlie Davison." He looked puzzled and said in heavily accented English. "I thought you were man?"

"No. I am definitely a woman," said Charlie thinking this was going to be a long journey.

"My name is Bora," said her taxi man with a grin, "and I can see that you are most definitely a woman. You book A-B transfer to Kuşadasi. She noticed how he pronounced Kuşadasi more like Cooshadasi.

"Yes that's right. The hotel Güvercin."

"Goovercheen," he pronounced it, still smiling.

"Please come with me," he said as he took charge of her case. The journey was actually only about an hour or so and would have taken in some impressive scenery during the final twenty or so minutes, if it hadn't been so dark. Bora had been chatting, practising his English telling her a bit about the place. Recommending a few restaurants and bars, although Charlie doubted she would remember them in the morning and she was starting to feel really tired.

She did learn that Bora was thirty five despite looking at least ten years older. The thick moustache didn't help, he had a wife and three children and thought the current Government was too right wing and would drive away the tourists with the taxes on alcohol. He was an intelligent man and Charlie wondered how he had ended up driving a taxi. She found herself warming to him despite his constant chatter. Most of what he said didn't necessarily require a response. His bright yellow taxi was clean and she was comfortable enough in the back. He had thoughtfully given her a bottle of water, whilst warning her not to drink the water from the taps under any circumstances.

It wasn't long before they were approaching the built up outskirts of the town. She noticed the landscape changing from agricultural, to views of the bay, then to the neon signs advertising bars and café's on the route into the town. As they finally drove along the seafront, along the coast road she noticed the expensive yachts and boats moored along the Marina, and saw the Kuşadasi Hilton with some surprise. She hadn't realised that there was a Hilton hotel, or she may have stayed there.

She had booked the Güvercin after spotting it on trip advisor. It had good reviews and it was central, right on the sea front and she could get around quite easily from there. She had her mother's address, but she didn't want to turn up at this time of night and after a tiring journey. Dee had said that she lived within walking distance of the town so it couldn't be too far. 'She may even answer her phone tomorrow,' Charlie thought optimistically. She hoped her visit would be a pleasant surprise rather than a shock.

The Güvercin has a glass front with a coffee shop and a bar with a terrace at the entrance. A drink was tempting, but a porter appeared to take her case so she followed him into the hotel foyer. It was a flurry of activity. She said goodbye to Bora who had also followed up the steps with her luggage and he pressed a card into her hand.

"If you need taxi or lift anywhere, let me know please."

"Thank you Bora. I may just do that," she half promised. She took out her purse and gave him a twenty lira note, worrying if it was enough or too much. This was a tip, the trip had been paid for online.

"Thank you Charlie Davison." He looked pleased, so it must be ok.

At the desk a young handsome Turkish man with impeccable English gave her a key and requested her passport to copy. She gave them and was soon being taken up to her room in the lift by the elderly porter who had taken ownership of her two cases. As they reached the third floor, he carried the cases to the door and she opened it with the large key. No key cards she thought, how quaint to get a real key.

She gave the tired looking man a ten lira note and he also looked pleased. She had worked out that it was around three pounds so it seemed fair. She wasn't mean, but she had an accountant's mind and could never quite be frivolous with money in the way her friends could. When she was growing up, money had been tight and now she always saw it as her security. She bought a flat in London as soon as she was able to, mortgaging herself to the hilt and getting a lodger to help pay the bills. 'Canny' her mother called her.

She looked around the Güvercin's room. It was bright and airy with a large king size bed as its focus. It was covered in a brightly coloured throw made of a thick silk-like material, all turquoises and reds with some cushions scattered around that toned in with the throw. It was very... 'Turkish,' she thought. The floor was tiled as was the bathroom and she liked the simple lines.

She could see the balcony, but decided not to open the door until the morning. The traffic in the street below was still quite busy and she was more tired than she realised. The drink at the bar didn't seem such a good idea now either. She hadn't even switched her iPhone back on. That was a first.

She took off her clothes and climbed into bed naked. After she had brushed her teeth and that was it, she was soon in a deep luxuriant sleep.

10

Yucel

Yucel Semir was a happy man. He had the world at his feet, or so he felt. Thirty three years old and he had just been promoted to the Chief of Police. He was a large, heavily built man, whose men nicknamed him 'Yogi.' Cartoon characters are known the world over, so it seemed. He took it well and was a good humoured man for most of the time. He knew that he was blessed to have a good marriage and a five year old son whom he adored. His wife was due to give birth to their second child in less than a months' time and coupled with the recent promotion he felt that life was good.

He had however been slightly irritable over the last couple of months, due to giving up smoking. He had smoked since he was sixteen and had found it more difficult to stop than he had anticipated. He finally felt he was over the worst and had woken up that morning with a smile on his face.

He loved his job, and for the most part liked his colleagues. His small office was cramped, but he spent most of his time out in the larger open plan space where most of the staff had their desks. He was sociable, and didn't pull rank. This made him popular. He could be officious when the situation called for it, but generally he didn't feel the need to pull rank. He himself had worked his way up from the lowest rung to his current position and he knew the job inside out.

He felt that today was going to be a good day. He was due to go to the hospital later with Ayla, his wife, for her check-up. She didn't drive and he liked to feel that he was supporting her. He couldn't possibly have imagined how the day would turn out. Not in his wildest dreams, or even his nightmares.

Despite the town being a busy one, especially through the summer months, it was surprisingly low on crime. A few pickpockets chancing their luck with the tourists were dealt with punitively and it gave out a message to the others. He wasn't exactly overworked, and most of his day was spent doing paperwork of some description.

Motoring offences were common place and the odd fight had to be broken up. Apart from complaints from tourists when they had been ripped off in a leather shop scam. Quoting prices to the customers in Turkish lira and then charging their credit cards with the same total but in Euros. If anyone complained it could be construed as genuine error. In essence though Kuşadasi is a law abiding town.

The local businesses know the rules. No hassling tourists for trade or they would be shut down for a week. They couldn't afford to lose a week's takings, so most respected the laws. Most are honest and like a banter with the tourists. Large numbers of visitors return each year so they must be doing something right.

Yucel made sure there was enough police presence in the town to keep an eye on things and allow people to feel safer. No foot patrols though, mainly cars and sometimes horses! His officers carried guns as did the security guards in the banks. Not taking any chances, it was sometimes a shock to the English and Irish who were not used to seeing weapons.

Some twenty kilometres away, the National park or Milli Park as it is known locally was getting busy. National Parks are scattered all over the country and generally are areas of great natural beauty that Turkey is very proud of and wants to preserve. The park nearest to Kuşadasi, is out on the Davutlar road and popular with the local Turkish families who drive out at weekends and holidays. Unspoilt beaches and picnic areas with only the basic amenities are enough. Large families occupy the tables with their vast picnics of bread, salads, meat, pastries and fruit.

Children play in the sand, the shallow waters stretching out to the sea. Simple pleasures with none of the commercialism of the towns beaches. No shops or restaurants here. Self-catering is the name of the game, but the Turkish are well prepared. No soggy egg and tomato sandwiches for them.

You pass through an entrance with a barrier, buy a ticket for a few lira and stay for the day. The parks close up at eight and everyone goes home.

Milli Park was busy on this September day. Weekends always prove popular and people drive from the surrounding areas for some precious family time. The children wear very little, but a lot of the women are covered in headscarves, trousers and cotton tops as they busy themselves with the picnics, usually sheltered under trees. Couples lay on the wooden sunbeds topping up their tans and heading into the water to cool off.

Kamil was having a very good day. He sat at the wooden table and looked at the spread his wife Almas had provided. Turkish Pide packed with cheese and spicy beef. Sarma, (Vine leaves) with fragrant rice fillings, huge tomatoes, juicy and sweet and some of his favourite aubergine salad. A glass of salty Ayran to wash it down with. He watched his two boys playing in the sand and felt blessed. He didn't get many days off and he appreciated the time with his family immensely.

From the corner of his eye he saw two wild boars. They were huge and they roam the park freely. The boars approached a pit in the earth, usually filled with soil and water. His boys loved watching them have a mud bath. They wouldn't harm you as long as you don't harm them. He shouted to his sons to come and see.

As the boars got closer to their destination in the dirt, he noticed that one of them had something in his mouth. The long snout held a piece of meat maybe? He looked again and sent the boys back to their mother, crying with disappointment. They wanted to watch the boars. He held his breath for a moment as he confirmed to himself what he thought he had seen. The boar had an arm in its mouth, a human arm and hand, still with a silver ring on one of the fingers. Pink varnished nails.

He felt the bile rise from his stomach and retched on to the ground. He couldn't process what he had seen. He told the family to go and get into the car. He barked at them, in stark contrast to his earlier mood. He found his phone in his trouser pocket and dialled…

Yucel took the call personally, directed from one of the female 'communications' staff. It bypassed his colleagues such was the gravity of the information received. This needed to go straight to the top. As he spoke to Kamil, his heart was racing. This must be a mistake. He put the phone down, after telling him to wait for him there and summoned his staff to mobilise them into action. His good mood evaporated, as he rang his wife to tell her to call a taxi to take her to the hospital. He had a feeling he wouldn't be home much in the next few days and cursed under his breath.

11

Charlie

Charlie's day began later than she'd expected it to. She felt as if she had slept for her normal seven hours, but the clock in the hotel room said it was nearly eleven. 'Damn, I've missed breakfast,' was her first thought. She hadn't eaten since the previous lunchtime at the airport and was now starving. She pulled the covers back and got into the shower. It was beautifully tiled Turkish style reminding Charlie where she was and why she was there. She thought of her mother again and wondered if she was mad coming all this way.

She rinsed herself and took one of the large fluffy towels. She pulled on some underwear and one of the shift dresses she had bought in a hurry at the airport. Running a brush through her hair she decided she would be low maintenance for this holiday. She slipped on her flat leather sandals, grabbed her bag and set off to find some breakfast and then hopefully find Dee.

There was a Starbucks near the hotel, but she carried on walking turning up a side street. She found what she had been looking for, a small traditional café with some old men outside playing backgammon. She asked the man behind the counter for a Turkish breakfast, and was happy when a plate of crusty bread, tomatoes, olives, a mild cheese and a hard-boiled egg arrived. The old man looked appreciatively at her in the red sundress. Perhaps she had brightened up his day. Two cups of strong thick dark Turkish coffee later and she was ready to find her mother.

She found a taxi rank and gave the driver the

address. Tütüncüler Sitesi, Charlie couldn't pronounce it but the driver seemed to know where they were going. She remembered her mam telling her about the place, it had been a tobacco plantation originally. She remembered Dee telling her it was two blocks from the main road, so she had been paying attention.

As the car travelled through the town centre and up a hill or at least winding upwards, Charlie realised that her mam had been in Turkey for three years and had a whole new life she knew nothing, or at best, very little about. She recalled the argument that took place after Dee told her about the proposed move to Turkey. Charlie hadn't lived at home since going to University, but she always liked to know she could 'come home' to their terraced house in a friendly street in Gosforth.

She had told Dee she was stupid and selfish. Moving to a foreign land at her age. For God's sake mam you will be telling me you have a bloody Turkish man after you next. Dee blushed a deep red and Charlie stared at her in disgust.

"Oh no mam, don't tell me you have fallen for that! I thought you had some sense. He will take your money and run, you will be in the Sunday papers by next week, I can just see it. Aw I thought he really loved me! I can't believe you woman, you're cracking up or having some kind of mid-life crisis."

Her mother's expression changed. She looked at her daughter and spoke in a voice that Charlie recognised. The one when she was a child and had been really naughty.

"Listen Charlotte Davison and listen well. Yes I am involved with someone. He owns a bar in Kuşadasi. He also owns a bar on the Marina there and doesn't need my money. OK? Not that's it's any of your business. I'm sorry if you don't feel I deserve to be happy or change my life. I've always been there for you and I always will be, wherever I am or wherever you are, but I'm not living my life for you. You're a grown woman now Charlie, not that you're acting like one today."

Charlie stormed out of the house and went round to Elsie's a few streets away, still fuming with her mother. Luckily she was in. As Charlie told her what Dee had said, Elsie looked shocked.

"But Charlie it's her life. You can't expect her to sit in that house waiting for you to visit twice a year can you?"

This wasn't the response she expected from one of her oldest friends. Part of her knew she was being unreasonable, part of her was angry and would stay angry for a long time. She was acting like a child, or at least the child in her was responding to her mother.

As she looked back on those days, she knew she was still punishing Dee. Why couldn't she be like everyone else's mother? Comfortably solid and stable. Not flitting to Turkey on a whim and a promise from a bar owner.

Her mother hadn't mentioned Deniz for a while. Perhaps it was all off. She hadn't asked her mother when she rang. It was all part of her 'I'm not interested in your life' stance.

The taxi turned onto a main road and up a road into the Tütüncüler Sitesi, there was an Iron sign over the road entrance so she knew she was in the right place. It wasn't far from town, though she suspected it would be easier to walk down to town than up to the flat. As they pulled up at the apartment block on the second turning, she asked the driver to wait. She rang the bell to flat six from outside. She waited for a few minutes, but there was no answer. She looked up at the balcony, but the third floor balcony was empty. Some of the other balconies had washing pegged out, so she rang flat 1 on the ground floor. An old woman came out to the front door instead of buzzing her in. Charlie asked her if she could come in to go up to flat six, but the woman stood blocking the doorway of the hall.

She didn't seem to speak any English and Charlie spoke no Turkish. She pointed at the buzzer for flat six, but the old woman shrugged her shoulders. They were getting nowhere. The woman wasn't unpleasant, but not very helpful either. She almost pushed past her and started climbing the stairs. When she had climbed three floors she found number six. All the doors had shoes outside neatly stacked. 'It must be a Muslim thing,' she thought. Her mother's flat had a bright mat outside, but no shoes. She knocked on the large brass knocker for at least five minutes, after ringing a bell that sounded like birds chirping.

Her mother clearly wasn't in, so she returned to the taxi and asked him to take her back to the Güvercin. Things were not going to plan at all.

On the way back down the hill she racked her brains to remember the name of the bar that Deniz owned. She knew it was compass points. North meets South, no East meets West that was it, she would start there. She asked for directions to it from one of the staff at the reception desk. Although she wasn't convinced, she followed them anyway. It was getting to the hottest part of the day and she wished she could slip on a bikini and head for the hotel pool. 'How did people work in this heat?' she wondered, but guessing it would be much hotter in July and August.

She headed along the front towards the Port until she came to a large stone castle-like building, the Caravasi perhaps it meant castle in Turkish. It was huge, and made of ancient stones with a huge courtyard inside. She saw the Port on the opposite side and was distracted when she saw the huge cruise liners that were docked in a line. It was busy and vibrant and she was starting to see what could attract people to this town.

She knew she had to walk down the main street behind the Caravasi and go down the alley opposite a Chinese restaurant. Then follow it down to the bottom and turn left. When she eventually found where it was, half an hour later, she realised she could have just walked along that particular alley from the seafront. It was very confusing and nothing seemed straightforward in this country.

All the cobbled alleys looked the same. Packed closely together these streets were filled with restaurants, bars and T-shirt shops. Ceramics, leather goods, jewellery, you name it and it's here. Handsome and cheeky Turkish men shouting, 'where you from gorgeous,' as she walked past. Strangely she felt much less hassled than when she had been on a long weekend in Morocco. This was much more civilised and less threatening. People sat outside their shops drinking apple tea, smoking and chatting. Charlie was fascinated by the colours, smells and sounds. There were a couple of seedy looking clubs and bars that didn't seem to be open, probably late night haunts she guessed.

She didn't feel uncomfortable or unsafe on her own in a strange country, despite the circumstances. Although it was September and cooling down, it was still hot and sticky and just as she started to despair that she wouldn't find the place there it was 'East meets West.' A big shiny Harley Davison was parked outside the wooden entrance that appeared to be open. She walked in to the empty bar and looked around. A noise came from the bar at the side and a figure popped up nearly scaring the life out of her.

"Can I help you?" He wasn't tall, around five foot nine. He was stocky with powerful arms and chest. His hair was impressive, long black and curly in a ponytail. He half smiled and his brown eyes looked at Charlie quite intensely for a moment.

"I hope so, I am looking for my mother."

12

Val

V al made the decision to report Mary as missing. She didn't know what else to do. She had worried all night and after trailing round just about every place she could think of and she'd run out of ideas. Her Dutch friend had returned home, promising to come back and see her one day and she was now missing Mary, as well as worrying where she was.

She didn't know the procedure and had no experience of the Turkish police. When she had applied for her visa to stay in Turkey she had found the process laborious and the staff officious. She was expecting the same from the Police.

The main Police station occupied a prime position on the front overlooking the sea. It was almost at Bird Island itself a small peninsular that you could walk around and admire the ruins. Still a prime spot and easy to find.

Val's Turkish was limited to the usual hello, goodbye, thank you and a few other phrases needed to get by and at least give the impression she was trying to learn the language. She had been to night school before leaving Newcastle to come here, but left after a few weeks; she found it too difficult. This included the alphabet which was so different. Val had decided she was too old to learn new tricks.

So she was expecting trouble in terms of translation as she went through the main glass doors. She decided that she would ask Tarkan to go with her if it became too problematic.

She was surprised to be ushered in to see the main man, Yucel Semir within minutes. Turkish bureaucracy normally involves lots of ticket taking, form filling and queueing, so this seemed a bit too easy. She remembered queueing for two hours to get her electricity connected, only to be told to go to another desk, with an English speaking assistant.

As she was taken through the main office to the smaller room that was the Chief's office, he came out to meet her holding out his hand in welcome. He was a huge man, not fat just large with big shoulders and hands. Val was pleasantly surprised. In the back of her mind there was a scene from a film where the Police chief, bald and sweaty, bites off someone's ear. At least she thought that was what happened.

Yucel ushered her into the room and she sat down on a green leather chair. She told him what she had told the desk staff when she came in. That her neighbour Mary O'Donnell didn't return from a night out three days ago and hadn't been seen since.

His English wasn't bad and she answered most of his questions without any problems. He was painstakingly writing everything down on a large pad with a fountain pen. She expected him to be filling out a missing person's form or something similar. Why was she being seen by the Chief of Police himself, she didn't think Mary's disappearance would be seen as important. Then again there wasn't a great deal of crime in Kuşadası as far as she was aware.

"So you are very worried about your friend Mary?"

"Yes," said Val, "very worried, she doesn't stay away this long, ever."

"So no-one has seen her at all since she left Adem's bar on Saturday night, that is correct?"

"Yes, that's about it."

As she gave Mary's details to Yucel, he was himself very concerned. His team had just cordoned off the entrance to the Milli Park near Davutlar where they had discovered the remains of a woman, probably in her sixties. The news hadn't gone to the press yet. This was important, the body had not yet been identified

Yucel asked Val, a seemingly random question.

"Did your friend Mary wear a silver ring with a turquoise stone?"

Val wasn't stupid. She recognised the question was in the past tense. Was it deliberate or was his English not as good as she first thought.

"No," said Val, "not as far as I can recall. She had arthritis in her hand; she couldn't get a ring on when they were swollen." She tried to remember Mary's jewellery box, but her mind was racing.

Yucel left the room momentarily to make a phone call to Seb his deputy and second in command, to tell him about Mary.

"Keep searching the area, I need you to find the rest of the body. We've got a missing woman out there somewhere and her friend doesn't think the arm you've got is her friend's."

"No I haven't told her yet."

"Seb, you have much to learn my friend. Because it isn't fair to tell her that all we have of her close friend is a limb... And it doesn't look too good on us, so get out of your vehicle and start digging!"

He prayed silently that this was not the case. Perhaps Mary was with a man, stayed away for other reasons. It was possible.

He went back into his office to face Val. His eyes looked tired and drawn and he seemed lost for words. He didn't have a lot of respect for some of the women who settled in his town. Scantily dressed, drinking too much and acting like teenagers, but he liked this woman. She was down to earth and obviously cared about her friend Mary. He wished he could re-assure her. He noticed Val had worn a long sleeved T-shirt and jeans for this meeting and in English terms this was respectful. Her long fair hair was tied back and although he knew her age from the paperwork, she didn't look it. She drank the tea he had given her and looked him straight in the eye. This reminded him of his mother who was a force to be reckoned with.

He sighed very loudly. "I will phone you as soon as I hear anything. But please let me know immediately if she comes back."

Val moved to stand up and something stopped her.

"Why did you ask me about the ring? Has it got anything to do with Mary?"

He handed her a card with his personal phone number on it.

"I don't want to alarm you unnecessarily, but we've found the ring in Milli Park in a strange place."

Val put his card in her bag. "Oh, okay. She wouldn't go there. Mary doesn't swim. And isn't it a family place?"

He saw the glint of tears in her eyes as she got up to go, but could offer no words of comfort. "Yes. It is a family place." He hid what he was thinking.

Yucel made his way to the crime scene with his most senior female officer, Lale. He wasn't looking forward to this, but knew what had to be done. His men were already searching the area and the park had been evacuated. That in itself would cause some kind of talk in the town. They could offer no reasons without alarming the public.

The National Park was quiet. More quiet than he had ever known it to be. It was almost eerie as the sun started to set. He had forty men out there looking for the person whose arm had been found in the mouth of the boar. The park was large he guessed almost seventy acres and the force didn't have all the appropriate lighting for a night search. They would look until the sun went down then stay in situ until it was light again. No one would be able to get in or out. It would be a long night.

13

Dee

D ee felt as though she was in a dream that she couldn't wake from. Or was it a nightmare. She had no sense of time. When you are sleeping, dreaming, having nightmares, it could be five minutes, fifteen minutes or any time really. Was she slipping out of unconsciousness or simply waking from a stupor. She couldn't tell. She was being given some water, was it through a straw. Her lips felt parched again and she found herself drifting off.

She was remembering the funeral. Her father Jack's funeral. He was a popular man, there were a lot of people there and she didn't recognise a lot of them. He had a lot of friends from work, from the club, from the church that's why it felt as if he was never at home, thought Deidre then felt mean. The coffin's wreathes spelled out DAD, just as they had spelt out MAM some seventeen years before. Much had changed since then. The twins had left for teacher training college, two of the boys had joined the Army. Her brother Terry had taken up an apprenticeship at the Shipyard.

Only Joan seemed to stay the same. She was the true definition of a rock. She had soon composed herself after hearing the news about her father. Her priority was the family and she rounded up the lot of them very quickly to tell them the sad news. They had all come home and the house was temporarily filled with the sound of family, a bit of laughter and yes, a lot of tears.

After the service, Jack was laid to rest. The wake was held at the family home in Heaton. Deidre helped Joan with food and drinks and generally kept out of the way. She wasn't socially confident in any sense. Going to an all-girls school didn't help and she felt shy around strangers. Her grandmother's voice could be heard above everyone else's and she started to fear she would have to go and live with her. Joan was having none of it and told her grandmother that things would be staying the same. The others stayed out of it, they had their own lives and Deidre thanked God for Joan, once again.

Terry called her over to him. He was perched on the end of the arm of the chair her father normally sat in. In the chair sat a young man with a shock of black hair and a twinkle in his eye, despite the solemnity of the occasion. He smiled at her and offered his condolences.

"This is Paul Davison, Deidre, he's the union rep at the Yard." His bright blue eyes gazed into hers. She immediately looked down. "He might have a job for you sis."

She was interested now. She needed work especially now, with Jack gone. She had been doing a secretarial course after finishing school. She knew she was no academic. But she wasn't thick.

"Will you come and see me next week Deidre? Say Tuesday?" His voice was deep and had a resonant tone. She was surprised. He must be older than he looks. He handed her a card with his name and office address printed on. 'Fancy,' she thought. 'He must be important'. She smiled warmly at him. "I'll be there."

She got the job. She started in the offices of the Shipyard, first as a filing clerk in the Union office then moving up to a secretarial post. She was quick and smart and started to see life in a different way. She learned fast and was soon regaling Joan with tales from the office, gossip and such.

Joan watched her bloom and smiled at her little sister with pride. Joan had no interest in going out into the world herself. She liked the sanctuary of her home and was a little scared of the real world. She was born out of her time. It was the seventies and she was still acting like a post-war housewife. But it suited the family. She made the house a home.

Deidre found herself thinking about her sister. It seemed like such a long time ago. So much tragedy in one family. It was almost too much to bear. Joan her beautiful sister was not even thirty years old when she died. Ironically, knocked down outside the house on her way to the local shop. One of the new fast cars driven by a young man who hadn't even passed his test. She hadn't seen him coming. He hadn't seen her until she bounced off the bonnet.

Paul Davison brought her home from work after she was given the news. Terry was on holiday with his girlfriend and was going to fly back from Spain. She opened the front door of the terraced house and had to stop herself from shouting for Joan. She collapsed into Paul's arms and that was it. He didn't want to let her go. She was like a small damaged bird. He held her for the longest time. She felt safe. He had waited for this moment, not daring to approach her at the office. Tragedy had brought them together. Nothing would tear them apart.

Dee's mind was wandering again. She wondered if she was already dead. Perhaps she was having these flashbacks on the way to the light. She'd read about the 'light.' She felt she was watching a film. She could sense danger though. It was an instinct she had always had. Flashing lights above her head. A man's face peered down at her, she could smell his breath. Then darkness.

14

Charlie

C harlie looked around East Meets West. It was cosy, with the usual tapestry seating and stone floor. It had some charm with album covers and memorabilia on the walls. There were some guitars and equipment in the corner where the live entertainment must take place. It wasn't exactly Stringfellow's and she wondered how wealthy its owner actually was. She had wondered about Deniz and her mother; was he after her for her money. She looked at the man in front of her. He was smaller than she imagined and looked as if he'd got out of bed on the wrong side that morning.

"Are you Deniz?" Charlie asked Mr Ponytail.

"Yes. Who are you? How can I help you?" That was his attempt at politeness, she guessed.

"My name is Charlie Davison, I understand you know my mother, Dee Davison I think she is your girlfriend?"

"You are Charlotte?" He used her full name, how strange.

"Yes I've come to see my mam. Do you know where she is?"

"This is first time you come yes?" He almost scowled.

What did he know about their relationship? What had her mother said to Mr Ponytail about her she wondered?

"I've been to her flat. She isn't there. I've been phoning from England and getting no reply. I was worried about her."

He almost snorted at this comment and gave an

unpleasant smile.

"That's strange Charlotte, she always says the same about you. She rings you but you don't pick up."

"Where is she Deniz?" Charlie was starting to feel angry that a stranger was making comments about her. He didn't know her for God's sake.

He laughed.

"She has gone back to England Charlie. For a holiday. Yes, she said she would be gone for three to four weeks, that was it."

"Have you heard from her?" Charlie's frustrated tone was almost aggressive.

"Yes of course," he replied.

"When?" Charlie was persistent.

"She called me a few days ago. She said she was having a good time. Said she would be back in a couple of weeks."

"Have you heard anything since?"

"No but she did tell me that her phone had a problem with it, so I didn't worry too much."

"Whereabouts in England has she gone?" Charlie now scowling.

"I don't know. London maybe or Newcastle?"

"You two are close then?" Charlie offered sarcastically.

"Yes," he said, "but we don't live in each other's pockets as you say. I just wished her a good holiday and I know we will see each other in October when the bar closes. We plan a trip to Istanbul."

Charlie couldn't understand what her mother was playing at. Why wouldn't she say if she was coming to England? How ironic?

"Do you live with her Deniz?" She didn't even know the answer to that question. She ought to know.

"No. We don't live together, but we spend lots of time together. I am feeding her bird Oscar while she is away."

"Oscar, oh yes," lied Charlie. "She told me about him."

"Has she not told you she is coming to England?" Deniz was looking at the young woman, puzzling that she looked nothing like Dee.

"Perhaps she wanted to surprise me, just like I was going to surprise her."

"Sit down and have a drink." Deniz moved behind the bar. This all seemed odd to him too.

He poured her a glass of wine. As she sipped it she winced. Turkey wasn't known for its wine and this was a particular vintage called 'vinegar.' They talked about Dee. Charlie found out they had been in a relationship for the last three years. He said they were happy. Dee didn't want another husband though. She liked her own space. Charlie smiled at this. This was sounding more like her mother. As they chatted she had an idea.

"Deniz can I borrow the keys to her apartment? I want to see if she has left any travel stuff to let me know where she will be. Perhaps I can find her. If her phone has played up she may have lost my contact numbers."

She didn't say that Dee was more than capable of phoning her work or turning up there or in fact going to her flat.

Deniz thought it sounded a reasonable request. She was Dee's daughter. 'What harm could it do?'

"I will take you." He nodded at the bike.

Charlie smiled. 'Well it would be quick anyway and she would get to see Oscar.'

"Let's go," she said, swigging back the last of the wine.

"Deniz, what does my mother drink here?"

He looked bemused. "Vodka, soda. Why?" Charlie knew her mother's favourite glass was white wine. Even she couldn't drink the stuff here.

"No reason, just curious."

He handed her a helmet and they set off down the alley.

They pulled up at the now familiar block of flats. Charlie didn't need to ring the doorbell this time. She watched as Deniz opened the front lock and followed him up the stairs. As he let them in to the hallway through the heavy metal door she heard some loud chirping she guessed was Oscar.

The flat was larger than she imagined. A wide hallway with an impressive Turkish rug runner on the floor she realised Dee had embraced the Turkish lifestyle wholeheartedly. There was nothing here to remind her of the terraced home in Gosforth, Newcastle. A large galley kitchen was painted in shades of cream and yellow and the sun caught the colours of the floor length curtains in shades of gold, blue and yellow. Her mother had good taste and the place managed to look stylish and cosy at the same time. Wooden kitchen units were painted cream and there were various Turkish ceramic pots and containers in all colours, giving the authentic appearance of the east. She noticed a massive spice wheel on the wall; she had seen some like it in the market she'd passed earlier. Dee had her home comforts as well, a huge fridge stood in the corner with photos all over the door attached by various magnets.

She noticed the first picture of herself and Dee taken just before she went to university. They had been to Jesmond Dene for the day and the autumn colours of the trees could just be seen behind the two of them laughing together. Wearing woollen hats and scarfs they had their arms around each other and Charlie fought back a tear. She remembered the day well. They had been to the craft stalls around the dene, drinking hot chocolate and eating sugary doughnuts. Dee had bought her some Indian notebooks and candles for her room and they walked around the markets with their arms around each other.

'Oh mam,' thought Charlie. 'What went wrong? We were so close.'

Other pictures included Dee and Deniz at various sunny looking locations in the area. Grinning and smiling at the camera, Dee looked as if she was enjoying her new life. Her eye caught a black and white snap in the corner. It was a photo booth picture. Four in one, the old style from the cubicles that used to be everywhere before everyone had a camera on their phone. Her mam and dad looking about twenty and blowing kisses at the camera and then each other. She had forgotten how good looking her dad had been when he was young. Jet black hair and perfect features gazing at the woman he adored. Why had she chosen this photo to put on the fridge? She had hundreds of photos of them, including the wedding album. Why this one? It was a small token of a previous life. One that Dee had left behind.

Her thoughts were interrupted by the noise from the corner of the room. There was a large enamel bird cage with an ornate pattern sitting on the bench. A yellow and green parrot, quite small with beady black eyes watched them both suspiciously whilst managing to squawk at the same time. He hopped around from perch to perch clearly glad to have some company.

"Mammy's home. Mammy's home," he squawked. "Hello pet. Hello pet…" It was so strange hearing him speak he had clearly picked up some of Dee's Geordie tones.

"Hello pet," replied Charlie, not quite knowing what to say to a demented Turkish parrot.

"Mehaba. Mehaba," he squawked again and Deniz grinned.

He fed the bird and Charlie let herself out of the kitchen door onto the large balcony outside. It was the size of their kitchen in a previous life and decorated in Dee style. There was a wooden table and chairs and a kind of love seat under a canopy probably with room for two. It was painted in a pale shade of blue with a beautiful tiled floor. Various wall ceramics decorated the back wall and Charlie could imagine her mother sitting out here with her coffee in the morning talking to Oscar.

She re-entered through another set of double doors leading off the balcony to the lounge. It was spacious with a large corner sofa and various Turkish throws and rugs. Candles and books were visible on the large dark wood coffee table and she recognised her mother's touch. The room had a large dining table and chairs in the other corner and she could imagine her mother socialising here. Making food and feeding people was one of her favourite things to do. She had spotted a wine rack in the kitchen with some decent looking labels on the bottles, not the vinegar that Deniz served up at East meets West.

Dee had clearly tidied up before she left. There was no mess and no papers anywhere giving a clue to her whereabouts. She noticed a large brass chest near the flat screen TV. It was locked and Charlie guessed some of her mam's personal stuff would be in there.

Large prints adorned the walls, some looked as if they were originals, a bit abstract for Charlie's liking, but striking and gave the place a modern individual look.

Deniz walked into the lounge and saw Charlie looking at the art work.

He smiled. "All her work," he remarked, as if Charlie knew her mother was a secret artist.

What else would she find out about her mother?

"I like them. Does she paint them here?"

"Yes," said Deniz, "she has a studio in one of the bedrooms, did you know she painted Charlie?"

His question was so direct that she couldn't lie. "Not really," she said. "I knew she did some classes in Newcastle, but I didn't know it had become a hobby."

"It's more than a hobby..." Deniz paused. "She sells to a gallery on the Marina. She has done well there, they love her work."

Another surprise. Charlie found herself feeling slightly ashamed that she knew so little about her mother's life here. She had always been 'crafty' in the early days, but that was more to make ends meet. She would make patchwork bedspreads and curtains for her daughter, long before they were actually fashionable. Charlie had been embarrassed as a young teenager when minimalist décor was all the range, but looking back her mother's work had been pretty amazing. She had been taught to sew by her sister Joan who died before Charlie was born and it all seemed to be quite old fashioned to someone who'd prefer to go to Ikea.

Guessing he spent quite a bit of time in her mother's flat she asked. "Where would she keep her paperwork and stuff Deniz?"

"In the bedroom probably. She isn't that organised, but she has a little cabinet in the spare bedroom. Charlie followed him back into the hallway through the connecting lounge door. The hall turned a corner and there were five more doors leading off the corridor. The

85

bathroom door was open and she could see a washing machine in there. She looked puzzled. "A washing machine. In the bathroom?"

"Yes. Of course. We haven't bashed clothes on rocks for a few years now…"

"No, I only meant… Never mind pet, it'll take too long to explain."

The shower and toilet looked quite new and a unit held a sink and a cupboard unit underneath. It was all spotless. That was Dee's way. She loved cleaning and found it therapeutic. Unlike her daughter who had a cleaner come in twice a week to sort out her Docklands apartment.

She found the spare bedroom, which was a good size, painted in pale green, a double bed, chest of drawers and wardrobe all in dark wood furnished the room and she saw the large blue patchwork quilt, that had been on her bed at home, covering the duvet and pillows. My room? She wondered. Perhaps her mam had always hoped she would come after all. The small bedside table had her old lamp from home on it too, whatever had possessed her to bring that she wondered. Given the luggage allowance, it must have meant something to her. Pale blinds were drawn and the wooden floors gleamed. Charlie liked the room.

Dee's room was twice the size and a large brass bed dominated it. She had continued the dark wood theme. The walls were painted turquoise, giving it an eastern exotic look. Huge silk cushions covered the bed and there was a chaise lounge in the corner. French doors led to a smaller balcony with a small cream ornate table and two chairs just about fitting. More of her mam's artwork could be seen on the walls here, a huge byzantine style painting incorporating gold and silver threads, again in an abstract pattern. Dee liked the painter Klimt and there were touches of his style in this painting, thought Charlie.

It was also very tidy. Her bedside table held some books and a few letters. They seemed to be friends from home and Charlie did not like to read them. It wasn't as if her mother was a missing person. The second drawer held some paperwork in a plastic folder. It seemed to be household stuff, bills for electricity and water and some bank books. Nothing of any significance. She turned to Deniz.

"Anywhere else you can think of?"

He went to look in the spare room, but whatever he expected to find there was missing or maybe moved.

"It looks as if she has had a clear out," he said. "There was a wicker basket in there with some travel brochures and stuff, but the drawers are empty now."

Charlie was puzzled. She opened her mother's brocade jewellery box, one she recognised from home. Dee didn't have much jewellery, but she liked silver bracelets and necklaces with semi-precious stones. Nothing valuable most had sentimental value. Turquoise and Emerald stones set in silver made up most of the collection, with some earrings hanging on a brass butterfly ornament. She found a brass key in the box and without knowing why, held it in her palm as she looked through the other drawers.

A plan was forming in her head. She turned around and spoke to Deniz who was sitting on the bed, probably wondering what they were doing there.

"Deniz? I know this sounds crazy, but can I stay here for a few days. I feel closer to my mother here and I am sure she will be back soon. I can look after Oscar and water the plants. I know she would want me to stay here. I can ring round all the Newcastle relatives and friends and find out where she has gone.

Deniz could see some logic in the idea. He was busy at the bars, including his new and bigger place on the Marina and he could do without the parrot duties. Dee wouldn't mind and when she did get hold of him he could tell her that Charlie was here. It would be a nice surprise. She talked about her daughter a lot and he couldn't understand why the girl had never come to Kuşadasi. He knew it had hurt Dee, although she said very little about her feelings in connection with Charlie. She was loyal. That was one of her best qualities.

"Okay Charlie. If that's what you want. There's a spare set of keys hanging in the cupboard in the hallway." He went to get them. "I'll drop you back at your hotel on the bike for now, yes?"

"That would be great thank you, I will come to the bar later and see if anyone else knows her movements. Does she have many friends here?"

"Yes, she does. There are quite a few English women here, but I can't see that they would know anything more than I do." Deniz was scowling again. She had hurt his male pride.

"Look," she said, playing along. "You know how women talk to each other. Men are not always interested in the details are they?" She smiled.

"I am more interested in when she is coming home." He was a man of few words.

15

Yucel

Yucel was in the dog house. It wasn't a Turkish expression, but the sentiment was the same. He hadn't been home and a terse phone call between him and his wife suggested that despite the enormity of what he was facing at work, it didn't equate to her anger at him missing the ante-natal appointment and failing to turn up for dinner.

He hadn't said too much about the case. He didn't want to frighten her at this stage and he had to keep things quiet for as long as he could. He guessed it wouldn't be long before the press found out about the body and journalists arrive from as far as Ankara.

In the early hours of the morning as it was getting light, his men went back out to search the park. They started around the entrance and the first beach in the park where the arm had been found. At ten to eight they had found a shallow grave behind a group of trees and the body of a woman probably in her late fifties. The grave hadn't been disturbed by the Boars and the corpse was intact.

Yucel's heart sank when he heard the news. He'd hoped the murder was a one off. Maybe a fight between a couple that had gone too far, and the killer had panicked and come to the park hoping to bury the woman where she would not be found. This corpse, now very dead, was wearing a stretchy dress in an animal print. Her bleached blond hair was shoulder length and she had some deep lines in her face. Make up smeared and looking as if she had struggled. There were no obvious bruises on her face, but around her neck, there were deep grooves where she had been strangled. He didn't need to wait for the autopsy to know this was how she had died. Her tights were ripped around the gusset and he guessed she had been raped or sexually assaulted as well. He felt sick. This woman was not much younger than his mother and could even be a grandmother.

His heavy heart told him that it was Mary O'Donnell. Val's description of her, and her clothes were close enough to match this woman and he saw the knobbled hands and fingers where arthritis had set in. Her hands were tied together with what appeared to be thick rope. As he looked closer, not wanting to disturb the body before the forensic team started work, he could see that the rope was attached to a round ceramic object around seven centimetres in diameter and decorated in yellow and two shades of blue. He recognised it immediately as the Turkish Eye, a symbol of luck and prosperity seen around the town in many forms. Usually given when someone moves house to bring good fortune. The streets of Kuşadasi had the eyes embedded into the stone work of the streets and cobbles. It was a cheap ornament that could be purchased in any of the gift shops in town. Had the killer just picked one up to use as a weapon or was it something more sinister, like a calling card?

It had been a long night and it was going to be a long day. He phoned the number Val had given him and asked her to meet him at the Police station that afternoon. The body should have been examined by then, but at least there could be an identification before the full autopsy. Not that it would be the end of it. There was still an arm to account for.

He ordered his men to continue the search as the

body was wrapped in plastic and removed from the crime scene. He wanted a cigarette. And wanted it all to go away.

16

Val

V al hadn't slept well at all. Tossing and turning she had gone over the events of the day in her mind. She had spent the evening in town, hoping to find someone who may have seen Mary. She had a list in her head of people who she hadn't seen since Saturday and who may be out in town this evening. She had gone back to Adem's bar and spoken to the bar staff who hadn't been at work when she went there during the day.

The two barman who were regulars, Erol and Gül, knew about Mary's disappearance. Adem had told them. Both were upset and worried about their regular customer. Gül whose real name was Gülbahar had known Mary the longest, since he had been a waiter at a large bar called the Drop in. Mary used to go there frequently before the owners sold up and it became a T-shirt shop.

Val suspected they'd had a fling at some point, although Mary hadn't confirmed or denied it. She had been coming to Kuşadasi for a number of years before she moved here permanently and Val didn't know everything about her.

Erol said that he had tried to persuade Mary to stay and have another drink on Saturday night. She had declined and he thought she had probably had enough anyway. She was slurring a bit and repeating herself, he remembered. He had also asked her earlier on in the evening if she wanted some food, but she said she didn't. Val remembered she had seen a half-eaten sandwich in her flat, so she probably drank on virtually an empty stomach. The lads were good here, Adem often sent out for kebabs and food and shared it amongst his customers. It soaked up the drink and people were often hungry as the night went on. Three or four am, was the norm so it was nearly breakfast time for some, by the time they left.

Gül remembered Mary talking about Tarkan and enjoying his set of music. She liked it when he played some Irish music as he had on Saturday. It reminded her of home, he said and she said she was missing some of her family. Val thought to herself, that drink and music from the old country wasn't necessarily a good mix. She had seen Mary get quite maudlin before. She was normally an upbeat person but alcohol is a depressant at the best of times if you're not feeling very happy to start with.

Both confirmed the time she left, and remembered that most of the regular customers had gone by then. Tarkan had an argument with Symmon, another singer although he didn't know what it was about. Symmon had stormed off, and Tarkan had taken some of his friends back to his flat in town. He remembered that some of the others had gone on to East meets West for more drinks and live music. Billy held Val's hand for a second and said he hoped Mary would turn up soon.

Val was feeling jaded. The worry was taking its toll on her and she was still spooked by her visit to the Police. She felt sure that Chief Yucel knew something that he wasn't telling her at this stage. She decided to go to East meets West on her way home and check out any news they might have there and see the boss Deniz. She knew him quite well and had been going there for many years herself. She remembered when she first went to the bar on holiday with her girlfriends. They had been entranced by the young singer Tarkan and the atmosphere in the small, loud, smoky bar was electric.

Deniz had done well for himself since then; his empire grew. She knew he had other businesses now. A bar down in the Marina, that was much more upmarket than East meets West, but not as vibrant. He also owned a beach bar down on the front, but Val had never been in. She didn't fancy prancing around in a swimsuit in front of all the staff. Her posing days were over she thought to herself.

She entered the busy bar and wondered if she had made a mistake. There wasn't a seat in the house. She pulled up a bar stool next to an attractive young woman of thirty, maybe. She smiled and Val smiled back. She looked radiant in a silver top and jeans and Val wondered if she knew her from somewhere?

17

Charlie

Charlie decided to spend one more night at the Güvercin and pack up and take a taxi to her mother's flat the following day. She would go into town, get some dinner and then later go into East meets West and try and locate some of her mother's friends. She alternated between feeling anxious about Dee, then angry that she probably had sloped off to the UK without even telling her.

When she got back to her hotel room she checked her mobile. There was fifteen missed calls from Ant on it and some seriously cheesy messages. 'What an idiot,' she thought. Does he seriously think I'll change my mind? On her departure he seemed to think a break in the sun with her 'sick' mother would sort her out. 'Men!' She rolled her eyes and wondered why she'd ever gone there. It was a mistake she wouldn't make in the future. Charlie was enjoying making him sweat and wondered what that made her.

Visiting Dee's flat had brought back some memories and she found her mind wandering to happier times. When she and her mother were a team. As a child she worshipped her parents. Her tall good looking dad, who always had time for his little girl. He changed his job to work at a large car factory in the Union offices and he was quite a militant in his own way. A socialist through and through, he would have been outraged at Charlie's opulent lifestyle and capitalist ways.

She remembered waiting for her father to come home from work. She would hear the gate at the front of the house and run down the stairs to greet him as he scooped her up in his arms. He could have gone to work in a suit, but he chose not to, preferring to dress like one of the workers with whom he spent most of his time. On the factory floor sorting out disputes and problems, proving to be a diplomat as well as spirited. They didn't have a lot of money but Charlie didn't go without. He provided for the three of them and the house was always warm and cosy.

Her mother worked part time in the local florist. It fitted in well with the school run, so Charlie was never a latch key kid. Her mother took her to school and picked her up. Deidre enjoyed working a few hours a day, but the time when Charlie came home from school was their time together. She would cook or bake in the small kitchen and Charlie would sit on the worktop and chat. Her mother tried to teach her to bake, but Charlie was more interested in licking out the bowl. She loved her mother's cakes though and when her school friends came round they were impressed too.

Most mothers worked by then and Charlie was unusual in that her mother was always home. She had negotiated the school holidays off from work and they enjoyed the days together, travelling on the metro to Whitley Bay or Tynemouth, for a walk along the beach and fish and chips afterwards.

When her dad took his annual holiday they would travel around Britain in the Camper Van that her dad had brought second hand and fixed up. Her mother had made the interior look fabulous in a sixties kind of way, long before retro was fashionable. They loved camping and travelled to Whitby, Scotland, even down to Cornwall. It was always an adventure and her dad would encourage her to try new activities and even new types of food. Charlie felt a lump forming in her throat as the memories came flooding back. Her mother had seemed to be so straightforward then. Simple needs and desires, a proper mam. Why do things have to change?

Charlie didn't spend much time thinking about the past generally. She was too focussed on the future or at least the present. She kept busy and with work, commuting, social life and Anthony she had little time to spend thinking about painful or even joyful memories. She was starting to realise that this needed to change, as she got into the shower. This break had made her think about her life, as well as her mother's and she wanted to make things better. But first she needed to locate her mother.

She tried to decide what to wear from her limited holiday wardrobe. Although she had taken two weeks off from work, she hadn't necessarily planned on spending the full fortnight here. In the back of her mind she thought she would find Dee, spend a few days then maybe travel to Istanbul and see some of the sights. Be adventurous and forget all about Anthony. It hadn't quite worked out that way and she realised that she may need to go clothes shopping.

She then remembered she was going to her mother's flat. Of course she could do some washing and iron her clothes. She hoped that her mother would surface soon, it would be seriously weird sleeping in her flat without her, but with that crazy parrot. What had she let herself in for?

She put a pair of jeans on and as a concession to the idea of night life, a silver short sleeved jumper. Heels weren't an option on the cobbles as she didn't fancy going home with a broken ankle. Charlie knew she was accident prone and had many in her childhood. Falling off her bike or twisting her ankle playing football or tennis was quite normal for her. They knew her by name at the hospital's A&E department.

She settled on her black pumps and quickly dried her hair. Lipstick and mascara was all that was needed in terms of makeup and she was ready.

On her way out of the hotel, she told the staff she would be leaving tomorrow. She had originally booked in for a week so they seemed surprised and somewhat disappointed. She reassured Mahmut the friendly receptionist who was also a dead ringer for the footballer Ronaldo that there was nothing wrong with the hotel. She was going to stay with her mother. She just neglected to say that her mother wasn't actually there. How odd would that sound?

Mahmut decided to chance his luck and ask her if she wanted to go for a drink with him after work, he was risking his job, as he wasn't supposed to be fraternising with the guests and he knew it. Charlie politely declined flashing him a smile as she let him down lightly. He looked disappointed and she wondered how old he actually was? Old enough she guessed, but she wasn't looking for a toy boy. Unlike some of the women out here. She had noticed on her travels the older women, dressing in much younger clothes than suited them, with Turkish men, well boys some of them, sitting in bars and cafés, holding hands or lying on the beach together.

That sort of behaviour made Charlie feel a bit uncomfortable, but she didn't quite know why. It was a free country. She had accused her mother of such crimes when she came out to Turkey, but Deniz a toy boy? Well hardly, he must be forty five at least thought Charlie, now almost defending her mother's choices in her own mind. That was a turn up for the books.

Charlie headed towards the Cactus restaurant. She had seen so many adverts for the place she felt she had been there already. She had walked past the place earlier on in the day and had nearly been kidnapped by the very young looking waiters hovering outside. She promised to return and as she didn't know anywhere else in the town to eat, she decided to brave it. She guessed there would be a lot of English tourists there but maybe she may meet someone who knows her mother. She was realising that it was a small town in terms of the expats and according to Deniz, the English tended to go to certain bars and restaurants on a regular basis.

As she approached the corner where the Cactus restaurant occupied a prime position on the main shopping street and bordering on the alleyway entrance. She heard the music long before she got there and it appeared to be heaving with large groups of tourists. She wondered if she had made a massive error of judgement, this wasn't her type of place at all. She preferred the look of some of the quieter more authentic restaurants she had passed on her way here.

Before she could turn around and head back up the alleyway, she was cornered by one of the waiters she had seen earlier. He caught her eye and before she knew it she was escorted to a small table a bit too near the stage for her liking. She was handed a giant menu and the young waiter who introduced himself as Halil, asked her what she would like to drink. She decided to try Efes one of the local beers and ordered a chicken shish from the Turkish section of what appeared to be a worldwide menu. There were so many regions of the worlds' dishes on it that she half expected to find Geordie specialities, in the 'Scran' section.

She wondered why people would travel to Turkey to eat Chinese, Italian, or Mexican food. Still that was the English for you and apparently Ireland has gone the same culinary way.

She saw the singer approaching the stage to start his set. Fortunately this meant that the sounds of Tom Jones singing 'Sex bomb' stopped at least for a few minutes. The manic waiters who were dancing around the stage area with various tourists led their 'prey' back to their seats. She had been advised by a woman she met at the hotel bar to go late to avoid the large groups and although it was nearly eleven, they were still finishing their meals. Obviously it was not late enough yet.

The singer introduced himself as Tarkan and his picture was displayed throughout the restaurant. This was probably his second or third set, she guessed and wondered how he could stand this night after night. She had heard from the oracle in the bar that he had a set to sing in the early part of the evening then he would sing some requests. He had his guitar hung round him and she'd been told he was good.

She looked at Tarkan and he looked straight back at her. Shoulder length dark hair, pale skin and large dark brown eyes appraised the new guest. He smiled at her almost shyly and she smiled back. He was certainly good looking but could he sing? Fortunately he could and he was popular with the audience and the waiters alike. He had a very deep voice when he spoke and the accented English was also attractive. She wondered if her mother liked listening to him too.

Her food arrived, delivered by the over attentive Halil who fussed round her more than her Aunty on a Sunday tea-time. He eventually left her to eat and she enjoyed the meal more than she thought she would. She hadn't eaten since noon and was ready for the dinner she had chosen. The chicken was delicious; charred but still moist. She sipped her beer and listened to Tarkan singing 'You look wonderful tonight' one of her favourite Eric Clapton numbers and a favourite of her dad.

He did a few more lively numbers for the larger groups who were now leaving in droves having eaten, drunk, danced and sung to their hearts content. He then played some acoustic guitar numbers setting the mood for a quieter moment and some couples started dancing together slowly. Charlie had made it clear to Hasan, the other child waiter, that she didn't want to dance and eventually he left her alone. She ordered a large red wine and relaxed for the first time properly in a few days. She made a mental note to ask her mother when she found her, why the wine was better in the Cactus than her man Deniz's bar?

Tarkan was singing some Turkish songs now and his voice sounded even better in his own language. She noticed the change in clientele, more Turkish couples and groups were coming in to have a drink rather than food and enjoy the music. Eventually he finished his set, announced he was having a 'short break' and headed off to the bar. She wondered whether to ask him about her mother, but decided against it, he might think she was coming on to him. She needn't have worried. As she sipped the last of her wine, the tall figure of Tarkan sat down beside her with a smile.

"Hi," Charlie said, suddenly feeling shy. He probably spoke to all his new customers, after all it was the Turkish way.

"Did you enjoy the music?" He asked her.

"No it was terrible." Charlie dead-panned it.

His face changed until he realised she was joking. "Well you shouldn't ask," 'she joked. "It's called fishing for compliments where I come from."

"Where are you from?" His heavy accent was incredibly sexy thought Charlie, whilst also thinking that he must have a different girl every night.

"Newcastle, but I live in London."

"Ah luv Geeorrdies me," he said in his best impression of a Tyneside accent, which wasn't that great, but it was so unexpected she nearly fell off her seat laughing at him.

"Stick to the singing pet. Your career as an impressionist still needs some work."

Now it was his turn to laugh. They chatted for a few minutes, she couldn't resist telling him the real reason she was there. He was easy to talk to and his English was remarkably good.

"I know your mum," he said, "I've known her a few years now, she used to come in East meets West when I worked there. She is a lovely lady."

He was diplomatic as well. He knew her mother was with Deniz, whom he clearly had fallen out with in the past, but he wouldn't say why. He simply said, he didn't go there anymore, it was a shame though. He told her about a bar he did go to, Adem's place and told her how to get there.

"I am there later if you would like to have a drink with me?"

She asked him if he'd seen her mother recently and he said no. He was surprised that they had not arranged to meet each other, but Charlie described it as a 'surprise.' She told him that Deniz had told her that Dee had gone back to England to see her. He laughed, obviously believing it to be a misadventure. Charlie couldn't tell him the real reason. She didn't know him well enough. Tarkan seemed like a lovely guy, but who knows.

"I maybe see you later?" He asked.

"Maybe," said Charlie as he headed back to the stage to begin his last set.

He was singing 'Bridge over troubled water' as she left. 'If only you knew,' she thought.

She found her way to East Meets West easily. It was on the adjacent alley to the Cactus; she felt that she was starting to find her way around. Deniz came out from under the bar and gave her a kiss on both cheeks. The Turkish way. The place was full and the singer was only a few feet from the bar. It wasn't too stuffy as the open roof dispersed any smoke and noise, but there was nowhere for her to sit. Deniz pulled up a bar stool for her and she was able to watch, with fascination, everything that was going on.

Charlie could not get over the change in the place. It had certainly come alive. It was buzzing. People dancing in the tiny space in front of the singer. He was belting out an acceptable version of Pink Floyd's 'money' and there appeared to be a group of Danish or Swedish students Pogo-ing around madly. Whatever they've swallowed was powerful enough to be the subject of a banning Charlie reasoned.

The seats and tables were overflowing with people and drinks and everyone was laughing shouting or talking. The poor waiter needed to be in three places at once, darting around taking orders and joking with the customers that would appear to be various nationalities. The singer looked like a Turkish 'Johnny Depp,' apart from his slightly dour expression and the fact he was about twenty; other than that he could have been the movie star's twin.

Charlie watched Deniz behind the bar, making up the orders with speed and dexterity. He was focussed on the task in hand and barely had a chance to speak to her apart from when he had a quick break between orders. She felt a bit out of the loop sitting up on the stool until a woman pulled up the stool next to her and asked Deniz for a beer.

"Hiya love," she said to Charlie in what sounded like a Gateshead accent. "God it's heaving in here tonight isn't it?"

"Hi to you too," said Charlie, "yeah I canna hear meself think, is it always like this?"

"Nah, not really," said the woman. She looked to be about sixty to Charlie, but wearing well. "These Danish lot have been in for about a week, it's their last night, thank God, they make Geordies look like teetotallers."

They both laughed. "Val," holding her hand out to Charlie

"Charlie," offering hers to Val glad to find someone to talk to. "I'm from Newcastle too."

"You sound like a posh Geordie though pet." Val laughed

"Not really, Gosforth, but I've been living in London for a few years."

The two woman managed to chat above the noise of the music and exchanged pleasantries. Val told Charlie she had been living in Kuşadasi after retiring early. Charlie started to feel excited, she was bound to know her mother.

Charlie told Val she had come to pay a surprise visit to her mother, but she was nowhere to be found. She expected the same response as Tarkan, a laugh, or a 'how ironic pet.' She got neither. Val looked at Charlie with a puzzled expression.

"Aye, I know your mam Dee. We are good pals. Us Geordies have to stick together. I haven't seen her for a bit though. I thought she'd gone back to England."

"Did she tell you that?" Charlie was trying to look casual about the question.

"Yes, last time I saw her in here. I think it was a couple of weeks ago mind. Time just passes here, you lose track of the days pet."

'What's wrong?' she asked Charlie

Charlie looked Val in the eye. I don't know Val. It just seems weird that she didn't say anything to me. We haven't got on well for the last couple of years. But she rings me every month. I think she would have said something if she was coming back to England.

Val considered what she had said. "Maybe pet. Maybe she just wanted a break by herself like? She seemed a bit fed up the last time I saw her come to think about it."

"Did she ever mention me?" Charlie was probing gently.

"Of course pet, she's dead proud of her clever daughter. But she and I wondered why you hadn't been out to see her?"

"I should have done Val, I realise that now." Charlie was warming to this woman she had only just met.

Val considered whether to tell Charlie about Mary and her disappearance. She decided against it for the time being, she didn't want the girl to worry herself sick. But it would likely come out soon. Surely Dee wasn't missing as well.

"So she isn't answering her phone either?"

"No. I tried again earlier this evening, but it's off

now. Maybe the battery's dead I don't know."

Val's blood went cold when she heard the words. Her thoughts were back with Mary. She couldn't speak to Deniz now in front of Charlie. Surely he must know where Dee is. They're virtually married.

"Do you know 'Adem's bar Val?" Charlie suddenly having a thought, almost out loud.

"Of course pet, it's just around the corner. Why?"

"I just fancied having a look. To see if anyone's seen my mam around the town maybe? The singer in the Cactus asked me to meet him for a drink there later."

"We can go together if you like," said Val. "It's a bit too much in here for me tonight. All these great Danes."

Deniz had vanished from his post behind the bar, probably to get more lemons and both women made a quick exit. They headed to Adem's bar in the next alley. Chairs and tables outside and the sound of a guitarist playing inside. It wasn't what Charlie was expecting. They went inside and out to the back area where there was more seating.

Adem came out from behind the bar to greet them. He gave Val a kiss and hug and put his hand out to Charlie. Val told him she was Dee Davison's daughter and he then decided to give her a bear hug. He was huge and when she could breathe again, she told him she had come for a holiday to see her mam.

"So where's Dee," said Adem looking around.

"She's not here," said Charlie. I think we've missed each other."

Val explained to Adem. He laughed loudly then suddenly stopped and looked at Val. Charlie couldn't make out his expression, it was as if he had just thought about something'

"Have you found Mary yet?" Adem said without too

much discretion.

"Who's Mary?" Charlie enquired.

"It's a long story. Let's get a drink." They ordered big Vodka and Sodas in very tall glasses. "This could take some time."

Charlie was concerned to hear about Val's friend. As Val recounted what had happened, Charlie could tell how worried she was, but was trying to play it down. Ever the joker, Val said, "I bet, as we speak, Mary's with some toy boy and she'll be having the last laugh."

Charlie wasn't convinced. Val was genuinely worried about her pal and rightly so. Even if Mary did sound a bit of a girl, she should have come home by now. She thought about Dee's empty flat and tried not to connect the two in her mind. For God's sake girl, pull yourself together. Your mam's probably living it up on Tyneside while were sitting here.

Charlie and Val chatted about everything and everybody for the next hour. Charlie loved hearing her talk, it was like voices from home. But it also reminded her of Dee and the fact that she couldn't find her.

They were both tired and agreed to meet up for coffee the next day. They exchanged mobile numbers and Val gave Dee's daughter a big hug as she left.

As they were leaving. Tarkan came in to the bar. He smiled at the two women.

Charlie spoke first. "About that drink…"

"Yes?" Tarkan, sitting down on a stool at the bar, leaned forward to hear her.

She needed to get back to the hotel, to think and to sleep.

"I'll have another vodka and soda please." Where did that come from? Charlie wondered

Val touched her on her arm. "See you tomorrow pet.

Don't do anything I wouldn't."

As Val rubbed her eyes the following morning, she wondered what had become of Charlie and Tarkan. He was a lovely guy, but he was Turkish and a singer and popular with the ladies. She was sure Charlie could look after herself. She didn't need someone old enough to be her mother fussing around her. Val looked at the clock next to her bed. It was nearly ten, so she got up to shower. The next thing she did was automatic.

Looking down to the balcony below, she shouted for Mary...

18

Yucel

P olice Chief Yucel Semir was preparing for the press conference. He was actually dreading it. He was also due to meet Val Neville in ten minutes and she wasn't aware of the reason. He couldn't say anything on the phone. He hadn't shaved, he had a ten o'clock shadow and he was still in his wife's bad books. It certainly was a bad time to give up smoking. He had dressed in a hurry, almost in the dark and realised that his trousers had a stain on the front and his shirt had a button missing. It really wasn't going to be a good day. Then he thought of Mary O'Donnell and felt ashamed. He had a job to do and he was going to do it to the best of his ability.

His men were still searching for a second body. He wasn't going to reveal anything about the arm, but then realised he had to. He had decided to play this down and mention the turquoise ring being found to see if it triggered any calls before telling the press about the severed arm. The press would have a field day anyway. 'Yogi,' this big bear of an officer was facing the toughest day of his career.

Val turned up half an hour early. She couldn't relax after getting the call from Yucel. He sounded strange on the phone and she knew something had happened. She took a Valium from the cupboard in Mary's bathroom, such was her anxiety. She fed the cat, Alfie, almost in a trance.

She rang her new friend Charlie and told her she was going to the Police and would see her at the Güvercin in a couple of hours for coffee. Charlie was moving out from there today, but hadn't yet gone, so it was a good central spot. She hoped she would hear something positive about Mary, but she couldn't see it somehow. Not if the Police were involved.

Yucel led Val into his office. He could tell that she was on edge. He was a polite man, with good manners and asked her if she would like a drink. She shook her head, wanting him and urging him with her eyes to get on with it.

"I'm sorry Mrs Neville," he started not wanting to make eye contact but instinctively knowing that he had to. "We found a body this morning at the National Park. It is the body of a woman who matches the description that you gave of your friend Mary."

Val gasped. Trying to compose herself, she asked. "Where is she? Can I see her?"

"I need you to identify the body, to see if it is your friend. Will you do that?"

"Of course I will, please take me now. I need to know if it's her."

He took Val into the small Mortuary where the body was being chilled to slow decomposition in the heat of Turkey. The body was covered with a sheet. Val took a breath, it looked too small to be Mary. As he pulled back the sheet she saw the blue-grey face of her friend shrunken in death, already looking like someone else. But it was Mary. Her face and cheeks looked hollow and Val realised her teeth were missing. Mary had always tried to hide the fact she had a false set. She was embarrassed and it made her feel old. It was too late for embarrassment now.

She saw the deep red lines around her neck. The horror of realisation hit her like a cold blast of air that wasn't coming from the chilled room's vents. She had been strangled. Some bastard had done this to poor Mary O'Donnell. The woman who wouldn't hurt a fly.

"Yes," she gulped. "That's Mary, without a doubt that's Mary."

Yucel already knew from her first reaction that it was her friend lying on cold stone slab, lifeless and alone.

"Thank you Mrs Neville. I am so sorry."

"Who did this to her? Have you caught him yet?" Val was angry now.

Yucel stared at Val and then at the body of the English woman who had come to Kuşadasi for a better life.

"No not yet. But we will. We will."

He led Val out of the room and back to his office. He explained to her that there was going to be a Press conference this afternoon. It would be televised and the newspapers would be following the case. He warned her they may turn up at the apartment. He advised Val to say nothing to them at this stage. She agreed, barely hearing what he was saying. She was trying to take it all in. Who would do something like this to her friend? What kind of monster?

"There is something else Mrs Neville, but you must promise me to say nothing to anyone at this stage. It may prevent us from finding the killer if you do."

"What are you talking about?" Val looked at the Chief, who was shifting his large frame from left to right in a nervous manner.

"We have found another body part from a second woman. An arm. My men are searching for the woman's body now. We are combing the National park inch by inch. We will find her too, if she's there."

"So there is a serial maniac out there? Is that what

you are trying to say? Jeezus Christ Almighty," the tone of panic was raising the pitch in her voice now.

"I will be advising all women to stay indoors at this stage, Mrs Neville, it may not be safe on the streets for a woman alone."

Val started to weep uncontrollably…

Yucel left Val with Lale, tea and a box of tissues.

Chief Semir entered the room that had been set up for the press conference. Some of them had got wind that there was something big going on at the National Park and it wouldn't be long before one of his officers let something out. This was the right time to come forward and ask the public for help.

He stood at the front of the room. He held a clip board with some hastily written words on it, to guide him through the ordeal. It was being televised by a small film crew for the national news. It had all happened so quickly, he wondered how long it would be before he was taken off the case and someone from Aydin or even Ankara brought in.

His hands were shaking as he started to speak.

"At seven fifty this morning, the body of a sixty two year old Irish woman was discovered in the Milli Park, National Park. We will be identifying her shortly when her family have been notified. She disappeared from the town centre of Kuşadasi during the early hours of Sunday morning. We believe she has been strangled to death, but that is yet to be confirmed by Autopsy. We are urging women to stay home or if you have to go out, be accompanied by someone you know and trust. Please do this while our enquiries are taking place and we are able to apprehend the person who has committed this terrible crime. We would also like to identify a ring that was found near the scene."

He held up the prepared photos of the ring and advised them of the details now on the police website. Or they should be if his deputy had done his job.

The room burst into life as the various journalists fired questions at Yucel like bullets.

"Where exactly was she found? Whereabouts in town was she last seen? Have you got anyone in custody? How did the woman die? What were the motives of the killer? How many suspects do you have?"

He batted off most of the questions without a straight answer. He could have been a politician, some of them were writing. His staff were in touch with Mary's family as he was speaking although it was likely that she had left a grown up son and an ex-husband. Maybe grandchildren, he didn't know at this stage. He should have asked Val, she would probably know. She didn't come from a large family, but he wanted to be sure that they were told with sensitivity and care. They would likely fly out to Kuşadasi, well the son probably would. He would surely want to know what happened to his mother.

"That's all gentlemen, for now. I will let you know the details of the victim as soon as I can. Please be sensitive when reporting this crime. We don't want to frighten the tourists."

He kicked himself, afterwards. 'Why had he said that?'

19

Dee

D ee realised she was drugged. She couldn't move her arms or in fact any part of her body. She felt as though she was in the limbo state before the body wakes and the mind is awake. It can only be seconds but it's a horrible feeling trying to move. The black and white movie taking place in her head began to play and she gave herself permission not to fight. If she was going to die she could do nothing about it. She might as well remember the good times.

Paul Davison, a patient man, waited for Deidre and he was always there. First as a friend, to her and Terry and a confidant. Then something changed. She allowed him to love her and she trusted him in a way she wouldn't have believed was possible. She was vulnerable and needed a shoulder to cry on. His physical presence was a comfort to her and although he wanted more, he was content to hold her and re-assure her. She associated love and security with loss.

Deidre was an emotional mess when Joan died. She couldn't grieve because she couldn't accept Joan had gone. Her sister and mother wrapped into one, they had been so close. The world became a place that was unsafe, nothing could be relied upon any more. She stopped going to work. She couldn't face the sympathetic looks from her workmates and couldn't concentrate on what she was doing. Paul came back to the house every lunchtime and tried to keep her in the loop. She would listen to his stories as she made him a sandwich, but didn't really care what was going on at the Shipyard.

Paul worried about her. He wondered what would drag her out of the deep pit she was in. Depression was a black cloud that hung over her.

In the end it would be love that saved Deidre. She slowly began to see that she had a place in the world and that this man, this worldly, handsome, decent man wanted her and would wait for her to recover. Finally spring came and Deidre started to bloom, literally. She found a job in a florists and found it therapeutic to make up the bouquets and arrangements with care and precision. Flowers were vital to every aspect of humanity, birth, death, marriage and she managed to use them to understand the ways of the world.

Paul took her to a posh hotel in Edinburgh for the weekend, enjoying the shops and the sights. They climbed up the hill that overlooks the City and lay on the grass at the top on a blanket. They had filled a picnic basket with some food and Paul had sneaked in a bottle of champagne and two glasses. She was twenty-two now and felt as if life was finally making some sense. When Paul proposed she couldn't speak. She managed to say yes in between sobs and he realised she hadn't expected the proposal. He wanted a life with Deidre and had been anxious she would say no.

Deidre remembered Paul on that day. He had worn a white shirt and black jeans. His shirt was stained with grass where they had lain on and off the blanket. He smelt of an aftershave she had forgotten the name of, perhaps it was Eau Savage, she loved that smell and he wore it for years. They found a little Italian restaurant later that evening and started planning their future. They would have six children and a dog. Deidre wanted a Labrador, Paul a Dalmatian. They would buy a house, all that was missing was the white picket fence.

20

Charlie

Charlie was feeling restless. She had agreed to meet Val in the late afternoon at the hotel but she was eager to get to her mother's home and unpack. She had been pacing around the lobby for a while now and eventually decided to send Val a quick text message to change their arrangements. She decided to invite Val round to Dee's when she had finished at the Police station. All this business with Mary was making her nervous.

She sent the message to Val, giving her Dee's address although she suspected she already knew it. She hadn't actually asked her if she'd ever been to her mam's home, but they seemed quite close so she guessed that she probably had been round at some point. As Val said, the Geordies stick together.

She found a cab outside the hotel and the driver put her case into the back. As they approached the street where her mother lived she wondered again, if she would turn up. Or at least phone her. She rang some of the Newcastle relatives while she had been in the Hotel, including Dee's twin sisters, but no one seems to have heard from her. The plot thickened when her Uncle Terry said he was due to fly out to Kuşadasi in a couple of weeks for a holiday. Surely she would have told him if she wasn't going to be here?

She took the small lift up to the flat with her case and let herself in. Oscar started as soon as he heard the door. "Hello pet! What's the problem? What's the problem?"

"For the love of all that's holy, what had possessed

her mother to buy this bird," thought Charlie, out loud.

The bird hopped around the cage a bit and Charlie wondered if mam ever let him out. She guessed that she did, but she wasn't going to risk it. 'What if he wouldn't go back?'

She gave him some seeds and water and shut the cage.

She wandered around the flat, not knowing quite what to do with herself. She decided to unpack and put her clothes in the wardrobe in the spare room. She ventured into the third bedroom used as a studio and was surprised to see how professional it all looked. Easels and paint set out and half finished work on a huge table that dominated the room. The light was good in here with a big floor length window explaining why she had chosen it. Charlie was impressed by the talent she didn't know her mother had. What other secrets had the new Dee held from her she wondered?

She remembered the key and went to get it from her purse. As she expected it fitted into the lock of the big trunk in the front room. She sat down on the sofa and started to look through the contents. It was mainly memorabilia and photos that her mam had collected over the years. Her wedding album was there and some certificates, including marriage and death. She rummaged through the cards and letters her mother had obviously kept for years.

Something caught her eye in the side pocket of the trunk that had been lined in a kind of fake velvet. She pulled out a small black clutch bag and remembered it from years before, when Dee had been going to a 'do' or something requiring an evening dress. She opened the small purse and something inside made her hold her breath for a second. The familiar maroon cover of a

British passport. She opened it up thinking and hoping it was an old one that her mother had decided to keep. Dee's face jumped out from the photo. It was dated from the early part of this year. She must have just renewed it a few months ago. This changed everything.

"Dee, Dee, Dee, Dee, mummy's home," squawked Oscar making her nearly jump out of her skin as someone knocked on the front door. She waited and the door went again, the birds chirping as the door bell was also in full swing.

She got up and opened the door. Val stood outside looking as if she had been crying. A lot. Her face was blotchy and her nose red. She looked distraught.

"Canna come in pet?" She looked at Charlie and burst into tears. As did Charlie. They hugged and Charlie led her into the lounge.

"It's Mary," Val sobbed. "She's been murdered. They've found her body in the National Park…"

Charlie just stared at her not believing what she was hearing.

"Oh my God Val, what happened?" The women sat close together on the sofa and Val started to tell Charlie what had happened at the Police station. She was clearly in shock.

Charlie went to the kitchen and opened a bottle of Dee's wine. Both women took a large gulp of their drink as the story unfolded. Charlie was horrified.

Val got to the bit about the ring, then stopped. She hadn't given the matter enough thought yet.

"Let's put on the news Val and see what they are saying," said Charlie, looking for the remote. She found the channel, but they had a while to wait for the news on the hour. They drank the wine and wondered what on earth would happen next.

21

Ömer

O mer Demar was not a happy man. He lay on the sofa in his beautiful flat furnished with the proceeds of his girlfriend's divorce. He drank from a bottle of Tuborg, spilling some on to the cream fabric without noticing. He belched and wondered where Josie was. He had rung her best friend here, who had denied she was there, but Karen was a lying bitch and he was sure she was there, moaning and groaning to her about him and his antics.

He swore in Turkish and went to look in the fridge for something to eat. It was full, but there was nothing to eat that didn't need cooking. She should be here to make it, the ungrateful bitch. He had kept her happy hadn't he? He was still angry that she wasn't waiting when he eventually returned home two days after she left him at the Orange Bar.

It was her own fault, she was jealous and paranoid about everyone he spoke to for fuck's sake; and anyway she didn't own him. He hadn't intended to go back with the Irish girl to her apartment in Ladies Beach, but hey, he was a man and she was a sexy young thing. She wanted him and he was sick of Josie and her constant moaning. She had brought it on herself when she had gone off to one of her friends, just to prove something. Well, Ömer wasn't about to go and look for her; she would come back eventually. Begging for it.

He looked round the flat. It was a tip. Bottles and pizza boxes. Dirty clothes and crockery everywhere. It wasn't his job to clean it up. He worked hard didn't he?

What did that lazy woman have to do, nothing, that's what? She didn't work, just idled around on the beach reading magazines and moaning.

Siobhan had been a joy. Her young firm body and tight little arse. Okay, she swears like a trouper and dresses like a tart, but she was happy to have him in her bed. Her parents didn't seem to care what she was doing. Seventeen going on forty, she had all the words in bed he liked. And double-jointed. Ömer could still remember the moment she had whispered that in his ear at the 'Orange.' He bet her fifty lira that she was lying. He paid up happily when he found out that she wasn't!

He promised her he would see her again. He wasn't a man to break a promise, was he? It wasn't as if he was married to Josie. The flat was in his name, let her try and take that from him. Turkish Law would be on his side. These English women are all the same. He was sick of her saggy breasts, her varicose veins, and her breath stinking of old smoke. She couldn't have thought it was forever surely. She couldn't be that stupid.

He picked up his mobile and rang her number. It went to voicemail, so he decided to leave another abusive message. Feeling slightly better he rang Siobhan, who answered immediately. Things were looking up.

"Hello Sweetheart, how you doing?"

"Hi OHHHMERRR." He loved the way that sounded in her Irish accent. "How are you big boy?"

"Missing you honey. What you up to?"

"Getting ready to go out baby. Where are you?"

"At home waiting for you, getting hard just thinking about you sweet lips."

"You'd better stay hard then, for when I meet you at the bar later. Hope you got rid of that old bitch?"

"Don't worry about her, sweetheart. She's gone."

He hung up and went back to the sofa. Time for a shower and shave then out to the Orange Bar for some more serious action. He switched over from the football to the news and opened another bottle of beer.

He saw the picture of Mary as the news switched to the police man talking about her. Murdered and found in the National Park. He sat up. He knew Mary, everyone knew Mary. One of his cousins had been with her for a while until he found out that she didn't have any money. What was going on?

He phoned his cousin and told him to switch on the TV. As they were talking a picture of a turquoise ring flashed up on the screen. Fuck. What's that got to do with it? It was Josie's ring. At least it looked like Josie's ring. He had bought it for her the week she came out on holiday. His brother had got it cheap from a dodgy jeweller and she had been thrilled. It was all part of his strategy. He looked at the picture again. It couldn't be her ring. She was wearing it when he last saw her.

He drank the rest of his beer quickly. He didn't know what to think now. Had Mary taken Josie's ring? Why? Where was the bitch? He had a bad feeling. A very bad feeling that he couldn't shake.

He jumped in the shower and dressed quickly. His motorbike, courtesy of Josie, was outside and he got on it and drove the few miles to the Orange Bar. His brother and cousin were already there when he arrived and everyone was talking about Mary. Some making jokes even. But all the women were frightened and there were fewer customers than usual. Ömer rang Josie again. No reply.

He told his brother about the ring. He watched the news again on the big screen in the bar. His brother was shaking his head.

"Was this bad? My brother? What are you saying? Is it the ring you got me?"

His brother stared at him. "You had better find her and find her quick."

22

Jenni

J enni Higgs was a happy girl. A very happy girl. She looked into the mirror now and liked what she saw. Auburn waves, almost pre-Raphaelite curls, pale skin, green eyes and a generous cleavage, Rubenesque in its magnificence. She smiled, showing a row of even white teeth, they're veneers, but they're worth every penny.

She spun around in her new swimsuit. Black Lycra, but in a Jane Russell kind of style. Fifties, with a push up top and a panel below to flatten and flatter, to deceive, but only a bit. She felt fantastic. Those months of dieting and exercise had paid off. The last four months had been frantic. But she was here now. At last she was here.

Parading around the bedroom looking in the full length mirror at herself, she finally felt like the woman she was destined to be. No longer Ginger Jen, or Chubs or any other nickname relating to her large breasts. She was free of it all now.

She remembered the day it all changed for her, as if it were yesterday. Forty years old and stuck in the same old job, same old life. She made her way to the Estate Agent's office where she had worked for sixteen years. She started there when her son Steven was three. She had brought him up on her own, his useless, idle, good for nothing father hadn't contributed anything apart from his genes. And if Jenni had bought them from him, she would've taken them back.

It had been a struggle over the years to put food on the table and pay the rent, but she had managed somehow, even if it meant going without things for herself. Her parents had tried to help, but when her mum passed away it all seemed to change. Her dad had a new Thai girlfriend and Jenni had to take a back seat.

She hated her job. She hadn't in the beginning. The car they provided and the buzz of showing people around their potential new home had been fulfilling and reasonably well paid. She was a natural sales woman and found the negotiations quite easy. Her targets were always met and the boss loved her. She should have been the boss by now, but had somehow been overlooked; deliberately because they wanted to keep her on the shop floor doing what she did best.

Knowing she was outspoken and for that reason wasn't always popular with the management, she wanted out, but wasn't qualified for anything else. After her fortieth birthday party she was starting to feel her age and that life was passing her by.

Jenni was a smart cookie though. In most areas of her life that is. One area that seemed to let her down was her choice of men. Steven's father had been a loser. A six foot, handsome, charismatic loser, but a loser all the same. He had no intentions of working for a living, or being a father to her son. He had to go, but the men who followed, seemed to be cut from the same cloth. She couldn't resist charm and a pretty face.

Jenni loved sex and she loved men, but couldn't find 'the one,' however hard she tried. As she kept on trying, her self-esteem was taking a dive. She put on weight and spent her evenings watching cooking programmes, rather than going out clubbing. Steven went off to university and her life became duller. Much duller.

Back to the day it all changed. Jenni arrived at work late. The other staff were already there and sitting at their desk. Alan her boss glared at her from the glass box in the corner he called his office.

"Morning guys," she said brightly, putting her bag down on the desk. A few grunted a reply and carried on working. She looked at her diary and saw her list of appointments. Luckily nothing until ten, so she switched on her computer and pretended to do some work. Checking her phone regularly, particularly as she had joined an Internet Dating site recently and wanted to see if there were any new faces.

'Reg' from Harlow popped into frame and she started to feel a deep sense of despair. Was this the best she could do? How can a fifty year old man have spots? She mused looking at his pasty ugly face. She liked her men darker and handsome, but she hadn't found much of what she liked on this site so far. Do they have a money back guarantee? She thought it an idea to check.

Looking at her Facebook didn't prove any more satisfying. She was fed up of looking at other people's lives, photos of their exotic holidays and so called 'fabulous' boyfriends or husbands. She wished she had something interesting to post. 'Having an early night, alone,' didn't really cut it. She saw her friend Carla had posted a picture of herself and her husband at the 'Shard' in London, having a meal. 'Lucky bitch,' she thought but clicked 'like' despite herself. There really should be a 'lucky bitch' button on there.

She checked her texts seeing that there were two new ones, probably from last night, as she hadn't looked at her phone since then. She had got up late and rushed around to get out the house. Then realised she needed petrol so it had been a mad dash to get to work in the first place. The first text was from Steven asking her to put some money into his account as he was running low 'pls mum. Just til nxt week. Love ya.'

She smiled. He knew she wouldn't refuse him, she was a soft touch when it came to her son. The second was the Lottery results text that came after the Wednesday and Saturday draw. She bought her tickets online. In fact she did most things online. She always did the same numbers, her birthday, Steven's birthday, her mum and dad's birthday and her two lucky numbers seven and eight.

She gazed at the screen without really taking it in. She could see the row of numbers 7 8 14 16 22 31, but she wasn't taking it in. Slowly, the realisation of what was going on, finally hit her and her hands started to shake. She put the phone down and went back to her computer terminal and logged into her private Outlook e-mailbox. There it was, an email from the National Lottery HQ. She had these emails before, over the years and had initially been excited, until it turned out that she had won a tenner and then subsequently, a slightly more life changing forty-seven quid.

As the email opened her eyes went straight to the figure at the bottom. £1,677.883 Her first thought was seventeen grand, whoopee! Long holiday. New Kitchen… She looked closer…

Her heart was racing. 'Oh my God, nearly two million quid.'

This was what she had been waiting for. This would change her life forever. After logging off, she got up and picked up her bag. Talking to no one in particular, she addressed the whole room.

"Well people, I wish I could say it's been a hoot, but it hasn't really. I'm off. I'm not coming back here, ever. But before I go I just want to say a couple of things that have been on my mind." She was on a roll now.

"Neil, you really need to do something about your

breath mate. It's vile. Sort it out! Sue, everyone knows that you're shagging Alan. He may be the boss, but he's pretty stupid too if he thinks we don't all know about it. Don't kid yourself love, you're not the first. Look at Gill's face!"

Gill was now turning a purple colour and she was glaring at Jenni.

"He was in her knickers before yours and he dumped her, and he'll dump you too."

The phone was ringing, but no one moved to answer it.

"Oh and Patrick, you may as well know that everyone hates you. You're an arrogant little prick and as soon as you leave the room they all start bitching about you. No one's got the spine to tell you to your face though, 'cause you're the boss's son. Anyway I am out of here. Enjoy what's left of your sad little lives."

Jenni literally flounced out of the office, not even stopping to inform Alan she was leaving. She went and sat in her car and found her e-cigs. She took a draw that would have persuaded a golf ball to pass through a hosepipe. Still shaking, she rang the number given in the email and they confirmed her winnings. She declined the publicity and slowly for once, drove home.

A few weeks later and her life was just getting better and better. Now a lady of leisure, she had plenty of time to trawl the internet and had met a very interesting man. Of course she hadn't told him about her winnings, she wasn't stupid. No he seemed to like her for her. She liked her men tall and very dark and he fitted the bill perfectly. His name was Khan, well it was short for Adskhan, which when she looked it up, saw that it meant 'knight or prince'. It was a sign and Jenni was very into 'signs.' She had been to see a fortune teller in

Southend who'd been recommended to her by her friend Lauren. The woman had told her that her fortunes were changing and she could see a man who was destined for her. He was 'far away,' but they would marry and be happy. Jenni was over the moon.

'Madam Zelda' also saw the letter A, and at the time Jenni only knew her man as Khan, so didn't think it was about him. When she found out his real name it confirmed her belief that Khan was the one.

At last her Prince had come. Though she had to go to him, as he couldn't get a visa. They are quite strict about that in Turkey. She understood. This was her chance to find happiness and she would grasp it with both hands.

Khan didn't disappoint. His emails and messages had melted her heart and had become raunchier as the time went on. When she met him at the airport he was over six foot to Jenni's five foot three and she fell into his arms. They got a cab to the Kuşadasi Hilton near the Marina and spent the next two days in bed. She felt young again, especially as she had spent the previous three months before they met, getting into shape. The sex was fantastic, he could go all night it seemed to Jenni. They drank champagne and smoked some hashish he had brought with him. She felt as if she was floating on air.

She loved Kuşadasi, loved Turkey and loved Khan. He wasn't a great conversationalist, but he was trying to improve his English with her help. She taught him some Essex phrases and laughed out loud when she heard him saying 'bling' and 'ream.' On the third day he asked her to marry him and she thought he was joking. She saw the look in his big brown eyes and knew he was serious. She had never felt this strongly about a man before. It was all consuming.

Jenni now knew all about his past. His parents were dead, killed in an accident. He had some distant relatives in a village near Aydin. He had come to Kuşadasi for work and was hired at the Cactus restaurant where he was a hit. His good looks and charm went down well with the tourists. He told Jenni, he loved the English and the English way of life. He had given up his job at the Cactus after breaking his foot. He told Jenni the cast had just been removed and he was planning on looking for work again, as soon as he felt able to stand all day.

She told him he didn't need to work. She stopped herself from saying 'ever again.' She wanted to be sure he wanted her and not her money. It was amazing how people had changed after they found out about her win. Suddenly she was popular and had friends coming out of the woodwork. She was fed up with it and even gave an interview to the local paper saying that money doesn't buy happiness. She also hinted she was giving a lot away to charity hoping that would stop the begging letters. She smiled to herself. It had certainly bought her happiness.

The wedding took place at the town hall, with a blessing on the beach. Jenni wore a cream dress off the shoulder and nipped in at the waist, with intricate lace up detail. It had cost her a fortune. It had been sent from London, the dresses in Kuşadasi were not her style. She flew back for two days for fittings, but couldn't bear to be away from Khan. He rang her constantly telling her how much he missed her.

Steven her beloved son flew in for the wedding. He looked fabulous next to Khan in his new grey Boateng suit. After winning the money she had bought him an IT business in Loughton. It was a fledgling company, but if anyone could make a success out of it Steven could. He gave up his business studies degree and was now doing it for real. He wished his mother well and seemed to like Khan. They were similar in age, laughed Jenni.

Her cup was full. Everything went to plan and the wedding was a success. She hired a local singer Tarkan who was popular and played in the Cactus. He performed with a band of musicians he knew; everyone was up dancing. Khan's family didn't come and she could see he was disappointed. He told her they didn't approve of him marrying an English girl. She hugged him and told him she understood. Her father hadn't bothered to fly in from Thailand either. His Pu-Ling or whatever her name was, obviously means more to him, Jenni told Khan.

Being married to Khan and being rich suited Jenni. They bought an apartment overlooking the Marina with its own pool and a view over the Aegean. It was magnificent and Jenni's interior design was pure Essex. White leather sofas and chandeliers completed the look. Khan wanted a boat and Jenni was excited at the idea. By now she had told him how much she was worth. After the wedding of course. She loved the look of surprise on his face, then delight. He still told her he loved her every day. He also told her what a great life they would have together.

Jenni like to think she had brought a little bit of Essex to Kuşadasi. They loved 'doing the town' and dressing up in the process. Khan had a collection of light coloured suits now, showing off his perfect tan. Horse and carriages operated as expensive and opulent taxis along the front and Jenni loved to take a ride with Khan. She liked to think of them as the Posh and Becks of Kuşadasi.

Jenni didn't want the bubble to burst. It was good. She had her man. Her son was settled. What could go wrong?

23

Yucel

Something woke Yucel up at three in the morning. He clicked his bedside light on, waking his wife at the same time. The mobile phone was glowing and he saw Seb's name flashing. He answered the phone and spoke in a hushed voice hoping Ayla would go back to sleep. Her bump was enormous now and she found it difficult to get comfortable. He felt for her, she couldn't get around easily and their son Seref was a demanding toddler. This case was taking its toll on them both. He had hardly been home and he was missing time with his wife and son, precious time before the new baby arrived.

He grunted into the phone. Seb, his deputy, was obviously outside somewhere and was shouting into the phone. He was on the night shift and they had finally rigged up lighting now to continue the search at the National Park.

He told Yucel that they had found a body. The body was missing an arm and the Boars had dug up the shallow grave. They had started to eat part of the body and Seb appeared to be hyperventilating as he told the news. Yucel told him that he would be there in forty minutes; it would take him that long to drive to the park.

He pulled on some clothes. No time to shower. He kissed Ayla softly on the cheek. She was asleep again despite the noise and he guessed she was exhausted. He hoped she would sleep through the rest of the night.

He slipped out the door and shut it quietly behind him. On the drive to the park he tried to envisage what sight would greet him. Wild Boar are carnivores and related to Pigs and like Pigs, will eat anything. He felt sick at the idea of the half devoured body. At least they found her before it was too late and there was no body at all. Who was this woman and why had no one reported her missing.

He arrived at the crime scene. One of his men was waiting for him in the car park and led him to where the body had been found. The shallow grave had been partially dug again in a woodland plot next to a group of large trees. This was becoming a pattern. His men were grouped around the body taking photographs.

What was left of the woman, showed her to be aged between fifty and sixty, but it was hard to tell. Long dark hair, quite slim, but that was about all you could tell without a forensic medical examination.

It was a shocking sight. The boars had chewed more than the missing arm. The body was missing breasts and the animals had started to bite through her thighs and torso. Yucel could see the now familiar rope and ceramic talisman around her neck, but laying to one side in the dirt. Presumably not left in that position by the killer, but disturb by the hungry carnage that ensued.

This killer was playing games now. It was the sign of someone who wanted to be famous; no, infamous. His calling card the Turkish Eye. His victims were European women of a certain age. What was the motivation here? Yucel's mind was spinning.

He had received the autopsy report on Mary O'Donnell. She had not been raped as first thought. The killer had not left his DNA on her. He must have worn gloves when she was strangled. Her clothes and tights had been ripped as if it was a sexual attack, but this may have been done after the murder.

Who was this woman? He watched as officers

combed the area around her body for any further clues to her identity or her death. Nothing significant was apparent, pretty much the same as with Mary's crime scene. He didn't believe they had been killed here. He suspected the deaths would be within a couple of days of each other. If the arm hadn't been found it would have been a long time before they found Mary. The shallow grave wasn't effective and the killer would surely have known that it could easily be disturbed. Was he aware of the boars in the park? Surely he must have known. Did he want the Boars to consume the evidence? Did these two women know each other?

He waited for the chilled van to arrive to transport the body to HQ and wait for the doctor. He checked with his men that he was on his way. Shaking his head he made his way to his car to make the drive back to Kuşadasi. He would ring his wife on the way and see how she was. Tell her he wouldn't be home early. Get the press on board and try to find out who the second victim was and locate her family.

It was going to be another long day. Yucel felt out of this depth. He was a man of action, not a strategist. If this was a serial killer he would need serious back up. Neither Yucel nor his deputy, were experts in psychology, yet both, no all the local Police wanted to catch this killer with whatever method they could before he struck again. They take pride in the lack of crime on the Kuşadasi streets, this maniac is hurting them and they need it to stop.

Driving back with his phone on loud speaker. One of his officers rang to say that the woman who was found today was probably a Josie Wilson, marital status unknown. Her Turkish boyfriend had been into the station to report her missing and said she had a ring matching the pictures we released to the media in conjunction with Mary's death.

Yucel wondered what had taken him so long. He couldn't have been that worried about Josie. Perhaps the news story regarding Mary changed his thinking. He would be asked to identify a body that may or may not be his girlfriend.

And explain to Yucel's satisfaction why it took him so long!!

24

Charlie

C harlie switched on the news on the hour. Despite polishing off a bottle of wine and opening another they both felt anxious and edgy. Adrenaline probably at maximum. Charlie had been pacing around the flat and eventually decided to tell Val about the passport. Val's eyes widened.

"You're kidding me? Why didn't you say pet? You must be worried sick."

Val was aghast, she didn't know what to say to Charlie. She hadn't really put Dee into the equation. She had been so busy being upset about Mary, she hadn't realised the extent of Charlie's anxiety. She believed Dee to be in Newcastle, or London. She couldn't be in either without a passport. What was going on? Charlie assured her that Deniz didn't think she was missing, despite not hearing from her for days. Wasn't that a bit strange?

Charlie and Val sat next to each other on the sofa to listen to the news. Something unusual was going on. The normally partisan TV channels had subtitles on the screen in English. The explanation, and rightly so, was that because the serial killer's attacks seemed to be targeted on European immigrants to Turkey, it was only fair to involve them as much as possible. It was Chief Semir's idea. Actually it was a condition of allowing the Media to broadcast it.

The item was headline news and the press conference was in full swing with Yucel trying his best to inform, without saying too much. He spoke of Mary without naming her, but the news reader had used her initials in the follow up. There can't be too many MODs in these parts, so at least the expat community all now knew who they were talking about.

Val hadn't been back to Mary's flat, but believed that the Police would have secured the place off and looked for evidence, in case the murder had taken place there. Val thought this unlikely. She had also been in the flat for the last few days so most of the prints would be hers. Anyway it was always that untidy, but maybe the Police would think there had been a struggle to cause that level of chaos.

Doubtless they would have taken her phone too with her contacts in it and anything else they felt was relevant. Val thought she would be asked more about Mary's habits soon, as part of the investigation, so didn't bother Yucel with it, just yet.

Val and Charlie listened as the Chief appealed to the public to come forward if they knew anything about the murder. Had they seen Mary that night walking around on her own? Had she spoken to anyone after leaving Adem's bar? Then at the end of the broadcast, the picture of the ring came up. Charlie stared at the screen and looked at Val both thinking the same thing. Dee loved silver and turquoise jewellery. That could have been her ring.

"Why are they asking about the ring? Charlie, if it didn't belong to Mary? Are they saying there was another victim?"

Val felt sick. She had been thinking about the arm that Yucel had told her about. It kept flashing back to haunt her like a vision from a horror film. She had to persuade Charlie to go and see him and tell him about her mother. She couldn't tell Charlie about the arm. But Charlie wasn't stupid. Not by a long way. She had picked up the issue of the ring being separate to Mary. She needed to know what was going on.

"Pretty baby. Pretty baby. Mummy's home.'' Oscar was making his presence felt. Charlie fed him. It seemed to quieten him, like a baby, she thought.

Val phoned Yucel on the number from his card. It went to answer phone. She rang the office and was told that he would be back the following morning. She didn't really want to talk to anyone else. She told Charlie and they agreed to go together in the morning. Charlie went through Dee's jewellery and found a turquoise ring.

"Surely she wouldn't have two?" She was trying to reassure herself.

"You wouldn't think so," said Val.

"There's hundreds of those type of rings in town pet."

It was getting late and neither of the two girls wanted to go into town. Val knew the news on the street would be all about Mary and she dreaded going back to the apartment. She thought about Alfie, she had fed him this morning. It made her want to cry again, but she held it together for the sake of Charlie. She couldn't have her go all hysterical on her and start to fret about Dee again. Until she saw Yucel and got more information she could only feel more anxiety. She knew one thing, if it was Dee, they would know pretty quickly.

"Do you want to sleep here Val?" Charlie imagined that she wouldn't want to go back to her own apartment, especially if the Police were still swarming all over her block.

"Do you mind?" Val felt relieved.

"Mind? No of course not. I'll sleep in mam's bed, it's made up anyway. Not that I'll sleep much. It's funny how much can change in twenty-four hours isn't it? Last night I was in Adem's with Tarkan, having a drink and talking about my mam. Joking almost. He walked me home; I'm glad he did now hearing all this.

Val smiled. "He's a lovely lad isn't he?" She thought of him as a lad, even though he was probably thirty.

Charlie smiled too for the first time in a few hours. Remembering the chat, the bonding over music, his voice in her ear and his kiss. Had she not been in the hotel, who knows what might have happened? But part of her was too pre-occupied to fully let herself go. And that was before today's events and hearing about poor Mary.

"Did Tarkan know Mary?" Charlie asked.

"Everybody knows Mary. Sorry, knew Mary," said Val sadly. "She was a character."

Val decided that she would spend some time to remember her old friend. She would adopt Alfie the cat. Well, she pretty much already had and try not to cry when someone else moved in downstairs and she would look down on to the balcony. She would never again have another cuppa with her dear friend, she had been snatched away. Her new life in Kuşadasi hadn't lasted very long. Val was almost feeling religious.

She thought about Mary's family. She doubted that her son would come over. They hadn't spoken for years. When Mary left his father, he took his father's side, apparently. Mary had never seen her two grandchildren and it broke her heart. She had only left his father after he had mistreated her for years. Her son thought his mother was ridiculous, in her new life. She told Val he had called her a disgrace. 'Mutton dressed as lamb.' She had been so hurt. Of course there was no money to be had. Mary had walked away from the marriage without a penny, but kept all her dignity and sanity, was how she explained it. Val thought she was brave. And right!

Mary O'Donnell lived on her pension and savings. Val started to feel angry, but motivated.

"Charlie, can we talk. I need to tell you about Mary. She's gone now but I want to remember her life."

Charlie was shattered, but she was developing a sensitive side that she was starting to embrace. Was it a Daughter-Mother thing? Valerie isn't her mother, she knew that, but in Deidre's absence, she's pretty damn close.

The words came out as…

"Val, of course," and went to get the corkscrew.

25

Ömer

O mer sat on the plastic seats in the Police station feeling uncomfortable, in more ways than one. When was this guy going to turn up? He paced around, and went outside for a cigarette. He had been told that Chief Semir would see him and he was on his way back from the National Park.

He saw the van pull up outside and wondered if he was inside. Two officers and what looked like a stretcher were taken out into a side entrance of the station. Ömer started to feel sick.

When he was finally taken into the big man's office. Ömer looked Yucel up and down. They were right he was like a big bear, 'Yogi' was a good name for him. The two men weighed each other up. Yucel saw a well-dressed young Turk the wrong side of twenty five. Deep tan, jewellery, hair slicked back and the confident look of the 'kept man.' By now everyone was beginning to look like a suspect to Yucel. He'd never been that way before. In the laid-back style of his usual authority he hadn't had to. Recent events were focussing his intuition.

"How can I help sir?" He wasn't going to give too much away at this stage.

They spoke in Turkish quickly. Ömer told him that his English girlfriend was missing. He explained that she had left the Orange bar, before he did, after an argument and had not returned to their home. This was a few days before and Yucel asked the obvious question why he had taken so long to report her disappearance.

Ömer shrugged his shoulders. The two men exchanged glances and Ömer admitted he thought she was staying with a girlfriend or someone just to punish him, and make her point.

"You know what women are like, she thought I was after someone in the bar; some young Irish girl."

"And were you?"

Ömer smiled. "It's hard you know when it's on offer. Ok, I did make a mistake maybe."

Yucel asked him about their financial arrangements and his suspicions were confirmed. Josie had bought the flat, but put it in both their names. She supported him financially. She had savings left, but he guessed they wouldn't last forever. Was this enough of a motivation to kill her?

'Yogi' wasn't in cartoon mood. "When Josie and yourself purchased your property, the 'Tapu' (Title Deeds) were in both your names?"

"Yes."

"Just the two of you? No children or other relatives included?"

"Yes."

"And did Josie have prior access to an English-speaking lawyer to explain about the complexities of Turkish inheritance laws?"

"Sort of." Ömer squirmed in his chair.

Yucel knew the answer. "That's a no then?"

"She just wanted to leave all that to me. I tried to get her to see someone, but she wouldn't. She trusted me…"

"And what about Mary." Yucel moved on.

Ömer told him that although he didn't know her that well, he had been shocked by news of her death. He also said that she had been 'going out' with his cousin for a time.

Yucel took his time to mention the ring. He wanted to know if this man had any idea his girlfriend was likely to be lying in the cold room.

Ömer stuttered when he talked about the ring. He agreed that was why he had come to the Police station. He had recognised the ring and thought it was the one he'd given to Josie, the week that they met.

"An engagement ring?" Yucel enquired.

"No, it was a gift, to tell her that I was serious and I wanted her to come back."

Yucel looked him in the eye. "So was it a fake ring for a fake promise Ömer?"

His words were profound. Ömer told him how he obtained the ring. Yucel pulled his drawer open and took out a box. He held out the ring and waited for Ömer's reaction.

"It looks like the same one," looking puzzled, "why would Mary have it?"

Yucel drew a deep breath "She didn't. The ring was on the hand of a second woman's body, also found in the National Park." He stopped short of telling him that the body had been half-eaten by wild pigs. Yucel is a fair man. One shock at a time.

Ömer looked up. It was finally sinking in.

"What?"

Yucel continued. "We found the rest of the body a few hours ago."

Ömer was too stunned to notice the word 'rest.'

"Can you come with me please Ömer? I need you to formally identify the body, if indeed it is Josie Wilson."

Ömer just nodded.

"I am sorry this may be difficult for you. The body was interfered with by some of the Milli Park wildlife." Yucel still couldn't say eaten. He ushered him into the temporary morgue, slowly pulled back the sheet and watched Ömer's face.

Despite his deep tan, Ömer went white. His hand went to his mouth and Yucel thought he was going to be sick. Then he was sick, coughing through it, "Josie, Josie." Then tears, now he was breaking down.

Yucel didn't need to ask the question. Ömer was becoming hysterical. Guilt maybe? Guilt at letting her walk to her death while he went off with a young girl. Or guilt because he killed her? Yucel arranged for the room to be cleaned and took Ömer back to his office.

"How did she die?" Ömer wanted to know.

Yucel wanted to say garrotted, but technically the man before him is a suspect, so the killer's MO is best kept secret as long as possible.

"We don't know at this stage. The forensic examinations and Autopsy haven't been concluded yet."

Chief Semir didn't sound cagey, just professional.

"I'm very sorry for your loss." He added as an afterthought. Ömer would be ok. He had an expensive flat paid for by this woman who obviously thought he was something special. He wasn't. Now she has paid another price.

"Can you let me have details of her family in England please?" Ömer nodded, remembering Josie when they met. A vision in a red shiny dress, eyes only for him. She had adored him. He knew that. Now half of her was lying in here and she wasn't coming back.

"I will need to speak to you again Ömer. I hope you are not planning any trips?" Sounding like a Policeman again. "Do you have a passport?"

"No," said Ömer. "Never needed one."

Ömer left Police Headquarters, his phone already at his ear. Yucel watched him leave. He didn't look like a serial killer, just a cocky little man praying on vulnerable women, who should know better. But he couldn't rule him out. Not yet.

He saw Val Neville and a younger woman waiting in reception and guessed they had come to see him. He wondered if she was a relative of Mary's. He welcomed them into his office. Mary introduced Charlie, saying that she was worried because her mother couldn't be located.

"Is she missing?" Yucel asked

"I don't know. I just know I haven't been able to get hold of her, since last Saturday morning. Everyone thinks she is in England, but she isn't. Her passport is still in her flat."

He wrote down Dee's details and kept the photo Charlie had brought with her. Then Charlie asked Yucel about the ring.

"It could belong to my mother," she said, looking anxious again.

"No," looking directly at Val. He realised she hadn't told her about the arm. Despite her fears for Dee.

"We know now who the ring belongs to. I'm going to tell you because it will be on the news tonight. We have found another body. An English woman, Josie Wilson. Her body was found in the National Park, a kilometre or so from where Mary was buried. We are sure that she too was murdered by the same killer."

Val took a sharp intake of breath. The blood drained from Charlie's face. Yucel sympathised. Surely her Mother couldn't be another victim. His men could be searching for weeks and not necessarily find her. If the killer had committed the crimes around the same period, perhaps he buried all the bodies together at the same time. That would make sense. Perhaps his men should be searching for Deidre Davison, not sitting in the room next door drinking coffee.

He tried to re-assure Charlie, but not very convincingly. "There could be another explanation Ms Davison. There is nothing to suggest any harm has come to your mother."

"There's nothing to suggest that she's okay either." Charlie fired back. "No one's heard anything."

The Chief took details of Dee's partner Deniz, although he knew of him already. Buying and selling bars like 'East meets West' brings him to the attention of the body who sanction Alcohol licensing, in which Chief Semir plays a part. He thought he could be an arrogant man when pushed. Still he had more to worry about. Once the English papers started reporting the details, he guessed many women would be cancelling their holidays.

One murder could be a domestic incident, a jealous husband gone mad. But two? And with a Turkish Eye hung around the neck. Strangled and buried. Left for the boars to devour. No that wouldn't go down well. And now there was a third missing woman.

Yucel assured Charlie he would do anything in his power to find her mother. As he said it, he knew the words were empty. What could he do? They had checked with English relatives. He could do a border check and see if she had left Turkey. He could check the passenger log of the ferry to Samos. But her passport was here, so how could she have got on it? Charlie gave him her mother's passport for him to check its validity. He would do the enquiries anyway and speak to Deniz, but he has a limited number of staff. Especially if half of them were doing manual work in the National Park.

Seb, his deputy rang through to say that he was being

bombarded by the English press already. The Sun, The Mirror, The Star all wanting to know what had happened.

"Tell them you don't speak English; and say it in Turkish." Yucel laughed as he said it.

"I tried that Chief, but they're not stupid, they get their Turkish speaking staff to ring me." Seb sounded bereft.

"Do what politicians do. Say a lot but tell them nothing. I've got to get on..." Yucel put the phone down, worrying what on earth Seb was going to reveal. He also needed to let the press here know about Josie Wilson and contact her family. So much to do and so little time. It had already leaked out to the local press about the Turkish Eye. He had a feeling he knew who was responsible, but there was no time for a witch-hunt. The Turkish press were now calling this the 'Ege' Eye Killer story.

"I'm sorry ladies. I have to do some urgent business. I have to speak to the deceased's family and inform the press of the second murder. I believe the English have a saying I might use and I apologise for my language, but the Shit is going to hit the pan."

Charlie said as she stood up, "it's fan."

"Fan?" Yucel looked puzzled, "how does that...

Val interrupted. "Never mind, pet," and steered the woeful Charlie to the door.

Charlie didn't know whether to be re-assured that the ring wasn't her mother's or terrified that she could be lying somewhere in the National park.

"Let's go and have a drink," said Val. "I think we need one."

147

26

Dee

D ee opened her eyes and looked around the room. Someone had cleaned her eyes and lids and she could see something now. A dark figure wearing some sort of green shirt loomed in front of her and she felt the needle go into her arm. Her consciousness drifted away yet again...

She was back in Newcastle and she was lying in a hospital bed. She looked down and saw her baby girl in her arms and the fear dissipated. Charlotte Joan Davison lay quietly and curiously looking into her mother's face.

Everyone agreed she was beautiful. Particularly her father who couldn't quite believe that she'd finally arrived. They had tried for years for a baby and it looked as if it wasn't going to happen. Deidre became paranoid as she started to think something was wrong with her. She couldn't bring herself to go to the doctor's as she didn't want to know the truth. This way she could always fool herself. Paul respected her views. He didn't go either, they just carried on their lives as normal. Closer than most couples, the infertility didn't tear them apart, it held them together. When he came home from work one night, he could sense something was different. Deidre was smiling, glowing almost. She had cooked him a steak and his favourite trifle for dessert. What was going on? She sat him down on the sofa and told him she had something to tell him. Not that surely? It had been too long?

"I'm pregnant!" She laughed as she said it, almost hysterically.

He picked her up in his arms and hugged her, the tears falling down his face onto his overalls. This was out of the blue, he'd just assumed it would never happen. Not that he didn't want it to happen. He had always wanted children. They had planned to have six. Well, one would do.

"You are an incredible woman Deidre Davison," he said laughing too.

And so the minor-miracle Charlotte 'Charlie' Davison arrived and changed their world. In a good way. Deidre loved being a mum or mam as she was known and thanked God for the safe arrival of her daughter. She loved breast feeding her whilst other babies were on their bottles, such was the trend. She was older than some of the new mums, but she always felt old fashioned for her age. She had hand stitched baby clothes and knitted cardigans whilst the other trendy mums were buying at Mothercare and Baby Gap.

It didn't bother Deidre, she would do things her way. Her brothers and the twins were thrilled for her and Charlie wouldn't lack in the cousins department. Paul's mum was over the moon and delighted to be Granny Pauline. It was a blissful few years. Perhaps Deidre only appreciated that when it was all over. The vision went dark.

27

Jenni

Jenni luxuriated in her sunken bath and felt like a cat that had got the cream. The wedding had all gone to plan and the flat was sorted, just the way she wanted it. She had her man and she had no more money worries. She would be comfortable for the rest of her life. She slipped into one of the soft towelling His and Hers robes. She smiled. Okay they're a bit naff, but she didn't care.

She had her morning planned. Hairdresser at twelve. Some lunch with a couple of friends then a pedicure at three. Maybe some shopping after that, then an early dinner somewhere nice. Perhaps that new restaurant with the walled garden.

She was on her own in the flat. Unusually, Khan had gone to see one of his friends and play some backgammon or go to the beach. Jenni wasn't a jealous woman. She had no reason to be. He was sixteen years younger than her, but she knew that made no difference. They were a couple and that was that. She had no reason to feel insecure.

She applied her makeup carefully. No sunbathing for her now. She needed to be careful with her skin being a red head, preferring the porcelain white look instead of withered prune. She went into her walk in wardrobe and looked at the arrangement of dresses. Actually, just the day wear section. It was quite casual here, but she liked to look her best. Her son had been amazed at the change in her since her win. Slimmer, more confident and not the down trodden Jenni she had become.

She heard the door. Don't tell me that he's forgotten his key again. She went into the hall way and out towards the front door. It looked as if it was ajar. What was going on? As she walked to the door in her heels and underwear she thought she had tripped. Then she changed her mind and thought she had felt someone grab her from behind.

And that thought was the last.

28

Charlie & Val

C harlie and Val walked along the front and down
one of the side alleys. Charlie was going to see
Deniz and tell him about the passport. She couldn't
leave it any longer. So much had happened in the last
couple of days since she had seen him last.

He was sitting at his computer behind the bar with a
serious look on his face. He attempted a smile as Val and
Charlie walked in, but he didn't manage to. Later on in
the evening he would cheer up, but now he was trying
to sort out some accounts.

The two women sat up at the bar. He asked them if
they wanted vodka and sodas and then poured them
efficiently. He went back to his accounts.

Charlie didn't know if she could trust him. She didn't
know anything anymore. But eventually they
interrupted him from his work and told him about
finding Dee's passport and the fact that there were now
two women that had been found, murdered.

His scowl deepened. "What are you saying, do you
think this man has Dee?"

Charlie looked as if she was about to cry. "Well, have
you heard anything from her?"

He admitted he hadn't, but wasn't that worried. It
had all seemed so normal when she went away.

"Why would she say she was going away if she
wasn't'?" This was all man's logic and Charlie winced.

"He has got a point," said Val. "I mean the other two
were presumably taken on their way home. Dee told
everyone she was going away.

Deniz was adamant she was okay. He couldn't contemplate her body in the National Park either, but he had been shocked by Mary's death. He had only just heard about Josie, on the internet news feed.

He also showed Val and Charlie the 'photoshopped' picture of Mary with the Turkish Eye around her neck. It was gross. Where had they got the photo? It was taken at Adem's and the people on either side had been taken out. Surely he hadn't given the photo to the press. Maybe everyone does have a price?

Val scolded herself for her bad thoughts. 'Don't make assumptions, she told herself.' Deniz though, didn't seem as upset as she thought he would be. He looked at them through narrowed eyes. "She will be back. I know she will."

Which was of little comfort to Charlie who, by now, just wanted her mother home. She had forgotten every bad thought she had ever had about her. She just wanted to see her. Hug her; smell her smell, 'Opium.' She had smelt it on her sheets the previous night and it had sent her mind in overdrive.

Charlie and Val had become a team. Somehow they bonded together in the tragedy of Mary and Josie and the missing Dee. Val asked Charlie if she would come back to her place, so she could feed the cat and see what mess the police had made. Charlie agreed, glad to be doing something rather than just thinking and worrying. She had a message from Tarkan whilst they were in the bar and he was asking if she would be going to the Cactus as he would very much like to see her. She replied with a quick maybe. Her mind on other things.

She walked up the hill to Val's flat, probably half way to Dee's place. It was smaller and more cramped than she'd imagined and the buildings around looked like a bit of a mishmash of architecture. Still the outside appeared to be free of the press and it wasn't cordoned off, so that was a good start. As they climbed the stairs, Val pointed out Mary's flat, the cat followed them upstairs. Val didn't have the key to Mary's on her, so she would have to feed Alfie from her own cupboards.

She found another tin of tuna and fed him on her own balcony. It felt really strange to be here. She didn't honestly know if she could live here anymore without Mary downstairs. Charlie looked around. It was lovely inside. Val was like her mother she knew how to make a house a home. She saw one of her mother's art work on the wall. It was blues and greens, a swirl of colour with silver leaf and a black background. Like the night sky, she thought. She saw the small signature DD in the corner.

"She gave it to me," said Val. "I wanted to pay her for it, but she was having none of it. It was before she started exhibiting in the gallery. She said she was just practising."

Charlie smiled. She loved the picture and it re-enforced that the women were close. Val asked Charlie if she wanted to go downstairs with her to Mary's flat. She said yes, but was apprehensive at the same time. It was a bit creepy. She didn't know Mary at all, but she felt somehow as if she did.

Mary's flat was starting to smell. Val opened some windows. It was stale and oppressive. The Police had clearly decided this was not the crime scene, so nothing much had been disturbed. Mary kept some personal papers in her kitchen drawer and they had been taken. Her bed sheets had also been removed although Val wasn't convinced that Turkish forensic science would reveal much.

Mary fed Alfie and he purred affectionately around their legs. He was missing Mary and the attention she gave him. She would have to get him settled in her flat. They went back upstairs and Val cooked some pasta and tomato sauce for them both. As she grated some cheese on the top, she saw Alfie curled up on her sofa. He had already made himself at home.

Charlie and Val ate their food on the balcony in a companionable silence. Both women had their own thoughts and eventually Val spoke.

"Look pet, we need to think about what to do next. Do you think it's worth going back into town and asking around? But this time, try and find out if anyone has seen your mam? Perhaps her and Deniz had a row? Maybe she wanted some time out. You never know, he's a dark horse that one."

Charlie agreed. "You're right, we can't just sit indoors for another night. I want to at least feel as if I am doing something to find her."

They walked back down the hill towards the town centre. The view was magnificent and for a brief moment Charlie forgot about her troubles. She could see why her mother loved this place. It had a charm of its own. It would be such a shame if people stopped coming here because of the murders or because they couldn't feel safe.

The Turkish people deserved better. She thought about London, the grime, the gangs and the crime. This town was different. But something had gone terribly wrong. She wondered about the Police in the same way as Val. Were they up to the task? How do you set about catching who did this? And how do you stop them? She didn't believe Turkey had a national DNA database as the UK did now. So forensic evidence would only help when they could match fibres or something like body fluids to a suspect in custody.

They decided to go to Adem's and hear the word on the street. It was a hotbed of gossip and activity when they arrived. She could hear people talking about Mary and Josie, before they got through the door. Clearly it was the biggest news in the town, since the bombings in 2004.

Charlie and Val greeted Adem and he found them a seat in the corner. Given that women had been advised to stay in the place was packed. The singer was almost shouting rather than singing and Charlie looked at Val.

"Who's that?"

"Symmon," said Val. "He used to sing at the Cactus when I first came to Kuşadasi." Charlie looked at the singer who appeared to be staring at her. He was about six foot three, with an imposing aura, shaved head and piercing blue eyes. Dressed in black leather trousers and a tight white shirt, he grinned as he sang. Charlie thought he looked pleased with himself. Singing 'Peaches' and old Stranglers' records, she didn't particular like his gravelly voice. His voice was too loud for the song and for the small bar.

They sat and chatted with a group of English who Val appeared to know quite well. An elderly couple from Liverpool expressed horror at what had happened to Mary. They all agreed she had been a lovely woman and a 'character.' How many times had Charlie heard that word? There was a group of three women from the midlands, who seemed to revel in knowing as many details as they'd been able to find out. The Turkish Eye featured heavily in their conversation and they told Val, they were only going out in a threesome now. Let the killer try and take on three of them!

Val looked at Charlie and wondered how she was feeling hearing all this stuff. It was inevitable, but she was in limbo not knowing where her mother was. She had introduced Charlie without saying who her mother was and gradually introduced Dee into the conversation.

The three women, Yvonne, Janet and Kath picked up on it when she asked if anyone had seen 'Geordie Dee.' Charlie hadn't heard her referred to as that and it made her smile. Yvonne told Val she had gone back to England for a while she thought. Janet said she had seen her in East meets West, last week she thought. But she was definitely going home.

"Best place at the moment," said Janet. She proceeded to tell Charlie and Val about all the expats who were going home 'for a while.' The couple from Liverpool, Alf and Alice said they had booked a flight back tomorrow. "You just don't know," said Alf sagely.

Charlie discovered that some of the group didn't have a home in England anymore. Some of the women, particularly the single ones, had sold up 'lock stock and barrel' and although they had family at home, didn't have a home to return to. She guessed their money went further here, though no one could have predicted what was going to happen.

Symmon came over to their table. He had finished his set with a rendition of 'Stairway to Heaven' that set Charlie's teeth on edge. He leaned over the table and grinned inanely. "Hello ladies." He addressed the group including Charlie and Val.

He sat down next to Val and Charlie without being asked and fixed his piercing stare on Charlie.

"Hi Beautiful how are you?"

"Okay thanks," said Charlie.

Val merely smiled and said, "hi Symmon, how's

you?"

"I am good my dear, very good. Apart from hearing the news about poor Mary of course and that other woman what was her name?"

"Josie," said Charlie.

He talked for a while with the group, mainly about the murders and then the conversation turned to chit chat. Charlie felt uncomfortable and told Val so, after he left. "What a creep!"

Val laughed. "He's okay when you get to know him; a bit full of himself, but he used to be worse when he thought he was a 'love god' at the Cactus."

Charlie looked at him, his stomach threatening to burst buttons. He may have been in shape once, but he was already going to seed.

Symmon was back on the very small stage. This time with an introduction that nearly made Charlie vomit.

"For all the beautiful ladies in here tonight, you know who you are," looking directly at Charlie. He proceeded to sing 'Hey, if you happened to see the most beautiful girl in the world.' It was beyond cheesy.

Charlie decided she couldn't take any more and told Val she was off to the Cactus to see Tarkan. The two women embraced. "Take care pet," said Val. "Ring me tomorrow."

The shops and stalls in the alleys were still busy. Charlie walked the few hundred yards from Adem's to the Cactus. She saw the back of Tarkan before he saw her. He was singing one of her favourite songs, REM's 'Losing my religion.' He was such a better singer than Symmon. No wonder he had been replaced. She smiled at Tarkan and sat down at a table for two to the side of the stage. Four waiters appeared simultaneously in a slightly oppressive way, buzzing around. She ordered a drink and waited for him to finish his set.

Left to her own thoughts, she thought about her mother and her own behaviour. She could see that she had treated Dee really badly. Things were so different now. Getting out of London and evaluating her life she could see how she had changed. She had made her mam suffer over the last few years and now she had that guilt hanging over her. She realised how selfish she had been in trying to control her mother's life and happiness. No wonder she only rang her once a month. She hadn't even deserved that really. Why had it taken her disappearance to make her realise all this?

Tarkan came over and sat down opposite her. He took hold of her hand and kissed her on both cheeks. She looked up at him and wondered what it was about him that made her feel so relaxed. They didn't even speak the same language, but they seemed to communicate better than most. He asked if there had been any news regarding Dee and she shook her head. They talked about the two women who had been murdered and Tarkan seemed genuinely sad about Mary. He said he was going to play some Irish music the following night at Adem's as a tribute to her. Adem had asked him today if he would

"It's a chance to remember her. It's not much, but it's all I can do."

He was sensitive and Charlie recognised that she needed him around while she was in Turkey. He made her feel safe and she wanted to feel safe. Mostly she wanted her mother, but she was still missing. Charlie liked to think of herself as an independent woman, but if she was honest, it was easy to be independent when you had friends and family to support you. She had always known her mother was there as a safety net, if she needed it. Until now.

"I'm finished now," said Tarkan. "Ekin is going to do a couple of sets tonight."

She was the attractive Turkish girl who had sung a duet with Tarkan the first time she had seen him. She had wondered initially if they were an item, but he laughed that off. She was a cousin who was trying to make it with her band in the town and he was trying to give her a break when he could. She was good, thought Charlie and you don't see enough Turkish women in this town.

Nearly all the bar staff and waiters were men. The same for the shop staff. It was a man's town in terms of employment and opportunities. All the singers she had seen in the bars had been men too. It was nice to see Ekin doing it for the girls.

"Do you want to go to Adem's?" Tarkan asked.

Charlie laughed. "Do you?"

"Not really", he said. "I know Symmon is playing there and we had a bit of a disagreement the other night. If I go, he'll just start again."

"Suits me, I was there earlier," confessed Charlie. "What was the argument about?"

"Women," said Tarkan. "There was a young girl there with him, she was only about seventeen or so. A student I think. He was coming on really heavy with her. Her friends were egging her on to go with him. I warned her off, when he was in the toilet. I've seen the way he treats women and once the sex is over he is... How do you say? Vile. This girl didn't deserve it and she was too young to see what was going on. When he came out and she had gone, he asked me where she was and I told him."

"How did he react," asked Charlie? "He didn't look

as if he was the sort of person to mess with. Those eyes."

"He went mad. He was holding the table on both sides in front of me, as if he was going to punch me. Adem had to sort him out. He made out it was a joke; a misunderstanding. But it wasn't believe me."

"He had to behave himself," said Tarkan, "or Adem wouldn't let him work there. He had already sacked him once for having sex in the toilet with another woman. She was drunk, he said he didn't know what he was doing. He is an animal."

"Nice," said Charlie sarcastically.

Charlie made a snap decision. "Do you want to come back to my mams flat? We can have a drink there. If you don't mind parrots!"

He laughed. "Yes please."

They took a cab back to the flat. Neither felt like walking, given what had been happening. As the cab pulled up she saw a light on in the window. Could it be Dee? Or had she left the light on when she went out earlier? As she put her key in the door she heard a noise in the kitchen. Tarkan went in first. It was Deniz, he seemed to be feeding the parrot despite knowing that Charlie was living there.

He scowled at Tarkan. "What's he doing here?" He asked Charlie.

"I could ask you the same question? This is Dee's flat not yours."

"I was feeding the bird. I can come here when I like. Your mother and I..."

"My mother and you what? You don't seem that bothered she's missing. Do you?"

"She isn't missing," said Deniz.

"Well she isn't in England. I told you her passport is here."

"I'm not going to argue with you Charlie. She will come back when she is ready. You shouldn't be bringing… him," he almost spat out the word, "here."

"That's my business Deniz and I'd appreciate it if you left now please."

He pushed past Tarkan quite aggressively, despite the difference in height. He was making a point to the younger man.

As he left Charlie turned to Tarkan. "What was that all about?"

"He is a control freak Charlie. He needed to know what you were doing here. What was happening?' That's his nature."

She opened a bottle of red wine and they went into the lounge. As they sipped their drinks, she asked Tarkan why he had left East Meets West and why he had fallen out with Deniz.

"It was about money Charlie. He would 'forget' to pay me; say it would be next week. The wages didn't get any better, even when the place was packed and he was making a fortune. He is mean, that's how he has so many businesses. He doesn't care about the staff, just about making money. I worked there from the age of eighteen; I saw him as a father figure, but as soon as I became popular he changed. I was the one who was supposed to change? Get big headed. But it was Deniz, he just started being strange with me. The pay was the final straw I suppose."

"Go on," Charlie encouraged.

"They had asked me to go to the Cactus, offered me more money. That was the joke. Even the year before they were trying to poach me away and I was loyal to him and the bar. I loved working there, but in the end I told him what he could do with his job. He still owes me money. He gets other singers, but they don't stay long. It's the same with the bar staff. He isn't a man of honour Charlie."

Charlie wondered what Dee saw in him. Were they still an item? She only had his word. Her mother hadn't mentioned him recently and when she rang the conversation seemed mainly to focus on the weather, and asking Charlie about herself. She realised how little she really knew about her mam's life. Was she happy? Did Deniz make her happy in the way she had been happy with Paul. She doubted that. He was very different from her father, physically and in every other way. Her father had lived and died by his principles. This puzzled Charlie.

Charlie looked at Tarkan. He had principles and she liked that. She also liked his smell as he moved closer to kiss her. Gently at first then with more passion. She groaned. She had known what would happen when she invited him back here. She wasn't a fool. He was stroking her nipples now, through her T-shirt and they were responding despite her doubts. She put her arms around his powerful shoulders and pulled him down on top of her.

The sex was as good as she had hoped. He was a patient and an enthusiastic lover. They moved to her bedroom and he pulled off his jeans and started to undress her. He kissed her neck and her shoulder blade and dressed only in a pair of Calvin Klein's his erection was impressive. She started to rub his cock and now it was time for him to moan, "Oh my God Charlie, come here." He pulled a condom from his pocket and asked her to help him. She obliged, sucking and licking his shaft at the same time. He felt as if he was going to burst, but he held back.

They fell on to the bed and he propped himself on one side as he started to lick her nipples, alternating with her mouth. His lips moved down and soon he was tickling her labia with his tongue causing the most fantastic sensations she had ever known. He worked his tongue inside her and hit the spot quickly, but with the lightest touch. She gave herself up and lay back. After he'd made her come for the first time, she pushed him back on to the bed and mounted him. It had become all about the moment, she had forgotten everything else at that point. She wanted him inside her. She held his cock in her entrance with her muscles, before sliding down and pulling him fully inside her. "Fuck me," she said, "that's good."

He began to move rhythmically, controlling himself and pulling her hips back and forth, she moaned and knew she was about to come again. It was exquisite and as he sucked her nipples, biting them with his teeth gently, her contractions began and she was lost. He followed, triggering his own climax that seemed to last for minutes as he pumped into her. They collapsed together on the bed and he continued to kiss her lips, her eyes and her face.

He looked at her in the half light. He hardly knew this woman, yet he felt he had always known her. She lay next to him her hair covering her breast and still breathing heavily. She smiled at him.

"I think you've done this before Tarkan," she teased. He laughed and began to rub her clitoris almost as an afterthought. She started to squirm and soon was speechless as she waited for the sensation of another climax. He carried on his caress until he felt her juices as she came for him again. He felt power and delight that he could pleasure Charlie so intensely. He had many offers during his line of work, but he was choosy with whom he spent the night.

She got up and brought back the wine and glasses with her. They were both hungry, but the fridge was empty apart from a few ice cubes. He rang someone from his mobile and a fast food driver on a moped soon appeared with a veritable feast of lamb shish, bread, salad and yoghurt. They ate on the balcony and talked through the night. His English was good, but he said that this hadn't always been the case. When he first came to Kuşadasi from Izmir he struggled initially.

He told her about himself and his family. It all sounded a bit idyllic to Charlie, who envied the uncomplicated relationships he appeared to have with his parents and siblings. He must think I am strange thought Charlie. Hardly talking to my mother for months on end apart from a quick phone call. Charlie thought she was mad too, and wished for the umpteenth time that she could turn back the clock.

29

Yucel

The Chief sat in his office with the forensic and medical reports. Confirming that both women had been garrotted, but not with the rope attached to the Turkish Eye. They would appear to be solely for decorative purposes. No, they had been strangled with some kind of wire. Nothing was found near the body so he must have planned the killings in the eyes of Yucel. Or at least been prepared to take advantage of a situation. Also the National Park was definitely not the crime scene.

Ömer appeared to be off the list of suspects. Yucel thought him to be an opportunist and a rogue, but not a killer. However, he could have prevented the death of his girlfriend had he taken her home that night and he would have to live with that. He had the apartment and he didn't think it would take him long to forget Josie. Her sister was absolutely devastated and had been hysterical on the phone. She suspected Ömer immediately, but for no other reason than she didn't like him. She hadn't trusted him and look what had happened to her sister.

Mary's family had been less interested. Her son was an unpleasant piece of work, thought Yucel. He was blaming Mary herself for her own death. He appeared to be quite religious and zealous with it, talking of Sodom and Gomorrah and his mother turning into a harlot. He clearly blamed Mary for leaving his father, even though Val had told Yucel she had been a victim of domestic abuse. He said he hadn't seen his mother for seven years, his two children hadn't seen her at all and he had no desire to come to Turkey to claim her body for a burial.

Yucel would have hated it if his children treated him that way. What had the woman done to deserve that treatment? She was still his mother and he should have had some respect for her. He certainly respected his mother. She was a force to be reckoned with and although like most Turkish women, appeared to take a back seat, actually she was very much in charge at home. She was proud of Yucel, her firstborn and what he had achieved in the Police. She was four feet eleven in her stocking feet and when she stood next to her giant son, she literally had to look up. She could have a sharp tongue if crossed, but no one crossed her.

Luckily for Yucel, she had taken to her daughter-in-law almost instantly. He thought she might think no one was good enough, but the two women got along famously. His wife Ayla would take his mother shopping to the new Marina and they would sit drinking tea in one of the café's. He guessed his wife would be complaining to his mother about him not being at home right now. His mother would be shaking her head and agreeing, but both women knew how serious this case was and had empathy with the women and their families. His mother had never heard of such a thing, she constantly told him on the phone. Her town was a safe town, what would people think about it? The killer couldn't be a Turkish man? Surely not.

He had tried to calm her. The Police were doing everything they can, he assured her. We will catch the killer. His mother said it had put her off going out. She still went to the market every few days though. Her routine wouldn't be changed. His father was close to retirement, but still worked for the government offices in Aydin. He was also a creature of habit, leaving home at eight every morning and returning at six thirty every night. He was a tall man, but not as well built as his son. He was a man of few words, but Yucel knew he could rely on him for anything. Both grandparents were looking forward to the birth of their second grandchild.

Val Neville rang him and said they were having a fund raiser for Mary tomorrow night at Adem's to raise some money for a decent funeral. He supposed that Val would sort out her few belonging and personal items. It was a difficult situation in a foreign country for these women. Most would have wanted to be buried in their home country and in Mary's case Ireland. But what could he do? There was no fund to pay for any of this, unless the Irish government got involved. But then again, she seemed to have more friends in Turkey.

Headquarters had sent a criminal profiler down to assist. Zeki was from Ankara and had studied forensic anthropology and psychology in America, gaining a double-first, apparently. He still looked about twelve years old to Yucel.

Zeki had a very serious demeanour as he looked at the case information and statements from those who had known the two women. Neither appeared to have any enemies, it all seemed quite random to Yucel. They were in the wrong place at the wrong time. This killer was a predator.

Zeki was currently looking at wire. Having examined the wounds in microscopic detail. He was sure that the ligature could be identified and that may give a clue as to the perpetrator. Yucel wasn't convinced, as far as the big man was concerned wire was wire. But what did he know. He hadn't been taught forensics at University, he had worked his way up the ranks. If he was honest he was a bit put out. It was a blow to his pride, although he'd half expected it.

Yucel's phone rang. One of his officers had initially taken the call. It was a man called Khan Emlak who lived in an apartment near the Marina. The officer said he was hysterical. Yucel spoke to him and he said that he had come home to find his wife, of three months, murdered in their bedroom. He said it looked as if she had been strangled with a Turkish Eye on a rope.

The Police were there in ten minutes. The Chief ordered the area to be sealed off and walked into the palatial hallway. Jenni Khan was lying on the floor in the bedroom. Her husband said he had put a sheet over her, he couldn't bear to look at her lying there. He was rocking and sobbing on the floor and almost wailing with grief. In between sobs he managed to tell the officers that he had been out since ten that morning and had returned home an hour ago, to find his wife dead in their bedroom.

'She must have known her attacker,' thought Yucel. 'She let him in, there was no sign of any break in.'

He told two of his trusted officers to check with the other residents immediately. "Find out who has been in and out of this building. Get all their details, any deliveries, anything."

Jenni was lying in a prone pose on the floor. She was pale and voluptuous and even in death, looked like an alabaster statue. She was showing the same signs of injury as the previous two victims. Her neck was bruised already and there were cuts and scratches along the lines of strangulation. The rope was still round it, with the Turkish Eye held on with a double knot. It didn't look by her nails and posture that she had struggled. She was wearing expensive looking underwear, but no other clothing. She had one shoe on and one off, it lay on the floor a few feet away. A dress lay on the bed that didn't look as if she'd had it on. It looked clean and ready to wear. New in fact. Why did she let someone in wearing only her underwear? He didn't think a Turkish girl would. He knew English girls were less shy about these things, but...

Unless of course she thought she was letting her in husband?

Khan wasn't much use to them in the state he was in. Yucel told him, as kindly as he was able, to pull himself together because he would need to answer some questions at the police station. He looked panicked at this point and he assured him he had nothing to worry about. Unlike the Chief who had a third death on his hands and a missing person. The killer had now moved on to killing women in their own homes, panic would now ensue, he was sure of that.

He rang his wife's number and started preparing how he would say that he would fail to turn up for dinner, yet again. He gave a deep sigh and wished he had some cigarettes.

30

Charlie

Y ou don't need an alarm clock when you've got that damn parrot, was Charlie's first thought of the day. She must have forgotten to feed him last night.

"Hello pet. Hello seedy. Hello seedy." It was really loud. She looked round and saw Tarkan sleeping peacefully next to her. Almost angelic in sleep, his hair flopped over his face and he looked younger. Oh Charlie what have you done, she chided herself, life was complicated enough as it is, without this.

She got out of bed and went into the bathroom. Cleaning her teeth she pulled on one of her mam's robes that hung on the bathroom door. She went into the kitchen and fed Oscar, who was maniacally squawking all kinds of rubbish now. She found the coffee maker and made a pot, realising there would be no milk as she hadn't actually bought any.

Tarkan heard her get up and stirred. He looked at his watch it was just after eleven. Quite early for him as he was a night person, given he didn't start work until the evening. He pulled on his CK's and went to find Charlie in the kitchen. It's always an awkward moment, after the night before, in the cold light of day. They hugged and he felt they had a connection.

"Coffee?" she asked smiling at his matted hair and four o clock shadow. He still looked good.

"Do you have milk?"

He must be a mind reader, Charlie thought.

"No sorry. I haven't got round to going to the supermarket." It sounded feeble as there was one only about two hundred yards away at the entrance of the Sitesi.

"Don't worry," he said.

'Oh I see,' she thought. 'He's going to make a quick exit.'

"I'll go down to the supermarket and get us some breakfast." Charlie smiled. Perhaps she wasn't such a bad judge of character after all.

Tarkan came back with crusty bread, cheese, tomatoes, some eggs, milk and orange juice. He made them scrambled eggs with the tomato and cheese and called it Menemen. She also saw him slip in some fresh chilli. For breakfast? He said it was his speciality.

"That means it's the only thing you can cook." Charlie laughed He pretended to look outraged?

"Excuse me Charlie, but I think you will be surprised at my skills in the kitchen."

"Well pet, if they're anything like your skills in the bedroom, you can make dinner too." Why was she so comfortable with this man?

"Okay," he said kissing her, as he grabbed her waist.

They had breakfast on the balcony and Tarkan suggested that they went to the beach. Charlie felt guilty at first. She should stay here for Dee, but he gently reminded her that it wouldn't bring her back quicker. He knew how anxious she was about the murders, but all he felt he could do at this stage was take her mind off things. He didn't want to believe anything had happened to Dee either. She was a lovely woman. Is a lovely woman he reminded himself?

Charlie agreed there was little else she could do but wait at this stage. She knew Yucel would ring her if there were any further developments. He had already told her that he had requested a high level check on whether or not her mother had left the country.

These last few days were so strange. They had gone so quickly. It wasn't like a holiday and yet in a strange way she felt as though she had been in this country for weeks, rather than days. It had embraced her and she had embraced Turkey. Despite the terrible events that were happening.

Tarkan suggested that she pack a bag for the beach and they would get the dolmuş to his place in town, so he could collect his swimming stuff. She had seen the small buses around the place with people hopping on and off, but hadn't been on one.

It was an experience. Tarkan told her that the word 'dolmuş' means 'full' in Turkish and this was an accurate description. People got on, filled the seats then simply carried on getting on, until no one else could fit on the bus. People handed small amounts of change to the driver and passed the money to each other. It was very different to anything she had experienced. The driver drove along honking at anyone walking on the street who may be a potential customer. Luckily she had a seat next to Tarkan, as the bus hadn't been full when it stopped at the end of the road where Dee's apartment was situated.

She held her bag close to her and watched as the bus filled with women, dressed in headscarves, going to the market or the shops. Children coming from school in their white shirts and the girls in smart tartan shirts. Older Turkish men huffing and puffing. It was a microcosm of Turkish life, she thought and like a lot of things here, looked chaotic on the surface, but it actually worked well. The traffic was crazy, but she hadn't seen a single accident. The buses seemed random, but you never have to wait very long.

She hoped the Police department operated in the same way. Appearing to lag behind, but would be able to find the killer of these women quicker than people would imagine.

They got off in the centre, near the Town hall, and where all roads appeared to lead into one massive noisy roundabout. Tarkan took her past some shops and restaurants she hadn't yet seen, before heading down a backstreet. She was a bit lost, but knew she wasn't far from the Cactus and the old town as they had passed the infamous 'Bar Street.' She had avoided the place after being told by her friendly taxi driver that it was full of young English and Irish shouting, vomiting and generally behaving badly in lots of other ways. He shook his head in such a way when he told her that she wondered what exactly went on there. She asked Tarkan as they passed the end of Bar Street, but he shook his head dismissively.

'It's for the younger kids really. Pricy drinks, and young waiters. Loud music with no opportunity to talk. It's what they like. He smiled. His music wasn't for bar street. They want new 'club' music to enhance the alcoholic stupor and judging by the quietness at two in the afternoon, it doesn't come alive till much later in the day. Charlie wondered what the Turkish really thought of the tourists here. Did they despise them for their loose morals or accept that the cultures were different. She guessed economics came into it. Much of the income in the beach towns was tourist hospitality and now hotels were being built further and further out.

Tarkan spoke of the expansion of the town in recent years and the 'all inclusive' hotels springing up. He told her they didn't bring much revenue to the town, because apart from the odd excursion the guests tend to stay in the hotels.

Charlie laughed, "to get their money's worth. It's an English thing." They didn't know what they were missing she thought. The town, the port and the harbour made an impressive picture and the character of the place was in the town itself, not in the sterile hotels. She herself had been to a few in her time and was realising that she could have been anywhere. It would be a particular shame in Turkey not to experience the real place.

Tarkan told her about the Milli Park. Now closed whilst the murder investigations were going on and searches were still being made. It was a place for the Turkish people to go to, without the trappings of tourism and tourists. It was their place where they could relax with their families, take a picnic, drive around and enjoy the views. Charlie wondered how it would change now. Would it put them off the place of natural beauty because some maniac had decided to attack European women?

They went up some narrow steps to Tarkan's small flat. A studio it would have been called in England. One room and a shower room. It was dingy and dark and she looked at him wondering how he could live somewhere so small and cramped. He saw her face.

"Believe me Charlie, this is good by Turkish standards, the Cactus owns this building and some of the waiters have a room with three or four beds in it. That's how they live; up and out at lunchtime until the early hours of the morning maybe. They just sleep and change here; wash and back to work. At least my place is big enough to bring a few friends back, chill, play some music."

He was right. She saw the guitars in the corner

against the wall. The big floor cushions and throws. The Turkish lived to their means and he went on to explain how most of their wages were sent home to their villages in the neighbouring areas. The work was intense from May to September but after that they were lucky to find anything other than agricultural. They flocked to Kuşadasi in April like migrating birds hoping to find work for the season.

Charlie asked Tarkan about his family as they headed out to find another dolmuş to take them to the beach. He told Charlie that his family lived in Izmir and they had a small farm there. Reasonably wealthy by Turkish standards he'd had a good education, but always wanted to play his music. He had learnt the guitar when he was seven and could also play piano and keyboards. He got very animated as he told her about his band, the 'Purple Otters' who he played with during the winter months in the bars in Izmir. This was his real passion not the stuff at the Cactus. But it paid well and raised his profile in the town.

They jumped on another dolmuş to the beach. Charlie smiled as she saw an advertisement for the Cactus Restaurant on the small TV screen on the bus. Tarkan told her this was a recent thing and the equipment looked as if it cost more than the bus itself. 'The Cactus... 'Good times, good food' and then a picture of Tarkan singing, looking unlike himself in a frilly shirt and black trousers. He looked a bit like a tanned Barry Manilow. She was laughing and he joined in. "You're such a celebrity here. Good job you've got your sunglasses on so you don't get recognised."

The dolmuş was heading out of town, past the huge supermarkets, Migros, Tansas and a DIY store called 'Koc.' Which had the same signage as B & Q in Britain.

Charlie wondered how westernised the Turkish were becoming and how much things would have changed, even in Tarkan's lifetime. He was thirty two. Older than he looked she thought looking at him. Even without a shave and lots of late nights he looked good. He smiled at her and went into tourist guide mode as they headed towards the beach. He also whispered into her ear, reminding her of the night they spent together and making her want more.

The bus headed off the main road and followed some dirt roads into a small area of beach houses with palm trees planted in between the properties. The bus stopped at a small supermarket and they got off. A sign pointed to 'star beach' and they headed off down another small road towards the beach.

Charlie didn't know it, but this was the beach where Jenni and Khan had their wedding blessing. There was a small café and a few sunbeds. Charlie was glad. She couldn't have faced a noisy place and she was glad she hadn't needed to point this out to Tarkan. A guy came over with an all year tan and put out some huge cushions on the beds and greeted Tarkan like a brother.

He must have been in his fifties, but he was lean and fast as a whippet as he found them a table and an umbrella. Not that it was needed. It was hot enough to lie out, but not to burn and Charlie guessed that for that reason September was a good month to holiday here. She remembered the holidays of her youth. Not much sun, but a lot of fun as they found various seaside towns and places to explore in the camper van.

She took off her dress and lay down next to Tarkan in her black bikini. She had bought some new swimwear at the airport thinking she would be spending some time at the beach with Dee. Her mother was a sun worshipper despite knowing it damaged her skin. She told Charlie she always felt better with a bit of colour. It was all those summers in the North East when the sun hardly made an appearance that had probably made her that way.

Two melon flavour iced teas and some nuts appeared delivered by their beach man. She lay back on the bed and admired Tarkan in his green swimming shorts. He wasn't that brown, but he looked good. He had told her that he didn't generally spend much time at the beach. He was a townie, he laughed, apart from in the winter when he became a farmer. He was kidding, she knew he didn't actually work on the farm, but gigged around Izmir and let his mother spoil him rotten.

They sipped their drinks and chatted as if they had known each other for years. He asked Charlie about her father and she took a gulp from her glass as she felt emotion rising in her throat. She hated talking about her dad and most of her friends knew it was a taboo subject, but this man genuinely cared and she wanted to tell him.

"My dad died when I was fifteen," she started. She hated saying the words. It made it so real and as if it was yesterday. She remembered the day as if it was. It had started like any other day. She went to school and had a normal day. She had said goodbye to both Dee and Paul without kissing them. She had been in a hurry, late as usual and Elsie was banging on the front door, to walk with her. She ran out of the house not knowing that would be the last time she would ever see him alive.

He had been in the factory apparently. He had gone to see one of the new workers who had complained about some of the glass cutting materials saying they were having to carry sheets of glass on their own. As usual Paul had taken the complaints seriously and rather than sitting in his office, he was straight on to the shop floor to check it out. He was much respected at the factory. His reputation from the shipyards preceded him and he was known as a no nonsense negotiator as well as a staunch Labour supporter and campaigner.

She didn't know exactly what happened but an argument started between Paul and one of the bosses over the issue of the glass. He was talking not shouting, when he clutched his chest and fell to the ground. They called an ambulance, but by the time he had reached the hospital he was pronounced dead. A heart attack. They rang Dee at work and told her to get to the Royal Infirmary. She was too late.

She rang the school and Charlie was taken out of class. She immediately knew something was wrong. Very wrong. The teacher who took her to the headmistress was looking at her in a strange way. She couldn't have known what they were going to tell her.

By the time she got to the hospital she was hysterical. Inside she was screaming, although outwardly silent, the scream was in her ears and her heart was racing in a way she had never experienced. She couldn't believe her dad, her lovely father who wouldn't hurt a fly and spent all his life helping others, was gone. He was forty-eight. That was no age. His life snuffed out in a second. He had been fit, that was the joke. Her mind argued the facts. He had a good diet, ate well didn't drink too much. Hadn't been to a doctor in years. It must be a mistake. Please God, let it be a mistake.

She met Deidre at the entrance of the hospital and one look at her mother's face and she knew it wasn't a mistake. Her mother had aged ten years since she left her that morning. Her face was ashen. She looked as if all the life force had been drained from her. Which in a way it had. They were the three musketeers. They fitted.

He couldn't leave them? How could he leave them?

Dee made a sound. It was a terrible animal sound, almost like a wail. She was trying to hold it in, but the sight of her daughter rushing towards her, pushed her emotions to the surface. Charlie was here. She held on to her daughter; both sobbing openly now.

"Can I see him?" Charlie asked in a whisper. They went back into the hospital together, to face what need to be faced.

The next few days were a blur. Organising the funeral, the cards, and the sympathy. Paul's mother trying to take over and just making things worse. The flowers, the phone calls that neither wanted to take. They wanted to be left alone, in the way an animal wants to be left alone to lick its wounds. They were grieving, but they couldn't grieve.

Charlie expected to see her dad walk through the door, every time she heard a noise. She sat in her parents' bedroom whilst Dee was downstairs talking to the constant stream of people who came through the door to offer their condolences. There were a lot of people. Work colleagues, Union members, the Labour Party lot, people he had helped in the past who had moved on to other jobs. His death made the front page of the Evening Chronicle and she saw his face smiling back at her. He would never smile at her again. She pulled herself apart. She hadn't kissed him goodbye, given him a hug. Told him she loved him on that fateful day. All the things she normally did.

She pulled his jumpers out of the drawers hoping to inhale his smell, anything. Everything made the pain worse, just being in the house without his presence. She took to going for long walks on her own. Round Jesmond Dene, just walking and thinking. She tried to comfort her mother, as she tried to comfort her, but the loss they had both suffered was too great for either to affect the other's grief.

Dee went into a catatonic state of depression. They got through the funeral. Four hundred or more people packed the little church in Heaton, where they had been married. People spoke about what a good man he had been. Dee spoke to a packed church and told the congregation of how Paul had saved her life, when her sister died. How he gave her a life, gave her a daughter the precious gift of life. Tears poured down her face as she spoke of his strength, his courage, his humour and his life.

Charlie was proud of her. But she couldn't get up and say anything. She sat on the pew next to her grandmother with a stony face and a heart that felt it had burst with sadness. Her friends had been wonderful, letting her rant and rave and say whatever she felt. She resented them even so, they still had their fathers. And none could hold a candle to hers.

She was crying now as she looked at Tarkan beside her.

"You must be regretting that you asked," she laughed through her tears. He just held her, saying nothing at first. He loved the fact she had been able to share this with him. There was so much more to Charlie than he had first thought. He let her compose herself before he spoke.

When he did, he said the right things. He also told her how brave she was. How she had coped at such a young age and made something of her life. Her father would be proud of her. This started fresh tears as Charlie thought about her mother and how harshly she had treated her. Perhaps she had expected too much.

She had expected Dee to go into mourning for the rest of her life. Never look at another man. Stay in the terraced house and keep it as a museum and tribute to her father.

What she hadn't expected was that her mother would grieve and suffer as much as she had. She would be depressed for months, not wanting to get up in the morning and face the day. It took every bit of determination and strength of character to carry on. She had lost her soul mate, her best friend, as well as her husband. She thought of the plans they had made for the future. Take the old camper and travel. They had both wanted to see Australia and Asia as well as Europe. It had all been snatched from her. She was distraught. The pain could be seen in her eyes. She seemed to age in a matter of weeks.

She had faced the day though in true Deidre Davison style, then went back to work and supported Charlie through her 'A' levels then to University. She worked extra hours so she could afford the things she wanted. Charlie had grieved too in her own way and she missed her father every day. But she was a teenager and teenagers are intrinsically selfish. She still had parties to go to, boys to date and spent hours in front of the mirror experimenting with makeup and hair straighteners with her girlfriends. She recoiled from her mother's grief; she realised that now. It was sudden clarity for Charlie. She could see now how she had behaved and even perhaps why. It didn't excuse how she had treated her mother. The tears that were now flowing, were they for Dee or for herself. She didn't know.

Eventually she sold the terraced house she had loved for so many years. Too many memories, most of them good, threatened to keep Deidre in a dark place. It was all about what she had lost. She knew she had been lucky with her marriage and her man, but it made it so much harder to bear. Neighbours, friends, family all looking at her with sympathy in their eyes and their voices. She didn't want to be a charity case. So she made the decision. She would leave the area, start a new life. For the first time ever, Charlie could see why now. This place was so different, she wouldn't have to be reminded every moment of what she had lost.

Sometimes they would sit and reminisce, take out the photos and sip tea. Charlie resented the fact that the house was going to be sold. It was another bone of contention between them. By then Charlie was at University, but wanted the security of her home to come back to. Her mother listened to her and understood, but ultimately she had to move on, or she would shrivel and die.

Tarkan listened to Charlie's story and was surprised at how Charlie had behaved, but he tried not to show it. How could he know how he would have behaved under the circumstances? Both his parents were still alive and they doted on him and his sisters. His grandparents were also still around and he was yet to experience the powerful feelings of grief and you feel as though your heart has turned to stone.

"Come on Charlie." He pulled her up from the sunbed. She was amazed, but she actually felt better having talked to him, a relative stranger, albeit an intimate one. They headed towards the water and soon she was in her favourite place. The sea was blue and she swam strongly through the waves alongside her new friend. He was a good swimmer too and they swam out some distance before floating on their backs holding hands. Her tears had been washed away by the salty water and she felt she had been cleansed somehow.

They spent the rest of the afternoon, talking and laughing together until the sun started to go down. Tarkan looked at his watch. "I think we need to go. I start work at nine and I think I need a shave."

She looked at his stubble and kissed him. "It looks fine to me, but okay. We can't let your public see you like this can we?" She grinned.

They packed up their towels and said goodbye to Yaşar who was still working hard. He was now packing all the sunbeds and cushions away. No wonder he was so fit. He didn't seem to stop. They walked back to the road and a dolmuş came almost immediately. They found a seat and Tarkan kept hold of her hand. She felt happier than she had for a long while. If only she could find her mother, everything would slot into place.

Charlie is at heart a pragmatist. However, she couldn't entertain the idea that something terrible had happened to her mother. She knew she should have been worried to death, but somehow she wasn't. She had felt more anxious when she was with Val mainly because their conversation centred on Mary and the other women. She thought that if something had happened to her mam she would know. In her heart she would feel something. They hadn't been close for the last few years, but they had shared a bond. A mother daughter bond. She must be okay.

She told Tarkan her thoughts and he agreed. Privately he wasn't so sure. It had shocked him to find out what had happened to Mary and the others. He hoped Charlie was right, but what were the chances. He liked this woman a lot, she had touched his heart. They arranged to meet later that evening at Adem's for Mary's wake or memorial or whatever they wanted to call it. Tarkan wouldn't be there until at least twelve, so

Charlie decided she would have a nap when she got in. How did they all keep up with these late nights? They put her to shame.

They parted in the town centre and Tarkan instructed Charlie which dolmuş would take her to the apartment or at least to the hotel opposite the Tütüncüler Sitesi. She wasn't sure. She didn't feel quite so confident on her own, but being Charlie she would give it a go. She managed to spot a number six dolmuş, flag it down and get on. As it took the unfamiliar route along the sea front and up to the hospital, she appreciated the fantastic view it gave of the town and the port. As the bus reached the top of the winding road, she looked down and it was breathtaking. Perhaps like her mother she was falling in love with the place. The bus continued on a long winding loop, high above the town, before it led back down to the familiar sight of her mother's nearest supermarket. She waved furiously at the driver and he pulled up sharply.

Their routes are weird she decided as she got off. There must be a quicker bus surely, maybe Tarkan had suggested this one for the view. She wondered for the hundredth time if her mother would be waiting.

She let herself into the flat, almost holding her breath. Nothing, just the shuffling and squawking of the parrot, who was delighted to see her and have someone to talk to. "Howay man. Howay man." He was now greeting her with a favourite Geordie expression. She'd taught him that one yesterday.

It heightened her sense of loss for a second and she looked at the little bird. "Don't worry pet, she will be home soon."

31

Yucel

Y ucel paced around his small office like a bear in a cage. His light blue shirt was stained with sweat despite his shower and a liberal spray of deodorant that morning. It was stuffy and close in the room despite the large fan that seemed to just waft the hot air around. His walls were now covered with paper and he looked at what he had. He had spent the last few days interviewing anyone who knew the three women.

It was easier with Mary and Josie than Jenni who hadn't been in the town as long. The list with Mary was long and Josie had known a lot of people in the town too. Everyone who he had come into contact with had been run through the Police computer to find out about any previous convictions or information. What he received was surprising to him.

He centred his original search on Adem and Adem's bar. These were the last people to see Mary alive. His men had also gone through the alleys and found out who was who and who she may have come into contact with during her last few hours. The same alleyways where Josie had likely met her death. Zeki his forensic guy didn't think either woman had been killed there or in the National Park. He suspected both had been killed near to where they disappeared and the bodies moved later.

By the time the killer had got to Jenni, he was obviously more confident. To kill her in her own flat when someone, namely her husband, could have come back at any time, showed either an arrogance or total stupidity. Had the killing become more urgent as the killer gained some sexual or instant gratification from his actions?

Yucel was worried about his wife and the forthcoming birth. She was complaining of pains and the hospital had told her that the baby was likely to come quite soon. Probably early and she was extremely tired and emotional. He knew he should be home more for her, but couldn't leave the office early, he had too much to do. He was trying to be strategic about the case rather than rely on instinct. He needed to focus the search on the alleys and the town centre, he felt sure about that.

His so called 'expert' from Ankara was still obsessed with wire and the type and origin of it. He had also established that Jenni had been strangled with the actual rope that still hung round her neck when they found her. Perhaps he had run out of wire or more likely the killing hadn't been planned in the same way as the first two. Perhaps it had been opportunistic, in which case why would he be in the area in the first place. His mind was spinning with thoughts and he wondered if he would get anywhere before the killer struck again. That was his big fear. This was a serial killer and it was likely he wouldn't stop now, he was getting away with murder.

His bosses were on his back constantly asking for progress and concerned about the effect of the murders on tourism and trade in the town. Cold hearted bastards, he thought to himself. The powers that be, didn't have the insight or the care for the victims to realise that these women were vulnerable. Their safety and the safety of others couldn't be guaranteed any more, until this killer was stopped and stopped soon.

He went back to his charts, as his assistant entered

the room carrying a cup of strong Turkish coffee. He looked at Yucel, he had never seen his boss look so tired or dishevelled in all the time he had worked with him. The shadows below his eyes told him that he hadn't slept much over the last few days and his normally calm demeanour had been replaced with a short temper and a constant scowl. He offered the Chief a cigarette, forgetting momentarily he had given up recently. Yucel scowled at him and had to stop his hand from reaching out for the cigarette he desperately needed. 'I must not weaken,' he said to himself. He promised his wife he would give up especially with the new baby coming. He could not let her down. He had done enough of that recently.

He went back to his criminal records check. Adem wasn't as clean as he made himself out to be and despite being asked the questions during a lengthy interview, he hadn't volunteered the fact he had been in prison, even though it was ten years ago. He had clearly had a misspent youth, car thefts and other petty matters culminating in a conviction for an assault. A nasty assault at that. He had wounded the man and used a knife in the process. He had told the Court the man had tried to rob him, but it didn't excuse the violence he had used. Two years in Buca Prison in Izmir, had obviously rehabilitated him; his criminal record stopped there. It showed Yucel though that he was capable of badly hurting someone. But would he hurt a woman?

As for the others, some petty thefts involving some of the bar staff, probably financially driven, but nothing to suggest that they would be capable of murder. Some had spent their national service in the Army using weapons and some had seen some active service. Perhaps that could be relevant. He was aware of posttraumatic stress, but no one on his list appeared to have anything on record to suggest they were unstable. He made a note to request more details of their activities. Any early discharges? That was always a sign that something was wrong. Not everyone was stable enough to fit in with the expectations of the military. Yes that was an avenue he could follow.

He picked up the phone to ring Ayla. She was at his mother's again today and he knew that she was safe. He couldn't bear it if anything happened to her. She was his world and he was looking forward to getting his family life back. That was another reason to find this killer and wrap this case up. His own mental health was suffering and he knew he wasn't at his best. It was testing him beyond the realms of his career to date. He was determined to find the person who had committed these horrendous crimes. His honour was at stake.

There was a knock on the door. Zeki entered looking sheepish as normal. This boy, well man, irritated Yucel by his very presence. He looked nervous as he stuttered something to the big man that he thought may be something of interest.

"The wire Sir. I think I know what it is."

"Spit it out then, I haven't got all day." Yucel was barking.

"It's guitar wire Sir, an 'E' string; a bottom 'E' to be specific. I have confirmed that both Mary and Josie were murdered with the same one. There were microscopic quantities of Mary's DNA on what remained of Josie's throat, Sir."

Yucel had two simultaneous thoughts. One was that 'E' string was saying undergarment to him and two was that young Zeki had just climbed a large number of rungs up the respect ladder. He could now see how he'd got such a sparkling University Degree. "Is there any more?"

"The other woman Mrs Khan, we know that one was rope and we have the murder weapon for that. No useable traces of anything other than the victim's own, Sir."

Yucel was now looking enthralled. "Carry on. Oh and stop calling me Sir."

"Yes Sir. Sorry Sir... Where was I? Oh yes. The guitar string is more interesting. I've been to the music shops in town and they both sell a type that matches the one used, s..." Zeki pulled the last word, just.

"Okay." Yucel said. "Just imagine I'm an idiot. Explain how you know all this."

Zeki's face lit up with the Chief's interest.

"The size and characteristic over-winding."

"The what?" Yucel didn't think they shared the same idea about idiots.

"The lower pitched strings need to be thicker to make lower notes. The way the instrument makers achieve this is, instead of making wire thicker in a single strand, they wind a second filament tightly round a central wire core."

Yogi nodded, "of course they do."

"I've looked at more than thirty strings and have identified the one used, as the murder weapon, from the distinct ribbed surface of the string."

The Chief wanted to speed things up a bit. "So, are we looking for a local guitarist murderer?"

"I would say so Sir."

"Thank you Zeki, can you type this up for me, by tonight. Just nod."

Zeki nodded and left Yucel alone with his thoughts.

His mind was racing now. There were a lot of

musicians in town especially at this time of year. Bars and restaurants hired them to boost their trade.

He got on the phone to Seb to tell him about the development. "Check out all the guitarists you can locate that are working in a ten kilometre radius of here. Interview them and see who you can link to the women.

Yucel went back to his lists and started to identify anyone who had already been interviewed that would have access to the guitar string that had killed Mary and then Josie. It didn't necessarily have to be a musician he realised. They probably left that sort of wire lying around near their equipment in the bars, but it was a start, and he needed this break.

32

Adem

A dem was making preparation for the wake. Informally it was intended to be a tribute to the woman herself, but also to raise some money for a decent burial. He couldn't understand why her family hadn't had the body flown back to Ireland. Whatever Mary had been, she deserved a decent funeral with her family paying their respects. He shook his head as he checked his stock. Jameson's whisky would likely be popular tonight even though Mary herself had been a vodka drinker.

Luckily one of his customers had brought a couple of bottles over for him only a few days ago and he hadn't opened them yet. He was partial to a drop of the hard stuff himself, but tried to limit himself to beer whilst he was working. It was a long night at the bar usually and he tried to keep a clear head at least for the hours before the bar started to empty. Sometimes he would sit out with a few favoured customers in the back garden and drink a bottle of whisky, if someone had bought one for him. Some of his regulars who had apartments, but didn't live in Kuşadasi, would present him with a gift on their return.

He knew he was a popular guy. The bar had grown in its popularity and although he had started with nothing, he had a regular clientele now and the place was busy even in winter. He wondered how the deaths of the women might affect his trade. Would the alleys be a no go area? He wondered. That said, Jenni the last victim, had been found in her own flat, so maybe not.

There was no street lighting here. Only the neon flickering of the lights that advertised the bars, shops or the local beer. He wondered why these women would walk about on their own when it was so late, but supposed that they had always done so, without fear. Men sat in shop doorways guarding the stock and it was unusual for no one to be around.

Whoever had done these crimes knew the area well he surmised, as he put out some flowers around the bar. Val Neville had made up a board of photos of Mary and her friends as a homage to her. She had found some of Mary in the flat when she was younger. There was also some pictures of her in the bar here, with the locals and the regulars. Usually with a cigarette in her hand and a vodka in front of her, smiling at the camera showing a gap in her teeth at the front. She hadn't been a rich woman, but she was well liked and always had a kind word for people. She didn't bitch like some of the women he knew. She would tell some tales of her life in Ireland, but she didn't seem to yearn to go back. Her life in recent years had been here. She had been free of the disapproving glances of her family, but someone had snuffed out the life she had made, in an instant.

He looked at the picture board again. Mary with a variety of younger men. Smiling as if she had been given a prize, glad of the attention. Adem wondered about the men in question rather than Mary. What had they hoped to gain from this lonely old woman? Perhaps they thought she owned her flat, had some money under the mattress. As she became more known in the area, the attention diminished, somewhat cynically, he thought. Then again, every year there were always new faces, on the lookout for a better life.

He thought of Josie as he arranged the flowers. He

didn't know her as well as Mary, but he had met her a few times when she came to meet people in the bar. He knew the set up in the Orange Bar and he knew Ömer, her boyfriend, quite well; not as a friend, he knew he was always on the lookout for a rich woman. He would spend their money and then leave them to wonder what had gone wrong. He guessed Josie was no exception.

She had become lonely at the weekends, in recent weeks, watching Ömer behind the bar and she had left there that night; was it to seek out companionship of the female kind. He wondered if she had been on her way to Adem's before she was murdered. The Orange bar was quite nearby a couple of alleys away. It was possible he thought. Who had been lurking in the darkness knowing she was vulnerable.

Adem wasn't a stupid man. He had made some mistakes in his life. Especially when he was younger, but he had put this behind him and thought of himself as a good judge of people. Perhaps these women had been lured to their deaths by someone they knew? Someone they trusted. He couldn't see how else they could have been murdered. Not in the alley, there would have been some evidence. Perhaps the stranger in the shadows had approached them with an offer of a drink or a chat. That was more likely.

As time passed the bar started to fill up. Val was early, she clearly wanted the evening to be a success. She had brought food with her that she had prepared for a buffet and Adem had been to the supermarket to stock up with crisps and snacks.

As the tables filled up and drinks were ordered. Symmon started to play. He beckoned Val to the microphone to say a few words and Adem could see she was choking with emotion of it all.

"Thank you to everyone for coming. Mary would have loved this, it would be her idea of a party. I know she loved coming here and felt welcome. So welcome that she didn't mind walking home on her own. She loved Kuşadasi and always felt safe here. It's ironic really, her trusting nature led to her untimely death.

Mary wasn't an angel. She wouldn't profess to be. She liked a drink, a smoke and sometimes a bit of the other." Everyone laughed. "But she had a heart that was bigger than her head and time and ears for everyone. How many of you here sat with her and told her your troubles? A few I bet.'" People nodded. "She gave good counsel, even if she didn't always take it. She listened and you knew she cared". Val's voice faltered and tears formed in her eyes.

"I have lost a good friend. I will miss you Mary my love. Raise your glasses for a toast please. To Mary."

"To Mary." Some of the regulars were crying now.

"Don't forget her. Look at the memory board that Adem has agreed can stay on the wall for a while. She had her last night here. Hopefully the monster that did this will be caught and quick." People started to clap.

"There's a box coming around now. Put in what you can afford please. Enough to give her a good send-off. I will let you know details of the funeral, as soon as it's arranged. Please put your name in the remembrance book and your phone numbers, so that I can contact you all. Thank you."

Val stepped down from the stage. She had said her bit. She re-joined Charlie at the table they were sharing. Symmon started to play 'You'll never walk alone' which seemed both strange and inappropriate to both women. Val started to laugh. "Mary would have seen the funny side pet," she said to Charlie. "She had a great sense of

humour. Oh God, I didn't even mention that."
    She started to cry again.

33

Charlie

C harlie had arrived at Adem's at ten thirty. She had arranged to meet Val there and most people would not arrive till later, it wasn't an early night spot. She hugged Val and the two women worked together putting out a buffet on the large table out in the back garden. It was a clear night with a few stars and wasn't cold. Charlie wore a black dress. She wasn't sure what to put on for the event. Val was also in black trousers and a chiffon blouse that tied at the neck. Both women looked at each other and smiled.

"I know, I didn't know what to put on either," said Val. "It should have been a leopard or cheetah print number really, that's what she would have liked bless her."

Charlie smiled. She felt as if she knew Mary. It was very strange. The whole event was surreal. She heard Symmon singing 'Road to nowhere' and wondered at his song choice. He had clearly researched his choices, but hadn't ran them past anyone English or Irish.

"What time is Tarkan coming," asked Val, as they winced at the song.

"About midnight," said Charlie. "He has someone coming in to the Cactus to take over then. He'll be sorry to have missed your eulogy."

Tarkan wore a black shirt and trousers. Both women smiled at him. He was respectful to the notion of death, although Charlie joked with him and told him it wasn't a Johnny Cash tribute night. He looked worried for a minute then realised she was joking. They felt guilty laughing somehow, though Val said that Mary wouldn't have wanted awkward silences.

Symmon and Tarkan exchanged looks as Tarkan took up position on the small stage and Symmon headed to the bar. Charlie had told him about the song choices and though English isn't his first language, even he winced. By comparison he had spoken to Adem and the regulars and decided to sing some of Mary's favourite Irish songs as he had done before, for her birthday, one year, in East meets West.

He opened with 'Wild Rover' one of Mary's particular favourites. The audience went berserk singing along and the party really started. Adem and the staff were busy behind the bar and although he didn't usually have to work much himself, this night was an exception it was so busy. As he predicted, the whisky was flying off the shelves and he had to send some staff out to find some more in other bars.

Tarkan sang his heart out. It wasn't his kind of music, but he was a natural. He spoke of Mary in between renditions of 'Galway Girl,' Christy Moore's 'Ride on' and other Irish anthems. The crowd liked his choices and everyone was singing along.

Val was pleased. It was going better than she'd imagined. The box was still being passed round, but she didn't doubt they would raise enough money for a funeral. She knew Mary would have loved this and maybe somewhere she was looking down on them and her Irish eyes would be smiling.

Charlie watched Tarkan sing and hold the audience. He spoke anecdotally of Mary and some of the conversations they had. He was warm and genuine and this came across. Val asked Charlie about what had happened between the two of them and Charlie told her the full story. Well, almost.

"Good for you pet." Val had noticed a change in her friend from the girl who had arrived, what seemed only days before. She was less uptight and more relaxed. Despite the terrible worry about Dee she seemed calmer somehow. They spoke of her mother and Charlie told her of her thoughts. She also admitted hating her mobile ringing thinking it might be news from Yucel, the Police Chief.

He had rung her, but only to say that there was no news. He had told her about Jenni before it was reported in the press, but again told her not to worry. She knew she ought to be worrying more if she was realistic. Nothing had changed since she had found the passport.

She looked for Deniz in the crowded bar. He was nowhere to be seen. She realised that he wasn't even going to come here to pay his respects to Mary. In a way she was shocked. She knew of the bad feeling between the two bar owners, but she didn't think that it was serious enough to prevent him from coming for this event. As she was lost in thought, her phone bleeped and she saw his name pop up.

He had sent her a message in response to her previous text inviting him to the wake. Val had agreed he should be invited, given the amount of time and money she had spent in East meets West.

'Sorry Charlie. I won't be there. I will happily give Val something for the collection though, if you want to call here afterwards.'

Charlie had no intentions of doing that. She sent him a reply. 'Sorry your pride won't let you come and pay your respects Deniz. I'll see you another time.'

She knew Tarkan wouldn't want to go to the bar after what had happened between them. There seemed to be a lot of bad feeling towards Deniz, but then again all the bar owners were in competition with each other and this appeared to be quite common. She had heard Adem saying disparaging things about the owner of the Orange Bar, so she knew that this wasn't a one off. They're all after the same customers at the end of the day.

As Tarkan finished singing he smiled at her. He could have carried on longer, the crowd were still up for it. She looked at her phone. It was after four. Where had the night gone? The last five hours had passed so quickly. She saw Symmon approaching the stage obviously wanting to carry on. Adem shook his head at him and he went back to his seat. It was late, a lot of the crowd had drunk way too much already. He put some 'nineties' music on the system, to guarantee people would start to leave.

Tarkan and Charlie said their goodbyes to Adem and walked Val back to her flat which was en route to Dee's. She invited them in for coffee, but they declined. It had been a very long day. Charlie wondered if he would stay the night. She wanted him to, but didn't want to push it.

He came up the stairs with her and kissed her in the doorway. "I have been waiting a long time to do that," he smiled as they shut the door behind them. Moving toward the bedroom, trying not to wake the sleeping parrot. Too late.

"Who's a lucky boy," screeched Oscar, "who's a lucky boy?"

34

Yucel

Yucel stretched out in the bed feeling for Ayla. She was groaning quietly and he felt the wetness in the bed beside her. He had slept so soundly having had so little sleep he hadn't noticed that her waters had broken and she was now entering labour. Finally the moment was coming. Nine long months with some initial problems between the third and fourth months; they had both worried desperately. Now the baby had almost got to full term and they would soon meet their newest child.

His phone rang next to the bed and he cursed. His wife was fully awake now and pulling at his arm. She looked enormous lying down, despite her small frame and her bump appeared to have a life force of its own. She seemed calm given the situation, but made a disapproving comment as soon as he answered the phone.

"What is it now?"

His staff had been working through the night, once the information was known about the wire. They had identified two shops locally that sold the same brand of string and although it could have been bought elsewhere in Turkey, it was nearing the end of the summer season. That made it more likely that it could have been bought here in Kuşadasi.

They now had a list of six guitarists who were performing in the town's bars and restaurants this season. Three of whom were probably known well to Mary and Josie, it was possible that the women had encountered the remaining four at some point. Yucel told them to arrest all six, bring them in for questioning and he would get there as soon as he could. He explained that Ayla had just gone into labour, so that might be some time. They couldn't afford for any of the suspects to find out that the murderer is likely to be a guitarist, in case the killer takes off.

He gave Seb his authority to issue arrest warrants, sign the paperwork on his behalf and pick them all up as quickly as possible, before the press got to know what they were doing. He suspected someone was supplying information to the press, but he couldn't prove it. The witch hunt would still have to wait.

Ayla had got up and dressed. Yucel turned his phone off for the time being. He was caught in a dilemma now, but his wife had to come first.

He showered and dressed as quickly as he could. Her contractions were coming now and luckily the hospital wasn't far away. She collected the bag she had packed. He could hear her on the phone to his mother and gave a sigh.

"Just don't tell her to come yet," he pleaded.

She didn't. She wanted her husband with her for the birth of their second child. He had been absent from the home so much over the last week or so and she had worried that he wouldn't be at the birth. This was their moment and she didn't want it spoiled by him disappearing off to the Police station.

Ayla wasn't a stupid woman. She heard part of the conversation and knew he was getting closer to catching the maniac that was terrorising the town's women. He had told her some of what had happened and she could tell that he might be on the verge of a breakthrough.

Yucel looked at her. She was radiant. He loved this

woman with all his heart. She was more understanding than any other wife would be. He was so excited to finally be taking her to the hospital. He couldn't think about what would be happening at HQ. That would have to wait.

They got into the car and drove to the hospital, passing through the centre of town and the police station on the way. Yucel made a pact with himself. Let everything go right with the birth and then I will get the bastard who has turned this town upside down. Ayla groaned and he increased his speed, narrowly avoiding a rubbish cart that appeared from nowhere. He growled like the bear he resembled and focussed on the task ahead.

35

Dee

D ee finally realised where she was, vaguely at least. She didn't know how long she had been under this time and her mind was fuzzy. She felt a pang of anxiety and wondered what the hell she had got herself into. You stupid woman she thought to herself. What the hell would Paul think of her stupidity? She often thought about him, more often than she would admit. He had been her life.

She remembered the day he died as if it was yesterday. The phone call, the panic in her gut that the life she had known dissipated in a breath. They had been a team; a good team that worked. She knew she had relied on him too much. Emotionally he was not only her rock, but his love for her gave her the strength to become the person she wanted to be. A mother and a wife. A good one she hoped. She had never experienced the insecurity she should have felt after her beloved sister passed away. She had clung to him like a limpet initially until his words of encouragement and support enabled her to find her wings.

She knew she would never know love like that again. She didn't expect to and in her heart didn't really want to. He couldn't be replaced. He was a man like no other. Charlie and Deidre clung together initially, their grief making the bond stronger. Then Charlie flew the nest. Rightly so, thought Dee. She didn't want her daughter to ever feel how she had felt. Her loss was palpable, but after what she could only describe as a breakdown, she had battled to save herself and save her daughter. Even if that meant letting go. She knew she had upset her daughter by selling the house and moving to Kuşadasi, but it was something she had to do. For both their sakes.

She wondered what Charlie would make of her current predicament. She would probably blame her in the way she had over the last few years. Everything was her mother's fault in Charlie's eyes. She would accuse her of taking unnecessary risks and not considering others in her now judgemental way. She was probably right, Dee was feeling frightened and alone. What the hell had she done? She wanted out, but couldn't move her limbs and her whole body felt tight and bound. If she ever got out of here in one piece she would make some changes, she decided. She would find Charlie and make her peace. Let the trust grow between them again. Explain to Charlie why she had made the choices she had. She must understand.

Dee said a prayer to her God, to get her home safely, and let her daughter know how much she was loved. She hadn't prayed in a long time. She remembered Paul's funeral and how she no longer wanted anything to do with the God that had let this man die. She hoped that her God was still listening and would somehow hear her plea.

36

Charlie

C harlie woke up to the sound of the parrot squawking for his food or maybe just squawking. She looked to her left, but there was no sign of Tarkan. Her heart sank; she assumed he had gone home without waking her. Then she heard him in the kitchen feeding the bird and talking to him in Turkish. She hadn't a clue what he was saying, but smiled to herself anyway.

She smelt coffee and lay back on the bed. It was eleven, but they hadn't had a great deal of sleep. Arriving home at five, Tarkan hadn't been too tired to make love to her for what seemed like hours. When they finally drifted off to sleep his arm around her waist, she saw the sun coming up through the curtains.

He walked back into the bedroom wearing a towel and not much else. She took the coffee he offered and he got back into bed. She thought he was beautiful, his muscle tone, his brown eyes gazing into hers. It was a cliché she told herself. Perhaps he is too good to be true. Her previous experience of men, including Anthony, wasn't particularly positive, but she felt less defensive, less demanding with this man. They gelled together and instinctively seemed to know what the other wanted. Whether or not that was sex or conversation or both.

She looked at her phone instinctively for a message from Dee. There was a text from Val thanking her for her help the previous night and suggesting they meet for lunch. She suggested Medums, a restaurant in the centre. She showed Tarkan the message and he pulled her back into his arms. "Okay, but tell her we'll be there at two. That gives us a couple of hours yet." He nibbled her neck as she was texting. "Stop it," she laughed. But she didn't mean it.

They eventually got up, showered and dressed. Tarkan leaving the shirt he had worn the night before, and just wearing the T-shirt that had been underneath. Charlie slipped on a white T-shirt and jeans and grabbed her bag. No makeup, she felt bronzed from the day at the beach. Tarkan ruffled her curls that she had just tried to tame in the bathroom. She hit him and he grabbed her round the waist. They started to kiss and she pulled away.

"Come on, we'll never get there at this rate."

Val was pleased that they were both coming. She had mentioned the restaurant to Charlie the previous day, saying it was run by a family of very good looking brothers. They had laughed about it and she told Tarkan about the conversation on the way to the dolmuş.

He pretended to be jealous and didn't pull it off. "Better looking than me?" looking aghast. "I don't think so. Their father looks like a sheep." It must be a Turkish joke thought Charlie as they hopped on the bus. "I like sheep," she said and he laughed again.

The restaurant was at the bottom of the old town and didn't take them long to get there. Val was waiting, her hair and makeup immaculate, looking brighter than the night before, dressed in a brightly coloured orange top and white trousers. Charlie felt decidedly underdressed. She told Val so, and she chided her "Charlie man, if I had your looks even at your age, I wouldn't have bothered with makeup. You're beautiful."

Tarkan agreed and put his arm round both women. He kissed Val on both cheeks and sat beside Charlie. Various brothers appeared and Charlie started to see what Val meant. The main man was obviously the eldest brother Hakan who greeted them first. Tarkan clearly knew him and they kissed as well. He greeted Val warmly and with humour asking her who Charlie was. Maybe her sister? They laughed and he sat down with them like an old friend.

Val asked him the question that had been on Charlie's lips. Yes he knew Dee. Lovely woman, he could see the resemblance between mother and daughter. No he hadn't seen her for a couple of weeks, but like everyone else thought she had gone to London. He said she hadn't come by to say goodbye though, which wasn't like her as she usually asked him if he wanted her to bring anything back from England. He said, without a hint of irony that she usually brought back bacon and sausages.

"For the Irish breakfasts," teased Val and Charlie looked bemused. He explained that most of his regular customers brought these items for the restaurant as they were hard to source in Muslim Turkey. He smiled at Charlie and she could see how he worked his charm.

"So were you expecting her?"

"Well I wasn't sure when exactly she was going, but yes I was. With everything that has been going on in the town, I haven't really given it much thought though." He looked serious for a minute and the penny dropped.

"Look I'm sure she's okay," Charlie reassured him, not knowing why she was saying it.

Hakan introduced Charlie to two more of his brothers, Koray and Serkan. Koray had the most piercing blue eyes and dark curly hair. Serkan looked more serious with glasses and longer hair, but with the same family features. They were certainly a good looking bunch. A younger brother appeared later who was probably no more than sixteen and introduced himself as 'Timur the youngest!' He started making Charlie a rose from a red paper serviette presenting it to her with a smile. She certainly couldn't fault the service.

They ordered fresh, deep fried calamari for starters and some of the house speciality for lunch a lamb stew with crusty bread. The eldest member of the family came over. It was dad, the man Tarkan had described as looking like a sheep. Nothing could be further from the truth and she nipped him under the table to demonstrate her point. He was grey haired with blue eyes and looked like old movie pictures of Paul Newman.

He presented their food to them and was utterly charming. His English wasn't as good as the boys, but he was up there with charm. Val teased him saying she was upset he was so happily married, otherwise she might have stood a chance.

They had a good chat and a few drinks. Charlie hadn't realised how hungry she was, but she demolished her food very quickly. Faster than Tarkan anyway, who teased her mercilessly about it. He told Hakan to bring some cakes as she hadn't had enough food yet. She stopped him and Val looked at them both thinking that they acted like a couple who had been together for years.

Tarkan asked for the bill and it was brought to the table in an ornate box complete with knitted boots inside. "Don't ask," said Val. "I have a whole collection at home. It's a gift."

Charlie wondered what to do with her gift, but took it anyway. The boys were busy with other customers, but still came over to the table to say goodbye.

Val saw the Police approach before Charlie or Tarkan

did. It all happened so quickly as they arrested Tarkan and handcuffed him, putting him into the back of the Police car. He looked bemused, but didn't resist and Charlie stood open mouthed looking at what was happening.

Val was quicker. "What's going on Officer?" She asked one of the men in uniform, without expecting him to reply. He didn't. She rang the number Yucel had given her, his private mobile or at least private work mobile. It went straight to answerphone.

"What the hell's going on?" Charlie was hysterical. The whole street had stopped to watch the spectacle and she felt embarrassed for Tarkan, who was well known in the town.

Val pulled Charlie aside. "Let them go pet. We'll find out the score. They must have a reason."

She hoped the reason wasn't what it appeared to be. Charlie hoped the same, but neither women voiced their thoughts to each other. Charlie thought to herself that this couldn't be happening.

They walked up to Adem's to see if he knew anything. It was nearly half past four by now, so he should be up and about. They found him in the bar reading the paper. His phone rang as they approached and they could hear shouting at the other end of the phone.

The call ended and he looked at the two women. He looked shocked.

"That was Symmon. He's been arrested and he's waiting to be interviewed by the Chief. It's in connection with the murders."

"Are you sure it's not for crimes against music." Charlie made sure that only Val heard the remark.

The two women told Adem about Tarkan. Perhaps

every singer in Kuşadasi has been arrested too. Val tried Yucel's number again. Still the answerphone. Where the devil was he?

Charlie phoned Deniz, he confirmed what they were starting to suspect. His singer, Musa, the young guy was also in Police custody. Charlie didn't know if this information made her feel better or worse. She couldn't believe that Tarkan had anything at all to do with the crimes. She couldn't doubt him for a minute and was sure he would be able to provide an alibi. He had told her himself that he'd gone back to his flat, with some friends, on the night Mary was killed. She just couldn't understand why they'd taken him in. Or any of the others come to that. This whole thing was getting more and more bizarre.

Again Val and Charlie were left with more questions than answers. Val rang the main phone number for the Police and was told that Yucel was at the hospital with his wife who was in the delivery room. Yes there were suspects being held at the station, but they would be there until Yucel had interviewed them personally. Val could understand his predicament, but it didn't excuse locking up Tarkan who couldn't possibly have harmed anyone. Even Symmon, unpleasant as he could be, was hardly a serial killer. As for the young singer Musa from East meets West, he was barely out of school.

The two women were speechless. Charlie felt as though she had the stuffing knocked out of her. Too much emotion; too much to take in. Poor Tarkan she didn't want to imagine how he would be feeling. There was no point in going to the Police station, until Yucel turned up, nothing would change. They decided to go home and see what had transpired by the morning. They got a yellow cab and Charlie dropped off Val on the way. Neither felt they were good company.

When Charlie got back to the apartment, it seemed eerily empty. No Dee, no Deniz and no Tarkan. Only Oscar for company and even he was quieter than usual. He squawked a few 'all right pets' then sat quietly in his cage, his beady eyes darting back and forth.

Charlie slumped back on the sofa. She had opened a bottle of red wine and sat sipping her drink wondering what else could rock her world. She had only just met Tarkan, but she felt instinctively that he wouldn't harm anyone. She had feelings for him in a way she hadn't had for her boss. She had the measure of Anthony right from the start.

Tarkan was different, they had bonded. Was she being ridiculous? Probably. He could be an axe murderer for all she knew. But those eyes. He was kind. No, she couldn't be wrong. She had been wrong about her mother and she could admit that now. She was stubborn and proud, but she wasn't a fool.

She picked up a magazine then a book. Nothing could take her mind off the events of the day. She switched on the TV, only to hear more news, but in Turkish and she couldn't make out what was being said. There seemed to be no mention of the arrests and she suspected there wouldn't be unless one of the men was actually charged. They could ruin a person's reputation if they published the wrong information. Now Charlie still wanted some answers. Ever since she landed at Izmir airport all she had wanted were answers.

She went to her mam's CD collection and took out a favourite for both of them. Her mum had eclectic tastes and loved Jazz. Ella Fitzgerald blasted out of the speakers and Charlie took some comfort from the words. As 'that ole devil called love' played, she wondered what her mum would make of Tarkan. She knew they knew each other. It was weird. Charlie felt as if she needed to keep the faith. Faith that her mother would get back and Tarkan would be released. She needed them both together. It was all she wanted. She had forgotten about work, forgotten about Anthony and his sad wife. Her flight back to Gatwick wasn't too far away, but she couldn't even contemplate that at the moment.

She rang her friend Elsie in Newcastle. She had to talk to someone. They spent an hour on the phone whilst Charlie poured her heart out. Elsie was crying at the other end. "Oh my God Charlie, I hope she's okay Hun," she sobbed. Clearly Elsie thought the unspeakable. That Dee was dead.

"My mam's not dead Elsie, I know in my heart she's alive."

"I only hope you're right pet," said Elsie, but Charlie could still hear her despair.

Charlie was tired. Emotionally tired too, drained in fact. She put on some Pyjamas and slid under the duvet. She could smell Tarkan on the cotton. Some kind of aftershave; some sweat. His smell. She inhaled it and sighed. Whatever tomorrow was going to bring she needed to be ready for it. She drifted into a heavy sleep. Nightmares involving Dee running round Adem's screaming. Naked and scared; her mother as she had never seen her before. Charlie woke up sweating. It was only six o'clock. She knew she wouldn't sleep anymore and got up to feed the bird and make coffee. She felt alone and it wasn't a good feeling. She couldn't call Val at this time.

Charlie pulled on a swimsuit and then some jeans and a top. She packed a towel and some underwear, her purse and keys and headed for the door. She wasn't sure exactly where she was headed to, but she needed to clear her head and she needed to swim. She wasn't sure she could navigate herself back to the beach she had gone to with Tarkan and didn't particularly want to go there without him. After walking down into town, she found a dolmuş that was going to Ladies Beach and decided that would do. She knew it wasn't as far as Star Beach and after a drive along the seafront past Bird Island, it didn't take long to turn down to its destination.

Hundreds of small holiday homes scattered around; a bit shabby in places, but not in a bad way. She eventually arrived at the entrance to the beach which was pointed out to her by the driver. It looked like something out of the past, as she walked along the path on the front. She followed the beach which was narrow and seemingly packed with sun beds. She could imagine in the peak of Summer, the throng of bodies filling the beach. Not this morning though. A few lonely joggers passed her and generally there wasn't a lot of activity, but it was still early. Boys on bikes laden with bread passed her on their way to various restaurants along the front, some advertising 'full Irish' or 'full English.' She couldn't imagine much worse in the midday heat.

She found a cove in the busy beach. A woman of around seventy was coming out of the water in a plain blue swimsuit and Charlie thought if she could do it, Charlie could do it. She stripped off and ventured into the water asking the woman if she would mind her bag for a few minutes. "Of course darling," she agreed in perfect Queen's English.

The water was cold as she ventured in. She didn't hesitate and ran into the water to minimise the shock. It hadn't had time to warm up and it was quite late in the season. She felt the icy spray cut into her body and she forced her way into the waves. It was exhilarating and woke up her senses quickly. She swam for a few minutes and her body became more accustomed to the cold. The vigorous front crawl strokes temporarily warmed her muscles until she made her way back to the shallow water and the beach. She came out of the Aegean Sea, her hair dripping down nearly to her waist and wondered how on earth she could dry herself in order to get her clothes back on.

The woman minding her bag introduced herself as Edith and directed her to a hotel almost in front of the beach with an old fashioned frontage. The Ladies Beach Hotel advertised itself as being built in 1968. Edith had told her that Mehmet, the owner would let her use the shower and facilities if she returned the favour and ordered a Turkish breakfast.

She found him inside and his English was good enough to understand. He saw Edith and waved to her. Charlie was eternally grateful for the hot shower and she dried herself off with the towel she had borrowed from Dee's apartment. Back in her jeans and sweatshirt she enjoyed a Turkish breakfast sitting on the terrace, looking at the sea and enjoying the peace. Edith came back with a small dog a few minutes later and sat and had a coffee with her.

Edith told her story to Charlie about how she had come to Kuşadasi in the eighties, after her marriage ended. She was a painter and sculptor and was now eighty two. Charlie couldn't believe it, she looked fantastic. Brown skin, white hair and a wiry body. She could have put some sixty year olds to shame.

They talked for a long time. Edith's background was upper middle class, but she seemed to be able to relate to anyone. She obviously had a lot of friends in the area, as

te told
Charlie she had met a Turkish man and been tempted to
stay. She had fallen out of love with the man, but not the
place. She said to Charlie quite candidly that she took a
lover now and then. Likening the sex to a bottle of wine.
Something to be enjoyed in the moment. She was a one
off, Charlie thought and they exchanged numbers. She
promised to come back and see her art work when she
had time.

Charlie headed back to the dolmuş almost like a
native. Her phone rang and it was Val checking how she
was. Val had just woken up and sounded amazed that
Charlie was down at Ladies Beach and had already had
a swim and breakfast. She yawned as they spoke and
Val told her she envied her youth and vitality. The two
women chatted so naturally that Charlie felt as though
she had known the woman all her life.

"I've rung the Police station this morning. They told
me that Yucel still hadn't come back yet, so I guess that
all the guys are still in custody?"

"That figures, I am getting no answer from Tarkan's
phone," said Charlie, who had rung him three times
already. "It goes straight to answer phone now, so I
reckon his battery's flat." They were both at a loss as to
what to do next.

"I feel useless. That's why I had to come and swim, to
try and get my head straight."

They agreed to meet at Adem's for a coffee in an
hour's time. Charlie jumped on the dolmuş and as it
sped into town she realised she would be early. She got
off the bus virtually outside the police station, just in
time to see the Chief's back disappearing through the
front doors. Thank goodness, thought Charlie at least
he'll interview Tarkan and the others and hopefully

216

release him soon.

She was still puzzled about why all the men had been hauled in. The only thing that seemed to connect them being they were all entertainers. Perhaps that was the only common factor. She was closer than she realised with this assumption, other than that the men themselves had little or nothing in common.

She headed towards Adem's and hoped that Val was on her way. Adem himself was nowhere to be seen when she arrived and only Tugrul appeared to be working. Charlie sat at the bar chatting for a few minutes about what had been happening and the barman seemed concerned about Symmon. He told Charlie he'd had a breakdown a few years ago when he lost his job and he feared this arrest could send him into a downward spiral again. Charlie thought not. He had an ego the size of a planet and she couldn't imagine him down and depressed in the way he was being portrayed.

Val arrived a few minutes later and they took their coffees to one of the outside tables where they could talk in confidence. Tugrul was all eyes and ears and they wanted privacy. Charlie told about the conversation she had just had and Val was equally dismissive.

37

Yucel

Yucel felt as though he was walking on air. A heady combination of no sleep and elation was acting as a stimulant to his tired body and brain; he felt as though he could conquer the world. His son Rifat had been born some two hours earlier at nine sixteen am. Weighing a good nine pounds plus, his wife had coped well with the labour and delivery and he'd been there holding her hand. They had both cried tears of joy as he arrived. He was perfect and Yogi held him with pride. As he cradled him in his arms he vowed to protect him and love him for all his days.

He was bursting with pride as he entered the station. His team crowded around him and a cheer went up as he entered the main office. He showed the photos he had on his phone and they all admired and congratulated him on such a handsome little man. They joked that he must have got the wrong baby, this one was way too good looking. He took all the teasing with the good nature that he had struggled to find over the previous few days and his staff wondered how long he would stay like it.

He felt as though his world was complete. He had a lovely wife, two sons, supportive family and a good job. Yes, the good job he now needed to put every ounce of energy he possessed into. To solve this case and find out who had murdered these women. He could do it. His confidence was renewed and he knew he could crack it. If it was one of the men currently being held in the cells he would sense it. Of that he was sure.

He went to his paperwork and looked at the list of suspects. Or were they suspects. Anyone could buy guitar strings and in more places than in the town. But it was all he had to go on and it was worth a shot. If someone had come into town from Izmir or Aydin or another big town though, it was likely they could slip back just as easily. Turkey was a big country, what was to stop them heading back to where they had come from. He felt a sense of panic and had to mentally calm himself. His gut was telling him that this was a local.

He didn't believe the first two victims Mary and Josie had been killed in the alleys. He had been thinking about this as he held his wife's hand and she puffed and panted. He was with her, but he wasn't with her. His mind had plenty of time to go over things whilst he was outwardly comforting and supporting Ayla. In the final moments he had been too distracted by his son's arrival to focus on the killings, but not before he had time to think about them.

There had been no evidence of murder in the alleys; no witness to sights or sounds. He wondered if the killer had somehow persuaded the women to go with him, either by charm or by fear. But where would he take them? Yucel guessed that this depended on whether or not the deaths were premeditated. Had he stumbled upon Mary then decided to kill her. And what about Josie? By the time he killed Jenni, he was becoming bolder. Or more stupid depending on your viewpoint.

He gathered his team together. He had asked Seb to sort out the paperwork for search warrants and put them in front of the judge whilst he had been at the hospital. There was an outside chance if it was one of the six men in the cells that they would find something in their accommodation.

Seb handed him the warrants signed by the officials just a few hours previously. Yucel sorted out the men into teams of two and gave them the addresses. They had confiscated keys from the suspects before they were placed in custody so it wouldn't be too difficult to enter the properties.

He looked at the list of singers. He knew Tarkan by sight as he and Ayla visited the Cactus occasionally. His wife had liked the young man's singing and he looked wholesome enough. But who really knows what's behind a stage persona? He was a tall guy who could have easily overpowered the women and certainly had enough charm to woo them back to his flat.

The second photo was Musa from East meets West. He was a young man with a very long ponytail and a look of angst on his face. He would have more angst if he had committed these murders. As far as Yucel was aware he was single and had a room in the alleys near both bars. He wasn't from Kuşadasi and like a lot of his counterparts had a family in one of the villages on the outskirts of the town. He knew of Deniz, the owner at East and West and wondered if he would have had access to the young guitarist's strings. In Yucel's head he was a more likely suspect. Surly and uncooperative with the police. His own girlfriend was missing. He was definitely one to come back to.

His third suspect was Asil, a popular singer in various bars for the last twenty years, he is at the most five feet tall and wouldn't push the scales past a hundred and thirty pounds. He looked the part, with his leather jacket and trousers, but he was tiny and Yucel doubted he could possibly have physically carried out the murders. He had no convictions, a wife and grown up children and a good reputation for being reliable. The

Chief couldn't reconcile this man with his idea of the killer. He put him to the bottom of the list.

Similarly Babar was an old timer; by Turkish standards anyway. He was around forty-five with black greasy hair and loosely based his act on Elvis. He was starting to look like Elvis did during the hamburger years, thought Yucel, who had seen him perform at one of the fish restaurants on the front. Jaded and tired, he should be hanging up his guitar he felt. Perhaps he was the one, but background checks suggested a strong family man, respected in the community and someone who raised money for local charities, especially during the winter months. He had four children, one still at school and he also owned a small business supplying popcorn and nuts around the bars. He wasn't rich by any standard, but he seemed to be a pillar of the community. Not a likely suspect in Yucel's book despite his slightly seedy appearance. He had a small apartment in Kuşadasi, but his family home was in Selçuk where his wife and children resided. Perhaps he had a double life wondered Yucel. He put him one above Asil.

Symmon was another has been, or so it was said. A big man, bald and imposing with a slightly creepy stare. There was nothing of consequence in his background search; should the lack of any history be troubling Yucel, he wondered. His 'career' was on the way down it seemed and he'd once been the star of the Cactus restaurant, the busiest and biggest restaurant in town. It had a prominent place in the old town attracting a lot of attention. He remembered seeing him once when he was courting his wife and he seemed full of himself and slightly pompous. His singing wasn't great, but his booming voice could be heard from streets away as he sang his way through the predictable list. Yucel knew he worked at Adem's bar sometimes and at another restaurant in Ladies Beach, but his star was definitely fading.

His final suspect was Billou aka 'Billy.' Originally from Bulgaria, not much of a singer apparently, but a great guitarist in the Carlos Santana vein. He played with other vocalists usually and had been known to play with Tarkan at Adem's and East meets West now and again. He also worked down at Ladies Beach on the restaurant circuit and had been known to play with at least three of the men in the cells. He lived alone, but had a long term liaison with an English woman called Tammy who was in her sixties. He was tall and gaunt with shoulder length greasy hair. If he was the killer, he would be surprised. He was known to be laid back to the point of being horizontal. Still he may have a record in Bulgaria, it would be worth checking with Interpol.

It was going to be a long day. He would time the interviews with the searches before he decided to release anyone. It wouldn't help for the officers looking for clues to be confronted by disgruntled and irritable occupiers.

He moved to the interview room and asked Seb to bring Tarkan to him. When he came in he looked wide eyed, tired and slightly frightened. Not the confident man he had seemed on stage. A night in the cells hadn't agreed with him and the big man sensed he was anxious to get out. He had no criminal record and Yucel guessed this was his first time in custody. He had prepared a list of questions, he would ask each man and he would tape the interviews with Seb present. He wasn't taking any chances if he managed to get a confession. It wasn't likely with this man.

He gave an alibi for the time frame that Mary was

killed. He had gone back to his apartment with three others and they had stayed there until around six that morning, playing music and chatting. One male friend had slept on the sofa that night and Yucel was satisfied that if this could be verified he would be off the hook. Tarkan clearly didn't know why he was there and seemed anxious that he could be considered a suspect. He looked Yucel in the eye and told him that he had been fond of Mary, and yes he had known Josie by sight, but he had no reason to want them dead. He was doing well professionally and no one seemed to have a bad word to say about him.

Yucel phoned the officers who had gone to Tarkan's flat. They had found nothing incriminating, apart from various guitars and equipment, but that was to be expected. No Turkish eye collection and no evidence that anything untoward had happened in that flat. He decided to release Tarkan who was starting to smell as if he could do with a shower and a change of clothes.

Tarkan shook Yucel's hand as he left. He couldn't wait to phone Charlie and let her know he was okay. He was given back his possessions that had been in his pockets at the time of his arrest. Apart from his door keys that were still with the search team. He was now free to leave, but he would have to return for them later.

Tarkan breathed a sigh of relief as he finally walked out into the sun. He could appreciate his liberty much more now after the uncomfortable night he had spent in the cells. It was explained to him that he was only being held because Yucel wasn't available to interview him, but he had been given no indication why he was a suspect. By the time he had answered questions about where he bought his guitar strings and how often, he put two and two together and surmised that the three women must have been strangled using the same kind of wire.

"Charlie," she answered him immediately.

"Tarkan, where are you? What's happened?"

"I'm okay, they have let me out. Shall I come to you?"

"Of course, come now." Charlie had never been so glad to hear someone's voice.

38

Apartment in the alleys

Officers Mutlu and Arin made their way up the narrow stairs. The apartment was situated above a dingy barbers and a lockup next door. The stairs led directly to the upstairs room with a door inside the landing and another at the top. It was grim and the door was sticky with years of grime and grease. The set of keys they held were confusing. There appeared to be at least four keys for what looked like three doors. It took them some time to open each lock. By the time they entered the small flat, there was a smell that neither could identify, but it was deeply unpleasant like rotting meat.

They looked around the flat quickly. It wasn't a flat more of a room with a kitchenette. Many of the workers lived in such conditions and some had to share this type of substandard accommodation. He could have cleaned up a bit and made the place more liveable, they thought. An unmade bed in the corner with a few creased sheets and a bare mattress gave a depressing air to the place. A small worn sofa with a guitar on it, filled one wall and there was nothing to suggest that the occupant spent much time here. In the corner of the room was a sink and a couple of rings to cook on. A door that was unlocked to the left of the front door led to a grimy shower room and toilet that obviously hadn't been touched for weeks by bleach or any other cleaning materials.

A large black bin bag was in the corner. Both men hoped the smell was coming from there and half expected or hoped to see some leftover food or some rotting meat. He clearly lived in this one room and the windows were tightly closed making it stuffy and airless. It was also claustrophobic.

They opened the rubbish bag and found it contained some fast food boxes and some beer bottles. Nothing significant. They looked around the room again. There was an alcove with a cupboard above it. A square door with a lock that they guessed one of the keys would open. It looked like one of the cupboards that go back some way and was probably the only storage in the place.

As they spent longer in the room, the smell was getting worse. They were both starting to feel a bit queasy. Mutlu the brighter of the two, started trying the keys until they found one that fitted. They opened the door and as they suspected it was a deep cupboard that went around in a corner shape about four foot high and six or seven foot deep. The smell was now overpowering and they could see what looked like a large package at the back of the cupboard wrapped in heavy duty plastic with rope binding it.

Both men were gagging and left the cupboard and shut the door. Arin said that he needed to get some air and they trooped back down the stairs. He was only twenty and had only been in the police for a year. He couldn't comprehend what he had seen, but both men knew it was a body. They made the decision to call for assistance rather than touch the package. Mutlu's hands were shaking as he phoned the Chief to tell him what they had found.

39

Charlie

C harlie opened the heavy front door to Tarkan as Oscar squawked his greetings for the day. "Morning pet, morning pet."

It was by now nearly afternoon. Tarkan hugged her and she felt safe for the first time in twenty-four hours. She had never doubted him for a second. They kissed and she drew back laughing.

"God you smell terrible." He looked distraught, but she carried on kissing him anyway, the touch of his lips making her forget the body odour and the scratchy beard. They eventually pulled apart and Charlie pushed him in the direction of the shower.

"I'll make you a Geordie breakfast this time, but no black pudding," she laughed.

"Black pudding?" Tarkan puzzled.

"Don't ask. If I said it was pig's blood made into a sausage you probably wouldn't want it! I know how about an omelette? Well that's the choice really," Charlie said when she looked in the fridge.

He showered and put his jeans back on. She guessed he was going commando, but tried not to think about it.

Charlie made coffee and they sat at their favourite spot on the balcony. "Come on tell me what happened." She was desperate to know the gritty details.

"So you think it was about the guitar wire." She quizzed as he told her what had happened and the questions he had been asked.

"Yes, and they had at least another five men in there." Tarkan still looked in shock at his arrest.

Charlie's brain was working overtime. Like Yucel, she wondered if it were too simplistic to expect the killer to be one of the entertainers in the town. She wasn't Miss Marple, but she told Tarkan she thought that the Police were looking at the crime simplistically and it was entirely possibly the wire could have been purchased elsewhere.

Charlie thought about the scenario and the killer. She went to the bathroom and looked in the mirror. She had been here for over a week now and she looked terrible.

There were shadows under her eyes and as she looked at herself she saw a different person than the woman who had got off the plane. She had been full of herself, her plans, her desires and the will to find her mother. It hadn't been about Dee though, it had been all about herself. She shuddered and looked back at her face, stripped bare in the strongly lit mirror. Tears were forming in her eyes and she realised she had been in denial since she arrived.

Despite the deaths of the women, she had wrapped herself up in the whole place, treated it all as a big drama and fallen for a Turkish singer. She hadn't really wanted to think about the possibility that her mother was dead, probably killed by the same maniac. It hadn't been a possibility to her, not really. She had again been naïve and stupid and probably not wanting to face reality. Some monster had murdered her lovely mother, kind and funny Dee, the woman who would help anyone and not hurt a fly. The possibility that she would never see her again hit her like a brick. Once she started crying the tears wouldn't stop.

Tarkan knocked on the door. He couldn't think what he had said to upset her.

"Charlie. Baby. What's the matter? Have I upset

228

you?"

She opened the door red-eyed and feeling stupid. He held her close and let her cry. She was trying to tell him, but the words wouldn't come. "Dee?" He said. He wondered when this would come. He had felt that Charlie had been too composed, too together over all this. She hadn't wanted to include her mother in any of the discussions she still maintained the fantasy she had created.

He comforted her instinctively and she knew he was aware of the source of her pain. Despite the language issues she didn't have to spell it out. The relief of having him back after the arrest and a sleepless night had compounded her emotions and it had all become too much.

40

Yucel

Yogi left Seb with Musa and went to ring his wife. They were both fine, she assured him, his mother was with her and the two women were in raptures over the new baby boy. He felt a pang of disappointment that he wasn't there and missed them all acutely. He felt a sense of responsibility for the new life they had created, but he had work to do. He wanted to succeed more than ever now, for his sons and heirs. He knew his father was proud of his achievements, but he wanted his boys to look up to him too. Be a good role model. He re-entered the room and continued questioning the young man.

Musa looked at the floor for most of the interview which didn't help. He confirmed that he worked at East Meets West and had been there for two seasons. He also agreed he had purchased guitar strings of a significant type at Hud's shop in the Bazaar. Other than that he was reticent. He may have known Mary, may have seen Josie, but wasn't sure there were so many different faces in the bar every night. He didn't believe he had spoken to either women other than superficially, but he couldn't be sure. He was sweating profusely throughout the interview which didn't help Yucel feel confident in his innocence. He was only twenty years old though, and whilst ringing his wife, a report had come through saying that nothing of any consequence had been found in his room.

The Chief put his nervousness down to his youth and inexperience dealing with the police. He couldn't help looking shifty he concluded. He smiled at Musa as he told him he could go for now, but that they would be in touch if they needed any further information from him. He still looked at the ground and didn't look at either Seb or Yogi on his way out. They both looked at each other and shook their heads. Seb crossed his name through on the sheet and wrote Charisma.

Asil was next. Yucel felt like a giant next to the diminutive singer. The man was very calm and very reasonable. He answered the questions with thought and didn't appear nervous or anxious in any way. He had earlier asked to ring his wife and said he was concerned about her and the worry she would be experiencing.

"Does she need to worry?' Yucel asked bluntly.

"No. Not at all," said Asil looking directly at the men. "I just hope you catch this monster and I will do anything I can to help you. He had provided an alibi of sorts, but was vague about the time he got home and his wife had been asleep. It was enough for Yucel to release him. There were still three more to go.

Babar aka Elvis was more than ready for his interview. His flick of black greasy hair had flopped onto his face and Yucel noticed his grey roots. A night in the cells had highlighted his sallow complexion and he looked older than his years. He was eager to please volunteering more information than was necessary. He had known Mary, seen her in various bars in the town. Wasn't sure about Josie or Jenni. He didn't go to the Orange bar and Jenni hadn't been in town very long. He described some various characters lurking around in the alleys that he suspected may be responsible including incriminating an old man who acted as security in the alleys; and a couple of men from bars who owed him money. He loved to talk and Yucel wanted him to shut up and listen. He didn't like him much, but doubted he was capable of murder. He had a wife and four children in Selçuk and said that he didn't generally fraternise with English women other than when he was singing. Seb told Yucel he thought he was sneering at the tourists even though they were his bread and butter. He seemed to think he was a bit superior to some of the other singers and on that basis could be described as delusional. Yucel thought Seb had been reading Zeki's psychology books.

Babar's flat in town had been checked. He shared it with two elderly waiters who were surprised when the Police let themselves in to the flat unannounced. Both thought they had been in the room at the time of Mary's murder, as was Babar, but they seemed unsure of times and dates. One night in Kuşadasi was pretty much the same as another to them. Yucel decided to let him go. This was going nowhere. He felt frustrated at the lack of progress.

Symmon was next. Yucel wasn't in any hurry to interview Billy until he had received some information from the Bulgarian police. He phoned through to Lale and told her to start harassing the Bulgarian Embassy in Ankara for answers. This was an important diplomatic incident, tell them.

Symmon sat back in his chair yawning loudly then apologising. He looked a bit dishevelled particularly his normally pristine white shirt. He had slept badly by the look of him, the cell beds were not made for comfort. He seemed confident in his replies to Yucel about the timing of his departure from Adem's bar and yes he had seen and spoken to Mary. He knew Josie by sight and had never heard of Jenni.

When asked about his history he confirmed he had

been in Kuşadasi for over ten years. Starting off like many of his counterparts as a waiter who was allowed to sing now and again. He had formed a friendship with the owner of the Cactus who admired his ambition and his work ethic. He moved back further in his chair and said that the rest was history. He expected Yucel to know of his success at the Cactus where he became the star of the show and told the big man he had seen him in there once or twice over the years.

Yucel gave nothing away, but nodded sagely as he continued. Symmon was enjoying the attention, Seb guessed. The man liked talking about himself that was clear. He played down the part of his descent from fame and tried to make out that he had tired of the routine and the late nights at the Cactus restaurant. Using words like musical integrity made Yucel smile inwardly. His ego was certainly bigger than his talent and he tried to convince the two men that he had been happy to leave and try his luck with his own music.

Yucel noticed a flicker of something in his eyes when he mentioned the guitar strings and asked him to confirm that he'd purchased the type of wire he described from the music shop in town. His eyes narrowed as he agreed that he had bought strings there, now and again. "They go out of tune," he said.

"So I'm told." Yucel trying not to laugh.

Looking puzzled, he asked the Chief why this was important.

Seb told him very little about the nature of their enquiry. He wondered how bright he actually was, he was down playing their enquiries about the wire. Tarkan and a couple of the others had asked the question directly, was the wire the murder weapon? Symmon either didn't want to ask or didn't get the connection.

Either way Yucel didn't trust him.

He asked him about his family and was met with a blank face. "What has my family got to do with anything?" He was defensive in his body language now, his arms crossed in front of him.

"Just answer the questions please and this will all be over quicker," Seb interjected.

Symmon told them that his family lived in Istanbul on the outskirts of the city. He has four siblings, two brothers and two sisters who had all left home and had families of their own. His mother and father owned a small hotel in an old mansion house. "Very luxurious," he added as if he was touting for business. Apparently his father had been a successful businessman prior to an early retirement. They were not hands on in the business though, and often travelled abroad.

He was relaxing again now. Back in control. Yucel wondered if his version of events was his own or the real one. He certainly liked to paint himself in a good light.

He felt that the interview wasn't going anywhere, he went to check on the progress of the search team. He left Symmon in the room with Seb, saying he was going to the lavatory. Seb knew the drill and wondered if the search would bring anything significant.

He returned quickly telling Symmon he could go. As soon he was out of the room Yucel told Seb to check that Billy was still securely under lock and key. He had a phone call from Officer Arin, to report that they had attended his room had found what looked like another body.

Yucel was excited and afraid at the same time. He wanted a breakthrough and this looked as if it might be the one. They set off to get the car, then decided it was quicker to go by foot. Three other officers were already on their way there from other searches.

He arrived at the property and climbed the stairs to see what awaited him. Seb followed and was talking on his mobile at the same time. They entered the room at the top which now seemed very small as it was filled with police. The 'package' hadn't been disturbed in the cupboard, but someone had opened all the windows, the smell was vile. Yucel had smelt a decomposing body before and had no doubt that there would be a body inside this packaging. The forensic and medical teams were on their way.

He ordered the crime scene to be sealed off and the package to be taken to the station to more sterile conditions. His heart sank as he thought about the phone call he was going to have to make to Charlie Davison. Perhaps Billy had killed her later than her disappearance suggested. Maybe he couldn't go back to the National Park because it was cordoned off by then. Perhaps he had planned to dump the body in a different place. The smell wasn't so bad she had been there for over a week that he was sure about.

He decided to walk back to the station and ring his wife on the way back. She was still at the hospital, he wished her well and told her to let his mother know not to make any food for him. Another body meant he wouldn't back home for the foreseeable. It would be another long night.

The Medical examiner and forensic staff were soon all gathered at HQ for the nasty bit, as they carefully unwrapped the packaging. It was heavy and the tape was carefully peeled back trying to do as little damage to the original materials that would later need to be forensically examined. Billy hadn't expected them to go to his apartment so may not have been so careful with this body.

As they unwrapped the final pieces of plastic and unrolled the body on to the slab, the doctor told Yucel straight away that the woman before him hadn't been dead very long. He would need to conduct tests to be accurate, but he guessed less than thirty-six hours. The smell would have got much worse over the next few days if he hadn't managed to bury her.

She was a petite blond haired woman, probably in her late fifties. She was naked apart from a pair of lacy panties and looked grotesque under the harsh lights. She had the now familiar marks to the neck where she had been strangled, but also had bruising around her thighs and her breasts. A thought came to Yucel, that he had progressed to 'playing with the victim' he had maybe held her hostage while he abused her, sexually probably. There was also bruising around her face, perhaps he had punched her into submission. Her mouth was taped up and some kind of gag appeared to be inside.

His heart sank. It must be Dee Davison. It matched the description given by Charlie, recalling the photo she had given him to look at when she came in. It had been taken a few years previously and she had aged a bit since then. He left the team to start the gruesome work of completing the examination and autopsy.

He wondered whether to phone Charlie straight away or to interview Billy first and to see if he would confess. He decided to be a coward and put off the inevitable. He doubted he would deny it, the evidence had him banged to rights.

Billy was looking nervous now. Seb and Yucel sat down in front of him and decided to go for a direct confrontation.

"Billy, we have just been to your flat. We had a search warrant and we have found a body of a dead woman wrapped in plastic, in a locked cupboard. We believe that body belongs to a Dee Davison. We believe that you killed her, just like you killed Mary O'Donnell, Josie Wilson and Jenni Higgs, by means of asphyxiation by ligature.

"Before I charge you formally, what do you have to say? Think carefully before you do say anything because this interview is being taped and will be used in Court."

"What cupboard?" Billy was now as white as a sheet.

"The cupboard above the alcove, you know what cupboard." The Chief was getting impatient.

"What alcove?" Billy said, almost frozen with fear.

"Stop messing. In the cupboard you put her in, probably less than two days ago. Have you forgotten already?"

"I don't have a cupboard or an alcove." Billy protested feebly.

'This is going to take a long time.' Yucel and Seb thought simultaneously.

"Your room above the Barbershop shop in Kemal Cadesi. We searched it with a warrant less than an hour ago."

A quiet voice said, "I live at Hazur Pasaji." He looked puzzled, confused and afraid all at the same time.

"We have got the wrong fucking address." Seb got up quickly scraping his chair. Yusel followed him out of the room closing the door quickly behind him.

They virtually ran to the front office to check the warrants' information sheets. The flat they had found the body in was on the list. But it didn't belong to Billou, it belonged to Symmon. Someone had mixed up the names and in the rush to get out there, it hadn't been double checked.

If Symmon went home, he wouldn't get in. He had been told to come back for his keys in a couple of hours like the others. But if he did go back he would have seen that it's now a crime scene and by now everyone will be talking about it. Once he knew they had been in his house he would be on his toes. He would know they would find Dee's body.

Yucel started to panic. He ordered every Officer on duty to get out there and find Symmon and find him fast. Go back and see if anyone has seen him around the area of his flat. Where would he go for a couple of hours? Adem's? Possibly. He prayed that he hadn't lost him. The shame of it. What a fundamental mistake. He started to feel angry at Seb. He had been in charge of that part of the operation. Heads would roll if this came to light. He had let a serial killer go. He would never recover from this, what would happen if he killed again?

Now that he had been found out maybe he would feel he had nothing left to lose.

Chief Yucel Semir had much to lose.

41

Charlie

Charlie was lying on the sofa with her head on Tarkan's lap. They were listening to some music. Dee's music. Pink Floyd to be exact. Charlie had smiled at her mam's CD collection. Most were albums she had bought as LP's in the sixties, seventies and eighties. She hadn't really moved on in musical terms. They had listened to Pink Floyd's 'Wish you were here' album. Poignant in the circumstances.

The curtains had been left open and they hadn't bothered to put the lights on. Charlie had lit a couple of candles. It was still early evening, but darkness had come early and it felt almost ethereal. The music was eerie in places and it seemed part of the atmosphere.

Tarkan was singing along to 'two lost souls swimming in a fish bowl,' and he thought an acoustic version would work well in his set. Charlie who didn't sing along, out of embarrassment, thought he was right.

They were sipping some good red wine (where did her mother get it?) and Tarkan was wearing one of Charlie's T shirts which was tight in all the wrong places. He had rung the Cactus and they had given him the night off after his ordeal at the Police station.

They snuggled together on the sofa and talked in hushed tones about the day and the past few days. Charlie had stopped crying, but felt a deep sorrow she couldn't explain. They rationalised what could or may have happened, but Tarkan couldn't rationalise Dee's disappearance any more. When Charlie's mobile rang she sensed immediately that it was going to be something significant. They both jumped despite the phone's low volume.

"Charlie Davison speaking. Hello Chief Semir. Yes I am with someone. A friend. What is it?"

Tarkan watched as her body froze. Her mouth stayed open for seconds longer than normal. She was gripping the phone so hard, her knuckles were white.

"Yes, of course. I'll come now."

"Yes. Please, send a car for me. Thank you."

She pressed the disconnect button. She looked at Tarkan and it was as if the light had gone out of her eyes. She stared at him for a moment. He said nothing waiting for her to speak.

"It's my mam. It's Dee. They think they have found her."

"Alive?" The words came out before he could stop them, but in his heart he already knew the answer.

"No. She's been dead for a couple of days at the most."

They looked at each other. Silent tears dripped from Charlie's face as her fears were finally realised. She would never get the chance to see her mam, tell her how sorry she was, tell her she loved her, and tell her to live her life any way she wanted, just live.

Just live. It was too late now. Her mam's favourite singer Carole King popped into her head.

'It's too late baby. Now it's too late.'

42

Val

V al had good and bad days. The last two had been bad. She had spent a lot of time on her own. She knew Charlie was spending time with Tarkan and she was glad. She had missed talking to her though and since Mary had gone, her flat just didn't feel the same. It had an emptiness and she felt vulnerable, something she hadn't experienced before. She now had the job of disposing of Marys belongings, her family didn't want anything. 'How sad,' thought Val, 'Mary didn't deserve that?'

She had sorted through her belongings. She binned most of her clothes. She gave away her books and trinkets to help the cat sanctuary and hoped some good might come from it. She had of course adopted Alfie the cat already and he now purred on her, as he had purred for Mary. 'Cats are fickle creatures.' Her furniture had been removed by some expats who needed stuff for their place which had just been rented. A few rugs remained and the big bed with the old fashioned candlewick bedspread that reminded Mary of home.

Val hadn't been out much over the past couple of days. She had heard about the arrests of course, from Charlie and she knew that Tarkan had been released without charge, she had texted her the news. She guessed all the others had also been freed by now. She kept in touch with a few people by text, but realised that gossip was rife at this time.

She was still mourning the loss of Mary and it would take time. She went down to Mary's flat to collect the last few carrier bags of possessions. So little to show for a life. Personal photos of her children and letters written, but not sent. She had started to read some, but she couldn't bear to finish them. Mary was apologising for her life and for herself; for not meeting 'their' expectations and for leaving. It was all too much. She had lived a life she had chosen, but felt she didn't deserve happiness. Her family had cut her off and it hurt her deeply.

Val walked around the flat, thinking this will be the last time. She planned to sell up; maybe buy a newer place near the marina. This place had some bad memories and subsequently her own flat felt the same. Her balcony where she shared time with Mary would always be difficult. Tainted. That was the word. Everything felt wrong now.

She heard a noise behind her as the front door opened and someone came quietly up the stairs. She mentally tutted to herself. People were always wedging that door open and leaving it like that. You would think they would be more careful given what had been going on lately. She turned around and shut Mary's front door behind her. As she let herself into her own flat she felt a hand on her shoulder and nearly jumped out of her skin.

"Symmon. My god you frightened the life out of me man. You shouldn't do that to people. I didn't see you coming."

He smiled. It wasn't a nice smile. It was more that his lips curled in the promise of a smile that didn't quite happen.

"What's up?" Val was perplexed. What was he doing here?

"Haven't you heard? They've arrested 'Billy the Bulgarian' for the murders. He is in custody now. I thought I would come and tell you myself. I know how close you were to poor old Mary."

"Thanks pet." Val was astounded. 'Billy? He wasn't the least bit like a killer. Surely that can't be right,' she thought. 'Why hasn't Charlie rung me?' Then she remembered her phone had been in the flat and she had probably been at Mary's longer than she thought.

Symmon looked strange. She couldn't put her finger on it. Spaced out, as if he had taken something. Then she remembered he had spent the night in custody.

"Have you not been to sleep pet? "You look tired."

"No, I didn't sleep very well Val. But thank you for caring. Would you mind making me a coffee before I go, perhaps that will wake me up a bit."

"Yes of course I will." He followed her in to the flat and shut the door. Why did she feel so uneasy? She had known him for years. She was just being stupid, it was Billy that she should have been watching out for all this time.

"Go and sit down Symmon and take the weight off your feet." She gestured towards the living room sofa.

She saw her mobile on the kitchen table. Something stopped her from going straight towards it.

She put two cups out on the counter and filled the kettle. As she was spooning out the coffee she realised Symmon was still standing in the kitchen staring into space.

"Symmon pet, go and sit down for God's sake you're making the place untidy."

He looked for a moment as if he didn't recognise her. Then in an almost robotic movement he moved toward the sofa and sat down.

Val was an intuitive woman and had learnt over the years to always trust her instincts. She felt something was very wrong. She carried on talking to Symmon normally, asking him how he was after his night in the cells. He grunted a response, but didn't engage as he had been when he approached her.

She needed to phone or text Charlie to see if she knew anything, but she didn't want to alert Symmon to the fact that she didn't believe him. Particularly as he was acting strangely. He'd always been a bit of a strange one. 'Moody,' Mary had called him in the past. One minute charming, the next dismissive. It was a bit unnerving.

She managed to pocket her phone as she was getting the milk out of the fridge and the large door blocked the entrance to the lounge. Perhaps she was over-reacting.

Symmon was staring at her from the lounge. He wasn't saying much unless prompted and she wondered why he had turned up in the way he had. She asked him, in typical Geordie fashion, if he would like a sandwich or some biscuits, but he declined. She took the coffees and put them on the table in front of them. She told him she was popping to the loo and would join him in a minute. She went into the small separate toilet, took the phone out of her pocket and found she was shaking.

She sent Charlie a text message, quickly.

'symmon in flat being v weird says billys the killer not at all comfortable'

She put the phone on silent so it would not alert him if she messaged back or rang her.

She flushed the toilet and washed her hands. Coming out of the toilet into the kitchen she picked up some biscuits whilst putting the phone on the worktop. She went into the living room and sat in the armchair opposite Symmon.

"What have you done Val?" he stared at her intently.

"What do you mean?" Val was properly worried now.

"Have you rang someone?" he continued to stare.

"No pet why?"

He stood up. He towered over her as she sat back on the armchair almost shrinking.

"Have you heard of a 'Swansong' Val?

Val's blood went cold.

"No pet." She lied.

Symmon told her in a monotone voice.

"Swans don't sing. But just before they die they make strange sounds almost like they are singing and then they die making no more sound again. Are you going to sing Val?"

"N…no pet. Why. Why would I?"

"Because you are going to die Val. That's why I'm here." He picked up his coffee again and drank it, thoughtfully, as if they were discussing philosophy. Yet his voice became very matter of fact. Emotionless.

"Can I tell you something about Mary?"

Val knew now. Perhaps she had known all along. Her instincts had always been good even as a child.

"Of course you can, I'm listening." Val was speaking as slowly as she was able. It was probably prolonging the inevitable, but even a few minutes more life would suit her right now.

"I didn't intend to kill her Val. You have to believe that." Val was silent now. "It was her fault all this started. She taunted me. Silly old bitch. I met her going home and she came back to my flat. She ridiculed me. I couldn't fuck her, I had too much to drink. I didn't fancy her either, but I wanted some company. I was angry. Tarkan upset me. I had a nice young one lined up. He told her something and she disappeared, so I was left with a hard on and nowhere to put it."

Val felt the tears welling up. She must not show fear. He would smell it.

"She started laughing at me. Me. How fucking dare she. She was lucky I even attempted to fuck her. She said I was a loser. A has been. Couldn't even sing, or fuck! She cackled like an old whore. I had to shut her up Val. You have to understand. I had a guitar string loose on a table and I wrapped it twice round her wrinkly neck. And then I pulled it. That stopped her noise. She was old anyway, she shouldn't have been out dressed like that. She was asking for trouble. Drunk and old. Fucking bitch."

Spittle was forming in the corners of his mouth and Val imagined the odour of his stinking breath on her friend. Mary would have found the whole thing funny at first, she wouldn't have thought she was in danger. She had a mouth on her at times and Symmon was pompous at the best of times. God she didn't know who she had gone home with this time. Val's thoughts were all over the place as he continued to rant in this strange monotone voice.

"Do you know the strange thing Val? The strange thing is I enjoyed it! More than I could know. I enjoyed it so much that I came in my pants. It felt fucking fantastic. That's her fault isn't it? I would never have known would I? Never known how good it would feel. I hate you English bitches. Your money and your ideas you are better than us. You think you can buy your men. Here you are all whores. Old whores. Saggy old whores." He was shouting now.

Val tried to calm him down. She wondered if this was it. This was her swansong. Had Mary realised what was happening to her. Had she suffered? Val tried to think if she could get to the door and get out. She doubted she could unlock the door with the key in it, and get down the stairs. He would be able to grab her easily. He saw her looking at the door.

"Don't bother whore. You won't get out. None of them got out, did they? Silly bitches. That Josie put up a fight I'll give her that. But it was too late. I had the best time with her. You should have seen the size of my cock Val." He started to rub himself almost unconsciously. "I couldn't stop Val, I couldn't stop even if I had wanted to…"

Val felt sick. He is insane she thought. Not just a killer. He is deranged. How has he covered it up for so long? Maybe Mary did trigger something. She tried to reason with him.

"Symmon," she almost pleaded, "what are you going to do?"

He smiled now. "Well after killing you Val, I will try to get to Samos. It doesn't really matter though. I guess they will catch me eventually. They shouldn't have let me out of the Police station. I was laughing all the way here. They think that stupid fucker Billy did it. Ha ha, stupid fucking Bulgarian, should have gone back to Sofia by now anyway…"

"What about your family Symmon?" Val was clutching at straws now. Anything to humanise the situation and make him think. He sat back down. She saw tears on his face and a faint hope welled up, perhaps she had hit a nerve. Then she looked closer at him rocking back and forth. He wasn't crying he was laughing.

"Val, I am going to tell you something now. It will make you laugh honey, honestly it will. No one else in Kuşadasi knows this. My real mother is English. Do you hear that? English. Fucking bitch left when I was two. She could be you Val, who knows? She could be Mary.

'She was Irish,' thought Val, but now wasn't the time to tell him.

"When I fuck you Val, I could be fucking my mother. She just upped one day and left. What kind of mother leaves her two year old son? She disappeared, leaving me with the old man and his new wife and all their brats. I was the weirdo brother, half English, not even a proper Turkish name. She called me Simon. Fucking hell she is lucky I didn't find her."

Val was sweating now. Profusely. Was it fear or a hot flush? She didn't know or care. This man couldn't be stopped, he was out of control now. He jumped up and the coffee went flying. He pulled her up off the chair and pushed her down on to the sofa. He had excited himself too much by describing the killings and his huge erection was pushing down on her stomach like a hungry python. He pulled her arms up and pinned them behind her head. He was so strong she couldn't believe it.

Was it the stimulus of the sexual arousal, or the thought of killing her that was driving him on? Anyone with any sense of self-preservation would have been out of town by now. But he was driven by the kill and had admitted himself he would never stop. She wondered if there was any point in fighting him, it seemed futile, he was a lead weight on top of her. She started to scream but no sound came out.

The next few moments were like a slow-motion dream sequence. Her captor had decided he could do the job better if he wasn't hindered by his tight fitting leather trousers. They were already unzipped, but it seemed he wanted to be naked to finish the 'I'm going to fuck 'mummy' one more time.'

Symmon let go of Val's arms momentarily to grab the waistband of his trousers. Val doesn't know what made her see her coffee cup on the table next to her, or how in the heat of battle she had the speed and dexterity to pick it up, but somehow she did. As he started to pull down his trousers, she aimed the full cup of hot liquid at his uncovered penis, accurately enough for Symmon to scream with the shock she'd caused to the sensitive area. He now had pain replacing desire. His ability to fuck 'mummy' had receded.

While he was momentarily distracted, Val made for the front door. She fumbled with the catch and Symmon now realised that she was planning to leave. He seemed hesitant, his prey or his genitalia?

He was spared of making the decision. Two armed Police came through the balcony doors. They had got into Mary's flat and climbed up from her balcony to Val's. Each armed with a baton and an un-holstered pistol they cornered Symmon who had now forgotten Mary and went for the taller of the two officers. The smaller officer swung his baton at his partner's assailant's groin.

Val meanwhile, had given up with the door and now that there was a full scale fight going on in her living room had dissolved into a tearful heap on the hallway floor and was sobbing uncontrollably.

Symmon was now lying foetal-like on the living room floor, yelping like a puppy. One Officer cuffed him with cable-ties, hands and feet, just to be sure, while the other Officer opened the front door before attending to the stricken Val, who was now trying to pull her blouse together where the 'killer' had ripped it.

Chief Semir came into the flat. His presence filled the

room and he came over to Val, now on her feet, but still shaking and to her surprise he hugged her. She was grateful for the gesture, however inappropriate and realised how close to death she had been.

Inside her head, she could still hear the madman's words...

43

Charlie

While Charlie was waiting for the car to arrive to take her to the Police station. She got a text from Val that sent a shiver down her spine. She rang Yucel straight away and told him that Symmon was in Val's flat and being threatening. She made that bit up. She thought that sometimes you need to embellish things to get a more urgent response. She'd discovered it works well in business. Otherwise you get overlooked. Perhaps it's an only child thing, she wondered.

Yucel had said, "shit, why does everything happen at once?" He then said he was going to send a patrol straight to Val's and he too would go there straight away. Yogi added, "I need to rescue your friend," and ended the call.

Charlie was grateful for the partial respite. It would presumably take longer now that the Chief was otherwise occupied and he had to detail his number two to look after her. Unselfishly she thought he was right, it was better to look after the living first. She told Tarkan she could pretend for a few minutes more that the body on the slab wasn't her mother. She was also worried sick about Val.

Charlie hoped to God that they would get there in time. Val was canny enough to send the message. She had sensed something. 'Val wasn't stupid,' Charlie thought. She paced up and down for the next twenty minutes or so, with Tarkan trying to calm her down.

She eventually got the phone call from Yucel, telling her Val was safe and Symmon was in custody. He told

Charlie they would have shot him if they had to, but he had been apprehended, alive.

At least this monster had been caught, he couldn't ruin any other lives. Was her life ruined? It felt as if it was over. The life force had been drained from her, adrenaline had been replaced with an anaesthetic numbing her feelings.

She heard a noise at the door. It was either the Police coming to pick her up, or Deniz trying to creep back in to see what was going on. Had he been told about Dee? She had forgotten all about him in the last twenty-four hours of madness.

It was neither. The door opened wider and a woman pushed her way in with a suitcase and handbag in each arm. She was in her sixties, but looked younger. Her face looked remarkably unlined, but bruised slightly she had the look of someone who had been in a car accident and survived. Charlie stared at the doorway, her mouth open.

"Mam!"

Then she fainted elegantly on to the floor.

44

Dee

D ee felt better than she had done for days. At times she had regretted the decision to be sedated following the procedure. The drugs that had been administered gave her the worst nightmares she had experienced for years, in fact since Paul had died so suddenly and her life had fallen apart. These last days were a blur, the medication she had been given to ease the pain left her feeling as if she'd been to Mars and back, whilst being poked continuously during the flight with a cattle prod. She was starting to feel a bit more like her normal self again though. On the inside at least.

As they were preparing her anaesthetic she wondered what the hell she was doing and why. She had thought long and hard, she wasn't a woman who made such decisions easily. The cost was exorbitant in itself although the prices for cosmetic surgery in Istanbul were a great deal cheaper than London or Newcastle.

The time spent lying in the hospital bed in the private clinic, not knowing where she was or what day of the week it was, had seemed like a good idea prior to her surgery. She knew the pain would be bad for a few days afterwards and she had spent enough money on the whole caper to get the best treatment she could wish for.

With no phone and contact with the outside world she'd been able to recover in peace and tranquillity, albeit induced by some strong morphine and five star service. When the bandages and dressings finally came off, she saw the results immediately and forgave herself for the moments of doubt.

Dee had spent the previous six months researching and planning the life altering operation. She trusted Dr Tarhan implicitly after meeting him at his clinic on two occasions to look at her options and see photographs of his work.

Dee felt as if she had undergone more than a physical transformation. Yes the face lift had taken years off her, and her skin was naturally good, but more than that, she felt as though she had changed as a person over the last few months. It was her time now and she planned to enjoy whatever time she had left. She had spent years worrying about Charlie, her lifestyle, her choice of men, and trying to cope with her indifference to her mother. God knows it had hurt at times. Really hurt. She had lived for her daughter for many years, not through her like some mothers do, but for her. Sacrificing to make ends meet and doing two jobs at one time to pay the bills. It had taken her until now to accept that Charlie didn't love her or respect her in the way she had hoped she might.

Moving to Turkey had been a huge wrench. Leaving her beloved North East and the friends and family who had been so supportive and kind to her over the years. Leaving the house full of happy memories and accepting that the life she had left behind had already gone. The house became bricks and mortar tying her to an existence she no longer recognised or wanted.

She had waited until she felt Charlie was settled enough in her own life. She was proud of her daughter's achievements and just wished they had made Charlie happy. The job, the flat, the boyfriends, nothing seemed to be enough for her. She had wanted Dee to stay where she was, and be the same person that she had always been. It wasn't fair. Dee decided after months of soul searching and counselling that she needed to move on to a different life. One that didn't remind her every day of what she'd lost.

She spent a year on a diet and exercise programme. She started to feel she could become the person she wanted to be. An independent woman, who could have a meaningful life and a new start in the town she felt was her new home. She had loved Kuşadasi from the first visit. A quirky place, but a place of acceptance. She had enrolled in an English Open University course in Philosophy and Politics. She started to realise how the world worked. Paul had tried to educate her in his own way, but she had been too busy being a mother and keeping house to really grasp the wider issues.

She'd tried to tell Charlie of her hopes and dreams. Of trying to be a better person and wanting to help the people who needed it. To give something back. She had worked tirelessly with Deniz to get a small shop in the alleys that she could turn into a drop-in centre, or maybe something more. To do charitable work with the underclasses, particularly the children. It was waiting to happen and Dee was excited that she was doing something positive. She couldn't lie around on the beach all day and become a lady who lunched. She'd had a fire in her belly that had been extinguished by loss and the loss of hope. She was going to re-ignite it.

She hoped that Charlie would one day understand. The face lift had been her last indulgence before she started her new vocation. She knew she wasn't deluded. She was still a woman in her late middle age, but she looked and felt so much better that it energised her for the work ahead.

She had come to realise that self-esteem was the key to everything, even though some of her friends told her that her beauty came from within and she shouldn't succumb to the knife. Despite their disapproval, she made her own decision based on her feelings of self-worth.

It had been worth it. The results were better than she had hoped for. She hadn't told anyone where she was going, apart from Deniz, who had been sworn to secrecy. She knew she could trust him to say nothing to anyone. He took that literally as she would later find out. Let the haters say what they wanted. She wasn't going to deny where she had been, but once her mind was made up, she hadn't wanted anyone to try and stop her.

As she boarded the train for Aydin, she used her phone for the first time to ring Deniz, who had offered to pick her up. She realised her battery was flat, but didn't care. She could get a Taxi and surprise him. Pop home and get dressed up, and cover the faint residual bruising with a bit of foundation. She wondered what had been happening whilst she was away. Nothing much probably. She smiled to herself, maybe a bit of gossip and scandal centred on her. If she was lucky there may be a missed call from her daughter although she doubted it.

Dee was always the one to ring Charlie and that was monthly at best. She couldn't find much to say really. Charlie usually did most of the talking filling her in on events at work and the latest with Anthony her boss. Dee wasn't judgemental, but she knew he wasn't the right person for her daughter. Maybe she would find that out, in time.

45

Yucel

Yucel looked at the man sitting opposite him in the Interview room. Symmon Yavuz, aka Simon was smiling at him. He didn't seem to care that he had been caught. Maybe he wanted to be caught, it was nothing short of reckless to go after Val when he had been released. Perhaps he knew he wouldn't get much further without his passport or money and had decided to have one last kill.

He refused to answer any questions. His lawyer, hired by his father had advised him to say nothing and he was happy to comply. He was asked about the deaths of the four women and he just sat smiling throughout. Yucel knew his confession to Val would stand up in Court. They found a Turkish Eye in his trouser pocket ready to leave as his calling card. He had become addicted to death and Yucel recognised the signs of a sexual sadist. Maybe he had managed to cover up his desires for years, or maybe he had killed others. That was Yucel's worry. Turkey was a big country and the powers that be in Ankara would want more information that they could compare with other deaths of women over the last ten years or so.

He hadn't given Yucel any information about the last victim. The woman in the cupboard had been identified as Theresa Wheelan. She had been held longer than the others in that cramped room and Yucel dreaded to think what she had suffered before he finally killed her. She lived alone without any family and Symmon had targeted her as she set off allegedly for a trip home. No one had realised she was missing and it would have been a few days more before it was reported. He was glad it hadn't been Dee Davison, lying there in the cupboard. 'Was this a terrible thought to have?' He wondered, but he had seen the face of Charlie Davison when she reported her mother missing. They had some catching up to do and a relationship to build, but he was glad her mother had returned.

Val had told Yucel about Symmon's family background and his mother, the English woman who had deserted him. Had this sent him over the edge? His madness had been concealed well until his life started to unravel. Yucel knew that Symmon hadn't planned the first murder. Mary had been in the wrong place at the wrong time, but he certainly had planned the others.

The experience of ultimate power and control had captivated him. The notoriety he had lost as an entertainer had been replaced by the importance of becoming a serial killer that no one would forget, long into the future. The token, the Eye perhaps meaning the evil eye, a parody in terms of its popularity as a gift and a symbol of Turkey. He was sick enough to want everyone to now associate the 'Eye' with the name Symmon Yavuz.

He continued to leer at the Chief and Yucel knew that he would get nothing from this man. He would go home now. Leave him with his own dark thoughts and move into the light. The light of his family, his wife and his sons. Symmon was behind bars now. That was enough for tonight. He felt a spring in his step and he walked out of the building towards his car. He couldn't wait to hold his son in his arms and smell the sweetness of his new-born innocence. Perhaps once Symmon's father had felt the same. It was a thought he didn't want to retain in his mind any longer. His sons would grow up to be people of consequence. Or at least kind men with good hearts, like their father and grandfather. His wife was ecstatic that the case would be closed. She would get her husband back. He would be able to see his baby boy, bathe him and enjoy the precious family time he had missed during this time of madness.

Kuşadasi would return to be jewel of the Aegean coastline, as it's always been. Women of any age or creed could walk the streets safely again.

46

Tütüncüler

Charlie awoke to find herself lying on her mother's bed with Tarkan and her mother leaning over her, wiping her forehead with something cooling. She could hardly take in the scene before her. She sat up, still feeling a bit dizzy, but desperate to hold her mother. Their embrace lasted long minutes and for the first time in many years it comforted both women. Tears were streaming down Charlie's face, as she tried to tell her mother she had thought she was dead.

"I know love, Tarkan's told me what's gone on. It's terrible. I'm still taking it in. Poor Mary, all those poor bloody women." Dee was still in shock.

"Why didn't Deniz say something?" Charlie continued to sob, with relief.

"Cause he's a man Charlie. I told him not to tell a soul so he didn't. Stupid sod." Dee was crying now. "Look what you have done, all this work for nothing. I will be a blubbering mess soon and my new face will be all botchy." They both laughed.

They had a lot to catch up. A lot of time and emotions to share. Tarkan grinned at them. "I thought it was your sister here Charlie."

Dee laughed. "Your charm school was certainly worth the money pet. And what's been going on here whilst I have been away I wonder?"

Tarkan and Charlie looked at each other and smiled.

"Nothing mam. Of course I wouldn't dare. Not in your house."

Dee thought Charlie had changed more than she herself had. Even with the surgery and the makeover; and the soul searching. Her daughter had come back. The real Charlie was back.

How long she'd been away...

"Mammy's home! 'Mammy's home!" Squawked a happy parrot, joining in the excitement.

"You're right Oscar," Dee said looking at her daughter.

"Mammy is home."

47

Khan

Adskhan Murat was a very happy man. He was possibly happier than his wife Jenni had been when she found out that she had won the lottery. Happier than when he had read about Ms Jenni Higgs in the Essex Chronicle and realised that he'd seen her profile on Dating sites. Happier than when he was able to establish on-line contact. Happier than when he thought of using his Turkish-Cypriot upbringing in North London to hatch a plan to lure the millionaire to Turkey. Happier than when she agreed to be married. Happier than when she left him to sort out the property and bank accounts. Happier than when he realised there was a serial killer on the loose targeting European women. Much, much happier.

Okay, he'd sweated a bit when he found out about the Turkish Eye. And again when he found out about the guitar string, but he needn't have worried. The crazy man Symmon Yavuz was happy to confess to all the crimes. Even the one he hadn't committed. Khan could go about his business without fear. Perhaps he might thank him one day.

He looked at the woman lying next to him. She wasn't as pretty as Jenni, or as lively, but she was rich. She thought Khan was rich too. This was correct. Having inherited all of Jenni's estate, he need never to work again.

'But you couldn't call this work,' he thought, as he casually caressed her breast, rousing her from her sleep. Not really.

We hope that you have enjoyed reading 'Turkish Eye.'
If you have, please tell your friends, or be kind enough to write a review on which ever website you favour.
Your comments, reviews and feedback are always welcomed by Beatrice, at this email address:

comment@obilium.org

Or tweet to: **@obilium**

Should you wish to be kept informed about future publications, send a short note to the above email address, or tweet to @obilium

If you haven't read any of Beatrice James's other titles, look out for the '**The Retribution Fantasies**' series.

'**An Artist's Impression**' – Volume 1 and
'**Sentence Expiry Date**' – Volume 2 are available now
'**Hammerkop**' and '**Baybe & me**' - coming soon!

10962214R00151

Printed in Great Britain
by Amazon.co.uk, Ltd.,
Marston Gate.